MOLLY OF THE MALL

HEIDI L.M. JACOBS

MOLLY

of the

MALL

*Literary Lass
& Purveyor of
Fine Footwear*

HER HISTORY AND MISADVENTURES

NEWEST PRESS
EDMONTON, AB

Library and Archives Canada Cataloguing in Publication

Jacobs, Heidi L. M., author
Molly of the mall, literary lass and purveyor of fine footwear : her history and misadventures / Heidi L.M. Jacobs.

(Nunatak first fiction series ; no. 50)
Issued in print and electronic formats.
ISBN 978-1-988732-59-6 (hardcover).--ISBN 978-1-988732-60-2 (EPUB).--
ISBN 978-1-988732-61-9 (Kindle)

I. Title. II. Series: Nunatak first fiction ; no. 50

PS8619.A2545M65 2019   C813'.6   C2018-904450-0
                                               C2018-904451-9

NeWest Press wishes to acknowledge that the land on which we operate is Treaty 6 territory and a traditional meeting ground and home for many Indigenous Peoples, including Cree, Saulteaux, Niitsitapi (Blackfoot), Métis, and Nakota Sioux.

Board Editor: Merrill Distad
Cover design & typography: Kate Hargreaves
Cover texture by shaire productions

NeWest Press acknowledges the Canada Council for the Arts, the Alberta Foundation for the Arts, and the Edmonton Arts Council for support of our publishing program. This project is funded in part by the Government of Canada.

201, 8540 – 109 Street
Edmonton, AB T6G 1E6
780.432.9427
NeWest Press www.newestpress.com

No bison were harmed in the making of this book.
PRINTED AND BOUND IN CANADA

THIRD PRINTING

For my mum, Merle Whyte Martin
(1940-2018)
"All of us are better when we're loved"
— Alistair MacLeod

May 1995:
Le Petit Chou Shoe Shop
The Mall, Edmonton

"My True Name is so well known in the Records, or Registers at *Newgate*, and in the *Old-Baily*, and there are some things of such Consequence still depending there, relating to my particular Conduct, that it is not expected I should set my Name, or the Account of my Family to this Work; perhaps, after my Death it may be better known, at present it would not be proper, no, not tho' a general Pardon should be issued, even without Exceptions and reserve of Persons or Crimes.

It is enough to tell you, that as some of my worst Comrades, who are out of the Way of doing me Harm, having gone out of the World by the Steps and the String, as I often expected to go, knew me by the Name of *Moll Flanders*; so you may give me leave to speak of myself, under that Name till I dare own who I have been, as well as who I am."

—Daniel Defoe, *The Fortunes and Misfortunes of the Famous Moll Flanders, &c.,* 1722

WHEN YOU'RE NAMED AFTER SOMEONE OR something you spend much of your life asking why. Why Rita? Why Sequoia? Why Wayne Gretzky? Most people are named after a grandparent, a favourite aunt, or, if you live in Edmonton, a hockey player. Your name might illuminate who you are, a historical moment, or what your parents wanted for you as they gazed lovingly into the tiny, squirmy wad of blankets you once were. Maybe your parents say, "You were named after my Great-Aunt Rita who studied art with Matisse, established a safe haven for feral cats in Regent's Park, and established an art school for underprivileged youth. We wanted to give you a name that conveyed her creative spirit, her compassion, and her commitment to social justice around the world." Or, maybe you are told, "I named you Sequoia so you would always be strong and deeply rooted to the earth." Or maybe you are told, "We named you Wayne because you were born the day they sold Gretzky to LA; it's the least we could do for Wayne after all he gave us." I am told, "You were named after the novel your father was teaching the day you were born."

And now, twenty years later, I find myself at Canada's largest shopping mall trying to explain to someone how it was that I became Molly. I was completing the paperwork for my new summer job at Le Petit Chou Shoe Shop and making small chat with Diana, the regional manager of the company that oversees four shoe stores in the Mall. Polishing my new name tag, Diana said, "Molly. That's a name you don't hear often. I was named after Diana, the Roman goddess of the hunt. Are you named after a famous Molly?" I looked up from my paperwork and saw she was well-named with her perfect hair and statuesque posture. I suddenly felt very short and in need of a haircut. I had to confess, "I was named after Daniel Defoe's novel, *Moll Flanders*. It was written in 1722." Without missing a beat, she said, "That is unfortunate, isn't it?" I had to agree. Perhaps I should have used this opportunity to say, "My name is Molly, but I go by Camilla. Or Lucinda. Or Isabella." Then I might not have had this hideous name tag in my hand with "Le Petit Chou Shoe Shop" sweeping elegantly across the top in a luxurious italic font, while "Molly, at your service" slumped in the middle in mundane Helvetica. After I signed the last piece of paper, Diana proclaimed, "You must be thrilled to be here, at the premier mall in the country. We think you should be delighted to be part of the Le Petit Chou family." I noticed she left no room for disagreement, so I nodded and attempted to agree wholeheartedly.

Working at the Mall would be very different from being an English major, but I was feeling up for the challenge. I was no longer Molly, soon-to-be third-year English major. I was now Molly, full-time purveyor of fine footwear, at your service. As I made my way home on the bus, toting a large pink binder with *Manual for the Purveyance of Fine Footwear* emblazoned on the cover, I was thinking about how my life might have been different had I been named after a Roman goddess instead of a character in a novel neither of my parents like very much. What I didn't tell Diana was the long story that led to me being named after Moll Flanders.

As the children of an English professor and an art historian, you might assume our names would have been chosen with a critical eye to symbolism. However, on the question of our names, there is a long answer and a short answer. I'm still working on the long answer, but the short answer is this. When my oldest sibling Tess was born, my father was a newly minted English professor, aglow and agog at the wonders of the British novel. The day she was born, he was preparing to teach *Tess of the d'Urbervilles* for his "The

Tragic Vision of Thomas Hardy" graduate seminar, and he thought Tess would be a lovely name for his baby girl. My mother, apparently sedated, agreed. She later confessed that she had not finished the book or read my father's dissertation (as she claimed she had). When she did read the novel, she sobbed for our Tess's future: "We named our daughter after a murderess?" If there is an upside to Tess's name it is this: had she been born a week later, my father's class was reading *The Return of the Native*, and Tess would have been Eustacia Vye and thus condemned to roam the heath she loathes. As Tess, she merely has dramatically flawed relationships with men, even when they're really nice. The downside of Tess's name is that my parents remained committed to using my father's class schedules to name their subsequent children.

When my brother was on the way, my mother was convinced she was having another girl, and she thought that Catherine would be a lovely name. My father, feeling perhaps a bit guilty about the whole Tess thing, succumbed to my mother's lobbying, and scheduled *Wuthering Heights* ("Love and Thwarted Lust in Victorian Fiction") around the due date. But Catherine was not to be; their second child was a boy. After emerging from sedation, my mother agreed to name her new baby after another flawed fictional character and they welcomed son Heathcliff. By the time I showed up, my mother had given up trying to stack the syllabus. Part way through his "Eponymy and Eponymity in the British Novel," I was born and named after Daniel Defoe's novel *Moll Flanders*. A class earlier, I would have been Clarissa and two classes later, Belinda. As my mother told me, "Your father first argued for Moll, but I got him to agree to Molly." I nodded gratefully, though noted that on every birthday card, note, or memo my ever-tenacious father spells my name Moll(y). I'm convinced that when he says my name out loud or even thinks it, he adds the y in parentheses.

In naming us after literary characters, my father, a rising scholarly star, started a bit of a trend in the English department. During Christmas parties at the Faculty Club, graduate students laughed—some with irony, some with compassion, some with derision—at miniature versions of their professors named Tess, Heathcliff, Molly, Prufrock, Pellinore, Isolde, Gawain, Grendel, and the twins Leonard and Virginia. By the time wee Chiasmus Widgett-Jones was born, people realized the trend had gone too far. Besides, newer faculty were rebelling against the old guard on all fronts. The next generation of departmental children had solid Old Testament names. In recent years, the children's tables at the department parties seemed less like living Norton Anthologies and more like Amish barn raisings.

It wasn't until I had to read *Tess of the d'Urbervilles* and *Wuthering Heights* for a class last semester that I gave much thought to our own names. Neither of my siblings has read their eponymous novels, and so I feel a certain degree of superiority, as if I hold a key to their inner worlds denied to them. I finally understand why Tess broke up with the perfectly acceptable Mark Forster: she was fated by her place in the syllabus to have disastrous relationships with men. I also look at my brother, an aspiring agronomist, with new-found insight. He was named after a brooding loner who wanders the moors in the rain and bangs his head on trees: of course he spends his days scouring prairie ditches for elusive and rare fescue. Whether or not my parents had considered the implications of their children's namesakes, these novels seem to have played a deterministic role in the shaping of their lives. As the third child, am I the one to prove or disprove my theory? I therefore approach my first reading of *Moll Flanders* with extreme trepidation.

Even though *Moll Flanders* is one of those novels every English major should read, I have gleaned enough facts from the back-cover blurb to make me fear it might reveal something horrible about my fate. Here's what I know: Moll led a life of "continu'd Variety ... she was Twelve Year a Whore, five times a Wife (whereof once to her own brother), Twelve Year a Thief, Eight Year a Transported Felon in Virginia, at last grew Rich, liv'd Honest, and died a Penitent." I may be even more doomed than Tess.

After handing in my final papers last week, I realized I had a whole summer ahead of me and decided I should use this time constructively to finally read *Moll Flanders*. I stared at it all last night, but couldn't bring myself to read more than the first paragraph and the back cover. Instead, I rewrote its back-cover blurb: "After several romantically melancholic years in Paris where the stunningly stylish Moll Flanders dated eighteenth-century equivalents of Jeremy Irons, John Cusack, and Alan Rickman, Moll moved to London where she became a cautiously respected artist, fashionably mis-understood novelist, and discreetly sought-after milliner. After a life-altering disagreement with her eighteenth-cen-tury Alan Rickman equivalent (who, while riding in a pic-turesque landscape in the rain, suffers a tragic fall from a very attractive dapple-grey horse, and utters 'Moll. Forgive me,' as his final words. The only one to hear his long-over-due apology was the dapple grey who promptly disregarded these words as inconsequential), Moll set out to make it on her own, possessing only her rapier-like wit and acute sense of style. In due time, she became an Augustan-era It Girl and found almost-true love with an eighteenth-century Noel Gallagher, and then truer love with a John Cusack equiva-lent." I wrote twelve more versions of the blurb, all of them involving Alan Rickman, John Cusack, rain in a picturesque landscape, and an attractive horse of varying colours. Some included members of Oasis.

No matter how many times I rewrote the back-cover blurb, I had to come to terms with the fact that this Moll does not live in London, or Paris, nor does she perambu-late within a picturesque landscape sodden with melancholic rain. Rather, this Moll lives in Edmonton where the men who love her are imaginary, fictional, or weird, the landscape is flat and snowy eight months of the year, and millinery is confined to the knitting of toques. Maybe instead of reading *Moll Flanders* this summer, I should write my own fortunes and misfortunes. And so, dear reader, I ask you, as Moll asks her dear reader on the first page, to "give me leave to speak of myself, under that Name till I dare own who I have been, as well as who I am." 🌸

*O*N THE FIRST CHAPTER OF *MOLL FLANDERS*, MOLL says nothing about the condition of her feet, so I am assuming this form of suffering is unique to me. True, she suffered, but was she ever required to stand nine hours in ill-fitting pointy pumps of questionable quality? Assuming not, I will take this opportunity to make a clean break from the trajectory of Defoe's narrative to note the misfortunes I endured today on my unpaid day of training.

While the *Manual for the Purveyance of Fine Footwear* promised that much of my first morning would be spent exploring the "art and nuances of excellence in shoe purveyance," my manager-mentor Maureen covered chapters two through six in under five minutes. Perhaps she assumed—rightly—that I had read the manual on my own for the "official" word on shoe purveying.

As we are required to wear only Le Petit Chou shoes on the floor, my first half-hour was spent purchasing a pair of shoes to wear on my training day. Purchasing shoes from Le Petit Chou Shoe Shop (with "a generous 25-percent discount on regularly priced items") was not just a way of enforcing a chain-wide dress code, it was also "an opportunity," the manual said, to "literally walk a mile in our customers' shoes." The manual went on to say that by purchasing a pair of shoes on my first day, my manager-mentor would model the excellence in shoe purveying that Le Petit Chou (and its four sister stores) prides itself upon. Early on, I was convinced Maureen had never read the manual, since my "shoe purveyance mentoring" amounted to having a box of shoes thrust at me without what the manual calls "relationship building verbal invitations." Instead she said, "Here, take these. They're black. They'll be perfect. We don't have 7 ½. They'll stretch. Where's your Mastercard? Oh, and you'll need polish and protective spray. They're not covered in your discount."

The remainder of my training was spent learning the unofficial version of what it means to succeed at Le Petit Chou, which, as far as I can tell, means not angering Maureen. Here are just a few things I learned. I will note them in case there's a quiz later. Maureen said there might be and I fear she wasn't joking.

- There are four nearly identical shoe stores in our retail family at the Mall: Le Petit Chou is the most prestigious store and I should be happy not to have had to work my way up. The next prestigious store is Prima Donna followed by Foliage. Tuesday's is so far away in Phase One of the Mall, it's almost not worth thinking about.

- There is a power structure that must be obeyed. At the top is Diana, the regional manager for all the prairie stores. On paper, Tim is the mall manager and oversees the four stores and its managers. In reality, Maureen runs all four stores, but I should never mention this fact to Diana or Tim because it makes them uncomfortable.

- If there are discrepancies between the cash in the till and the closing figures, I should assume the mistake is mine. Maureen's tills are always balanced. She has never made an error. She is never wrong. Shortages will be taken off of my paycheque, and overages should be put into the empty jar on her desk.

- I must never be late. I must be on time when starting my shift and when coming back from any of my "generous breaks, lunch, or dinner hours." This is especially true when she is working, because she has very important things to do. The last full-time employee made this mistake a lot. I shouldn't try it.

- Maureen's boyfriend is named Gordon and all women immediately fall in love with him when they see him. I should not make that mistake. I am not his type, not at all, so I shouldn't even think of falling in love with him.

- The last full-timer also made the mistake of saying Maureen took "smoke breaks" when they are, in fact, "business breaks." Actually, they're not breaks at all, because she is still working. They are important business networking opportunities that she must undertake, because no one else will. And she smokes during them. But only because she has to. I wouldn't understand. I shouldn't even try.

- I must never speak of the last full-timer. Ever. I don't need to know about her.

- The only reason I have my own name tag is because I'm "seasonal full-time." I should be grateful to have a name tag because part-timers don't warrant one until they've worked here six months. If we get a new part-time employee, they can use Karen's name tag. There's also a "Ken" if we have two part-timers on at the same time. They don't mind being called Karen or Ken. Sometimes it's easier not to have to remember their real names. (For contradictions, see chapter ten in the manual for the discussion of "managing personnel.")

- On the matter of selling shoes, "they practically sell themselves." But here are some helpful hints. If they're too big, sell them inserts for the front of the shoe. If they're too small, tell them they'll stretch.

- While a customer was in the store, Maureen said, "And another thing: never refer to those really high-heeled shoes as 'f____-me pumps' in front of the customers." The customer and I exchanged mortified looks before she scurried away to another store.

- Maureen contradicted everything I read in chapter eight about the importance of polish and protective spray: "I have no idea whether they work, but push them with every pair of shoes you sell." She then

offered this "how to get ahead" gem: "Polish and
protective spray separate the forest from the trees—
sell a lot and you'll go far."

- Maureen was emphatic that we're "not allowed to
use protective spray in the bathroom with the door
closed, ever. That's not what the spray is there for." I
did not see mention of this in the Health and Safety
chapter of the manual, but assume there is some tale.

I am starting to worry that even if there isn't a formal
quiz, every day will be a test with Maureen. Maybe the sheer
agony of standing in those shoes all day will numb whatever
Maureen might throw at me. The other girls seem very nice
and they assure me that my feet will become accustomed
to this routine within a few weeks. They are silent on the
issue of Maureen. I have eleven hours until I have to be back
at the Mall. Until then, I will let my toes return to a non-
pointed state and keep my heels on the ground, just as nature
intended. 🦋

*T*ODAY I TURNED TWENTY. I DIDN'T TELL ANYONE at work that it was my birthday. I just carried on and tried to live up to Le Petit Chou's high expectations for excellence in fine shoe purveyance. I broke my record of polish sales in one day: I sold three. But now I am home and celebrating my birthday by myself.

I remember turning ten and my excitement about being a double-digit age. I thought it was pretty neat to have a one in front of my years for a whole decade. And then my years would have a two in front of them. When I was ten, I could picture my twentieth birthday perfectly. I would live like some of Mum and Dad's grad-student friends in one of those walk-up apartments off Whyte Avenue with misleadingly elegant names like The Alhambra or The Loch Lomond. I would be grown-up and elegant and my hairstyle would no longer be an anarchy of curls but a sleek, effortless bob. A copy of my first novel would be sitting on a rattan coffee table, my paintings on easels in my hardwood-floored apartment. I would have a Siamese cat named Suki and a best friend called Saskia. Or maybe I would have a calico cat named Saskia and a best friend called Suki. At any rate, I would have a cat of my own and artsy friends with guitars. I would have lots of batik throw pillows. I would make my friends tea from a whole shelf of exotic teas in colourful boxes with names like Hibiscus Siesta or Rosehip Zinger, served in an array of mismatched teacups. My artsy boyfriend would sing me happy birthday as he strummed a guitar. He would have bought me an aquarium with four lovely angel-fish (what I wanted, but didn't get, when I was ten). I would have told him I liked him very much. There would be mirth and cake. I didn't really know about alcohol then.

It's probably a good thing you can't see into the future, because my ten-year-old self would be pretty disappointed to see how my twentieth birthday turned out. I'm still sitting on the same chesterfield I sat on when I opened my gifts as a ten-year-old and I still don't have an aquarium. I'd also be devastated to see that our ginger cat, Hodge, has passed on to kitty heaven and has been succeeded by Hodge the Younger, a tabby.

The new Hodge is my only party guest. My parents are both at the annual Learneds Conference (or as Heathcliff and I like to call it The Stupids), Heathcliff is out on a work field trip to scour ditches for fescue, and Tess is still in France. And none of my friends is free: Susan's out of town, Genevieve's working, and Glenda has to babysit her cousins. My parents left a card and some presents for me and put a decorated cake in the freezer. I was supposed to take the cake out to thaw this morning, but I forgot. When I got home from work, I made myself a nice dinner of pasta and peas, and opened my presents. I got the vintage purse from Zoryana I've been eyeing and a gift certificate for Le Château (Mum), and a Robbie Burns T-shirt with a distinct late 1970s styling (Dad). Heathcliff left me a book of poetry called *Seed Catalogue* by a Canadian, so no craggy moors or heroic knights. Tess sent me a tiny bottle of Chanel perfume. I am now eating a frozen piece of carrot cake, and feeding Hodge the Younger tastes of cream cheese icing. I have a Miss Jane Austen novel beside me for company. I keep looking at the card from my parents. My dad wrote: "Welcome to your twenties, Moll(y)! We know this is going to be an exciting decade and we can't wait to see where your adventures will take you." Today doesn't strike me as a particularly auspicious beginning, but I have cake, a cat, and a blooming lilac tree outside the dining room window. Happy birthday, little self. ❦

I'VE BEEN THINKING ABOUT *MOLL FLANDERS* and what it might mean for my future. Having read only one chapter, I need to be cautious before pitching myself into the depths of deterministic despair. Is, for example, my life determined by Moll Flanders, the character, or by *Moll Flanders*, the novel? Am I predetermined to become a 1990s version of a Twelve-Year Whore, a five-times Wife (whereof once to her own brother), a Twelve-Year Thief, an Eight-Year Transported Felon who eventually grew Rich and died a Penitent? Or, will my life follow the trajectory of Defoe's novel? Will I endure a life where I am respectfully validated by a small segment of the professoriate, but shunned and despised by just about everybody else? Since I was not born in prison, and the chances of accidentally marrying my brother are non-existent, my life may not be that of Moll Flanders. Instead, my existence will be determined by *Moll Flanders* the novel: my life will be respectable yet thoroughly unromantic. However, some hope remains. The back-cover blurb of my Oxford edition suggests there may be some raciness, irony, and rich sociological detail to which I may look forward.

It occurs to me that if I were to rewrite *Moll Flanders*, I might be able to thwart my destiny, and live a broodingly romantic life after all. Given the agonizing monotony of the first chapter, rewriting *Moll Flanders* with a Canadian setting seems to be my only hope. Here is a first draft of the plot summary:

- Moll's sublimely romantic life begins with the publication of her watershed Canadian, coming-of-age novel that establishes her as a sultry, much sought-after yet enigmatic authoress: think Barbara Stanwyck meets J.D. Salinger. She refers to herself as "authoress," sometimes she might be a "noveliste," but never writeress.

- Edmonton is magically transformed into an urban landscape of heaths and moors, punctuated with cobblestone lanes, vintage clothing stores with affordable Dior hats, and cappuccino bars with exposed brick walls. Snow arrives sporadically and functions decoratively. It melts before turning grey, and there is never ice, so you can wear nice shoes and sit on a Vespa year-round. No one wears Petro-Canada toques, ever.

- Moll receives and rejects proposals of marriage from a spectrum of eligible men. She will roll her eyes at inelegantly insistent proposals from Liam Gallagher. As this will be a Canadian novel, 30 percent of her proposals will come from Canadians as per CRTC regulations. Thrice weekly, she will write succinct, but compassionate rejections to her ardent suitors, while sitting at an antique, mahogany writing desk with multiple secret compartments. She will use sepia ink on lovely Devonshire cream-coloured note cards.

- Moll will mail said rejections in the early afternoon while walking her seven well-behaved and immaculately groomed Yorkshire terriers. Each dog will be named after a Miss Austen character, and each will have its own multi-season Burberry wardrobe in his or her own custom colour scheme. Moll will say things like, "Ah, Mr Darcy! You are incorrigible, but you simply must put on your alizarin crimson rain slicker. Look, Lady Catherine de Bourgh has her burnt umber ensemble on already, and Lydia Bennet is waiting to get into her vestment green rain cape. Chop, chop, Mr Darcy!" Moll is admired by some and envied by most for having sufficient *je ne sais quoi* to carry off dressing her terriers in Burberry ensembles without appearing to be a crazy dog lady.

- After critical and commercial success, Moll eschews her publicly sublime and romantic life, and becomes a mysterious yet stylish recluse. An anonymous fan bequeaths her an airy, tasteful flat near Hyde Park. Furnished with Edwardian antiques, the flat is also equipped with an espresso machine so complicated it comes with a full-time Italian barista named Alessandro. Alessandro writes poetry when not making perfect espressos.

- She will continue to avoid the "solitary woman with too many dogs" cliché by becoming "stylish reclusive authoress with canine companions," and will do so with aplomb. She will wear fabulous Fluevog shoes in all weather conditions, and will never slip on ice because that fatal flaw of Fluevog shoe soles will have been corrected at her insistence. She will ignore repeated pleas from *The New Yorker* for "any old scrap of your writing."

- While appearing to be reclusive, Moll will secretly write historically accurate, gothic bodice-rippers under the pseudonym Cynthia Lodgepole. She will employ a cabal of stealth librarians to ensure historical accuracy. Subsequent editions of her work may feature yellow stickers on the covers saying "Now Even More Historically Accurate!" She will sell enough copies to allow her to purchase a small cabin on a craggy shore of Scotland where she and her Yorkies will reside. She will make significant, anonymous monetary donations to orangutan sanctuaries. She sleeps better knowing endangered baby primates are safe, well-fed, and nestled under blankets she has personally crocheted for them.

- Reaping the benefits of her outpourings of a high literary quality, she will stroll the sublime shores of her Scottish hermitage. Her aging Yorkies follow along; no longer dressed in Burberry outfits, they wear drab yet durable rain gear in inclement weather. One

day, while grieving Mr Collins, who has just shuffled off his mortal Yorkie coil, she will walk along
the shoreline carrying the last of her aged Yorkies
(Willoughby!). It is there where she will meet her
true love, Fergus, a sheepdog trainer. Love at first
sight is inevitable. Under his nurturing attention,
Moll returns to writing Canadian *Bildungsromans*.
She receives many national awards for her canon of
respectfully misunderstood fiction.

- Living in a cozy stone house on their craggy yet
verdant piece of land, Moll and Fergus tend their
herd of well-trained and ethically treated vegetarian sheepdogs, each named after a character in Sir
Walter Scott's novels. They live blissfully ever after.

- Note to self: I will need to reconcile Moll's vegetar-
ianism with the life of a sheepdog breeder's wife—
ethically tricky, but likely do-able. Is vegetarian dog
food readily available in remote areas of Scotland?
Could dogs thrive on porridge? These are things to
consider. 🐾

I KNOW THAT WORKING AT THE MALL AND being born into the home of an English professor isn't quite like being born into Newgate Prison. But I have to be candid, dear reader. Issues of personal liberty, overcrowding, and abominable sanitation standards aside, no one in Newgate had to endure being the child of an English professor. If I were to write of my childhood in my own version of *Moll Flanders*, I would begin with the tale of my father on Career Day. My mum came to Tess's and Heathcliff's Career Days, but had to teach during mine. My dad, on the other hand, was not only free, but eager to rise to the occasion. My mother was a tough act to follow: a Career Day legend, she was. The kids loved her because she showed beautiful pictures and gave them colouring sheets and crayons. In his own way, my dad became a bit of a Career Day legend, if only in my mind.

As I recall, my father was one of three parents scheduled for the afternoon and was to speak for five minutes between Rocco Bertolli's mother, who was a veterinarian and brought kittens and baby bunnies for us to pet, and Marissa Simpson's father, who drove a cement truck and brought a model truck that made sounds. My father, not to be outdone, brought overheads, forgetting, it would seem, that grade-two classrooms generally lack overhead projectors. A true professional, he made do without them.

He began his Career Day talk rubbing his hands together excitedly and asking, "Who here can tell me what eponymous means?" Unfazed by the cattle-like stares of my classmates, he commenced a roving and energetic overview of Samuel Richardson and his oeuvre, stopping only once to crouch down and spell out "oeuvre" in pink chalk on a diminutive chalkboard. Used to speaking uninterrupted for eighty minutes, my father surpassed his time leaving Miss Abernathy ahem-ing, Mrs Bertolli tapping her sensibly shod foot, and Mr Simpson playing with the wheels on his cement truck. Throughout, I whispered "please stop please stop please stop" to myself. Just as I grew convinced my father would keep us until grade four, Tracy Kaplansky's finicky bladder created the diversion I had been praying for. I was sad for Tracy and I felt even worse for being happy I was not the one teased at recess for the next week. I don't think she ever knew the level of gratitude I felt toward her incontinence. I do hope things have improved for her on that count.

At the supper table that night my mother chirped, "What did Daddy talk about at your school today?"

When I said, "Eponymity," she wilted.

"Oh Hamish! You didn't."

"Yes, I did," he replied proudly, "And I think it went off crackingly. Didn't it Moll(y)?"

My parents and my siblings looked at me expectantly. I did not know what to say. I knew I couldn't lie. I knew I couldn't tell the truth. I moved carrots around my plate and finally I said, "Tracy Kaplansky peed on the floor." My siblings groaned in fascinated horror and wanted all the details; Tracy and her pee had saved me once again. My father ate the rest of his supper in silence, and when he finished his red Jell-O, he put his bowl in the sink and retreated to his study.

Later that night, my bears and I sat in our bed waiting to be read to and tucked in. I had *The House at Pooh Corner* balanced expectantly on my lap. I could hear my mother talking to my father at the dining-room table.

"Of course they don't know what eponymous means—they're seven years old. Seven, Hamish, not twenty-seven." I couldn't hear what my dad mumbled, but my mother responded, "I know Molly knows what it means, but that's not exactly normal, is it? I don't want her turning out like one of those faculty freak children like...." She whispered a name or two that I could not hear, but I assumed it was Prufrock and Pellinore. After a moment or two, I heard my dad slide his chair back. As he was leaving the dining room, my mother added,

"Hamish, could you give Robbie Burns a rest tonight and read her some Winnie the Pooh instead? Kids like that. Molly likes that. Please?" It took my father longer than normal to climb our stairs, and when he came into my room, he did so with a faux flourish.

"What do you say Miss Moll(y)? Want to hear about Winnie the Pooh and the Honey Tree?"

To this day, I remember the thin veneer of enthusiasm he wore. He knew that I knew his talk had not gone crackingly. It had never occurred to me that parents had feelings and that a child could hurt those feelings. But that's exactly what I had done at supper. I wanted Winnie the Pooh, but I said, "No, read me this," and passed him *A Child's First Robbie Burns Treasury* opened to "Tam o' Shanter." He kissed my head and began:

"When chapman billies leave the street,/ And drouthy neebors, neebors, meet;/ As market-days are wearing late,/ An folk begin to tak the gate." Although I fell asleep part way through, I know he recited the whole poem without even looking at the page, and that the sounds and rhythms of Burns worked their way deeply into my dreams. 🙢

*I*T'S 12:38, AND I'M EATING MY TUNA SANDWICH on a bench near the fish tanks by the dolphin show. I suppose it's cruel to eat a sandwich made of their distant kin in front of them, perhaps in the future I should bring peanut butter. It is the end of my first week at Le Petit Chou, and I feel like I'm starting to get the hang of being a purveyor of fine footwear. I've made some good sales this week and Tim, the supervising manager, is pleased with my progress, especially my polish sales. The one thing I am not quite adjusting to is the forty-four hours a week of standing. My feet and back are killing me. I am also not sure how to stave off the dulling monotony that I am already sensing. There might be a reason why all my co-workers are obsessed with break times and leaving not a fraction of a second late for any coffee, lunch, or dinner break.

I am often bored and find myself making excuses to go into the stockroom to check in with Fanny Price in *Mansfield Park*. I am also a little lonely today and find myself composing letters to Miss Austen. Here's one:

My dear Miss Austen,

I hope you are well. I recall you advising your niece Anna, regarding her writerly aspirations, that "three or four families in a Country Village is the very thing to work on." I too am seeking advice. As you know, I am a young woman not

only living in the south of Edmonton, but selling
low-to-mid quality footwear in Canada's largest
shopping mall. Where am I to find three or four
families in a country village? Without three or
four families or a country village, will I ever be
able to write fiction? Would living in Edmonton
negate any writerly genius I may develop? In
short, is there any hope for me, Miss Austen?
With best love, &c., I am affectionately yours
and somewhat despondent, Molly.

It's 2:09 and Maureen has gone on her "competition
analysis rounds" where she visits other shoe stores. In my
careful reading of our employee manual, I have seen no mention of such an activity. Eugenie, the other full-timer, rolls
her eyes at the phrase "competition analysis," and confided
in me that these rounds have nothing to do with shoes. She
says they're actually "flirt breaks." Maureen apparently is
quite taken with Gordon at Nova's on the main floor. This, I
hasten to clarify, is not her boyfriend Gordon: there is apparently another Gordon.

"The only competition she's checking out is whether the
new part-timer is prettier than she is," Eugenie tells me with
a laugh. Oh, Miss Austen, how I yearn for a country village.

5:10. I am on my dinner break and Miss Austen has not
responded to any of my letters. I will attempt to channel her:

Dear Despondent Molly,

Your life is indeed bereft of romance, not
to mention the sublime, the beautiful, and the
picturesque. However do you exist? But, that is
not your question. Perhaps given your situation,
three or four shoe stores in a prairie city might
instead be the very thing. I hope this adequately
answers your question.

I am aware that you have attempted to
contact me eight times already this week. I would
be most appreciative if you could kindly desist

from summoning me from the afterlife unless it's absolutely necessary. Best wishes &c., Miss Austen

P.S. As per your earlier queries: I do not find Yeats sexy at all; Wordsworth is even more boring in the afterlife; and never trust a poet with a monocle. 🙰

*M*ISS AUSTEN'S SUGGESTION THAT "THREE OR four shoe stores in a prairie city" might indeed be the very thing for me to write about. Indeed, it could become my oeuvre. Maybe my mall novels could become Edmonton's equivalent of Sir Walter Scott's Waverley Novels.

Granted, I do not have stunning highland and lowland landscapes to draw on, nor do I have the lingering tensions surrounding the Jacobite uprisings, but here's what I do have. At the centre of my narrative is Le Petit Chou: a pink shoe store making a nod to Parisian chic in name only. It is not a mere retail outlet, but "a purveyor of fine footwear." If I stand outside my shop's doors and look left, I can see a replica of Christopher Columbus's ship, the *Santa Maria*, which sits under a massive set of skylights. Beside the ship is a lagoon featuring submarines, a dolphin tank, and the Sea Life Caverns. Although I cannot directly see it, I can hear the screams of joyous children flying down slides at the Waterpark and the whoosh of water from the wave pool. If I go around a corner, I can see the accompanying indoor beach where Edmontonians, desperate for a more hospitable clime, lounge on the fake sand. Should I turn my head to the right, I can see the skylights that cover the NHL-size skating rink where, a few times a year, the Oilers practice. If I choose to stroll from my shop, I am not far from Europa Boulevard where I might leisurely perambulate, imagining myself in a quaint, climate-controlled, non-winding, European street.

Nor am I far from Bourbon Street where a lone female such as I might stroll safely around the nightclubs, after picking up a cute new skirt at Le Château, and having a cup of Daiquiri ice cream at Baskin-Robbins. I might also choose to take a longer stroll over to Fantasyland where there is a roller coaster, carousel, giant swing set, flying galleon, and a passel of shifty, suburban carnies.

Above me are lengths of skylights and below me are aviaries containing some small tropical songbirds and three or four peacocks. Evidently, whoever had the idea to put peacocks in an aviary in the world's largest shopping mall never spent much time around peacocks—beautiful, yes. Melodious, hardly. They alarm mall visitors daily with their piercing calls. There are also emus in a glass pen near Entrance Fifty. They appear agitated and bewildered at all times, though that might just be their demeanour. And the dolphins.... I worry about them. I also worry a little about my fellow mall employees. Many of them have the same look of agitated bewilderment as the emus, and I am hoping it is just a coincidence, not a result of spending much of one's waking life in this mall.

My Waverley Mall Novel will need dramatis personae. Maybe I'll create dramatic tension by pitting the managers and employees against each other. Hardly the makings of the Battle of Culloden, but perhaps it will do. In terms of romance, intra-store fraternizing is discouraged, but there seems to be a bit of intra-store something going on between Maureen and Rick, the manager of Prima Donna. I am reluctant to imagine much more on that front but I could certainly summon up something more suitable. The noble and virtuous heroine could be modelled after Eugenie who is nice, gentle, and kind in spite of Maureen's tyranny. There is also a seemingly endless supply of part-time employees and trainees who could supply the rich, sociological details vital for engaging historical fiction.

Lively subplots could be supplied by my fellow mall citizens. Beside Le Petit Chou is a Perkies! clothing store with an extensive staff of really friendly girls who, like their store's name, seem to end all of their sentences with an exclamation point. Most are part-time. On the other side is another shoe store and we never talk to them. There has been a long-standing feud between the stores since Phase Three opened. None of the original staff still works there, and no one knows what the feud was about, yet we still talk about them in whispered tones and never make eye contact. Directly across from us is an upscale fur and leather store with a small staff and a fair bit of attitude. The manager, in particular, seems to have issues with our sub-par leather goods. Down the way is a men's clothing store that appears to cater to men with upscale mullets and a penchant for shiny, metallic-hued suits. Nearby is a brand-new store called The Ottoman Empire that sells only ottomans. On its windows, it has big signs that say "No Chairs!" and "Only Ottomans!" I talked with Kevin, a new employee there, who is already looking for a new job. Three or four stores in a prairie city may not rival Scott's Waverley Novels, but it does give me hope. 🃏

I HAVE NOT HEARD MAUREEN MENTION GORDON the First for some time now. I am starting to think she is flirting with Gordon the Second from the rival Nova store down the corridor to make Rick jealous. It is unclear whether she is trying to enrage Rick on a romantic level or a shoe-selling level. When I asked Maureen, she banished me to the backroom to alphabetize the shoe polish. This is fine by me as I am tired of watching customers roam through my store like sullen, ruminating buffalo searching for bargains (you don't want to make sudden movements or startle them lest they stampede). Plus, I cannot endure Maureen imitating Blanche DuBois when flirting with Gordon any longer. I don't have the heart to correct her when she flutters her mascara-clumped eyelashes and says, "I have always depended on the kindness of strange men."

In recent days, I have become earnest in my attempt to become a novelist, and to read author biographies on my morning bus rides as a way of becoming more literary. This morning I was reading Emily Brontë's biography and learned she died of consumption at the age of thirty. I realized I might only have ten more years to write my equivalent of *Wuthering Heights*. I too could die of consumption. I have no idea what consumption is, but it strikes me as the most beautiful sounding cause of death. The most romantic and beautiful writers all appear to have died from it. I bet it's what happens when you are out walking in the moors, or in the Lake District, and you just get consumed by some overwhelming passion. I could not expect Miss Brontë to have died from anything less romantic. I want to die of consumption too.

I can imagine how Miss Brontë became consumed. Her house is cramped, loud, and smelly. She sits at a table gazing out a window, her pen poised over a bottle of ink. She looks out over the moors. It's probably raining. She is wearing lots of grey wool—shawls, wraps, long skirts. She is writing by candlelight. She sees the moon, although it's probably cloudy. She sighs. She imagines some swarthy, brooding Heathcliffian man wandering the bleak landscape, pining for her. He has the worldly swagger of a young Montgomery Clift and the voice of Alan Rickman. She sighs again and absconds from her cramped, smelly house pursued by her dog, Keeper, who may or may not have the mange. Outside, she can see her breath in the gloomy gloaming. She would say, "Alas, my trusty, canine companion, Keeper, I am consumed by my overwhelming and unrequited passion for this alluring man with his velvety voice. I will wander the moors, pining for him, even though it is very cold and rainy and I am wearing wool that, when wet, will be as smelly as you. Perchance I will succumb to an all-consuming illness in this bleak landscape that mirrors my brooding soul." And in this way, Emily Brontë will be consumed by her passions and will die a short time later of consumption, Keeper by her side. Could anything be sadder?

It is 3:30 now. Maureen came in with Rick while I was thinking about Miss Brontë's dog, and yelled: "What the hell are you still doing back here? Why are you crying?" I couldn't begin to explain about the death of Miss Brontë and the steadfastness of her dog. I told her I was overwhelmed by whether "blue" should come before or after "blue-black." She and Rick were very impressed with my alphabetizing. They were so impressed that they left to visit Prima Donna and consider alphabetization there as well. I am now free to provide shoes to the wandering masses undisturbed by Rick and Maureen.

4:10. I wonder if I could contract consumption through sheer boredom. Could my wandering the bleak, mirrored corridors of the Mall lead to postmodern consumption? How come people don't die of consumption these days? Are we that passionless a society that no one dies of consumption anymore?

5:15. Sigh. Only four more hours to go. What would Emily Brontë do if she worked in a shoe store?

7:45. I think Emily Brontë would eat shoe polish because consumption would take too long to kill her.

7:58. I wonder if Emily Brontë would eat the shoe polish alphabetically.

7:59. If so, would she eat "blue" before "blue-black"?

8:10. I wonder how much polish you'd have to eat until consumption sets in. I really must look up consumption in the encyclopædia.

10:15. Home now. I just looked up consumption in my dad's *Encyclopædia Britannica*. Consumption is just another name for tuberculosis. Suddenly consumption doesn't seem romantic at all. The *Encyclopædia Britannica* is inconclusive about whether boredom can be an actual cause of death. I fear I may find out by the end of the summer. ❦

*I*T IS 6:50 PM. THIS IS THE SLOWEST PART OF the shoe-selling day, and I am alone in the store tonight. Day shoppers have left and night shoppers have yet to arrive. I tell myself there's a buzz in the air tonight, the kind of buzz that suggests two-toned pumps are going to be flying off the shelves, and the evening will be over just like that. Whooosh! That's the sound of an evening vanishing. Whooosh! If I say it enough maybe I can jumpstart my evening.

Is it really only 6:58? I thought for sure it would be at least 7:20. Hmm. Well. Assuming I won't have any late stragglers or any cash-out discrepancies, I should be out of here in two hours and twenty minutes. I expect time will start whizzing by any time now. Whoosh. Whoosh?

It's 7:03 now. I've just returned from peeking down the mall corridors. The only people you can see are other nightshift employees standing outside their shops looking for customers. I waved to Radio Chalet Enrique and chatted with Nancy next door. I danced a few bars of the Charleston to amuse dear, sweet Stephen at Aloysius & Flint, and when I looked up from my curtsy, my eyes met those of the manager of the fur store across the way. He returned my coquettish smile and wave with a stern furrow. He rolled his eyes, turned his back to me, and continued to smoke. "Ouch," gasped Nancy. Enrique shook his head, and walked back into his Radio Chalet. I too have retreated—wounded—to the confines of my shop. Not only does he sell fur (so cruel!) and smoke (so gross!), he is also surly (so rude!). And while I have never admitted this out loud before, he also looks a little like an angry Pekingese dog. But that is not his fault. And I won't hold it against him. The fur selling is between him, his god, and PETA. But the second-hand smoke, I take personally. Not to mention his rude rebuff.

7:20. I have dusted the non-dusty shelves, refilled the receipt paper in the tills, replenished the credit-card slips, and designed a new Machu Picchu–inspired polish display to accent the new Incan-inspired espadrilles that just arrived. My feelings are still hurt by the rebuff from the surly Pekingese, and there is nothing to do, but sulk and furrow at the cigarette fumes that are skulking across the corridor into my shop. He has been standing outside his shop smoking for the past half-hour, and the smoke is really starting to bother me. He seems oblivious to the fact that my scowl clearly communicates, "There are peacocks and quality shoe purveyors inhaling that smoke!" I am too afraid to go ask him to stop. The only time he's stopped smoking was when he had to go in and answer his phone. Hold on. I wonder if Le Petit Chou has a phone book. We do. I have a plan.

7:23. There is indeed a listing for The Fur Emporium. What a simple solution to my problem. His phone rings, he butts out his cigarette, he scuttles back to his lair, and I hang up when he reaches the phone. The air is breathable. I am happy. The peacocks rejoice in the clean mall air. Brilliant.

7:38. I realized I had overlooked a vital error in the internal logic of my Machu Picchu polish display: you cannot polish an espadrille. As I was tearing down my display (really not my best work), I got another whiff of cigarette smoke. He's out there again. This time he has a coffee too. I've done it before and I can do it again. I moved over to the counter, knocked the receiver off the hook, assembled lots of spreadsheets and shoe boxes on the counter to make it look like I'm working, and then I hit "redial." As predicted, he butted out his cigarette, put the lid on his coffee, and then attempted to run without spilling said coffee to catch that possibly important call. Ohhh. Missed it. Too bad. What a shame.

7:40. He's out there again. This is getting too predictable. Redial, butt out, run, missed it, darn. And you were so close this time. Must be important if they keep calling.

8:10. Really? Another cigarette. For the love of peacocks, Sir. You must realize you are compelling me to do this for the greater good. By now my timing is getting impeccable. He's just got that pesky lighter to work and finally lit his cigarette and, ohhh, there's the phone again. Better go get it. Run, Sir! Who could be calling? Can't be me. I'm building a Greek-themed sandal display in plain sight.

8:40. Now he's just out there with a coffee. And I am bored. I can't get my shoebox and protective spray Acropolis to stand, and my cardboard Aristotle looks like Diefenbaker in a toga. I want to hit redial just so I can see him scuttle. But he's glowering like a seething, rabid Pekingese. I dare not do it again. It's 8:46. Maybe just once more. Careful, Sir, don't spill the coffee, it looks hot.

8:52. Two minutes until I can begin to close the doors. Maureen told me there are sensors on the doors that transmit to head office precisely what time the doors open and close, and we'll all be fired if we open late or close early. So far I've seen nothing that would indicate such sensors, but I've killed three minutes looking. One minute left.

*I*T WAS, FOR THE MOST PART, A TRYING DAY AT LE Petit Chou. I have learned that one woman's taupe is another woman's beige, and one woman's beige is another woman's off-white, and yet another woman's biscuit is another woman's ecru.

Here is my day. The first customer came in soon after opening. She was dressed in what is normally marketed as "cruise wear." Her frosted hair and designer makeup were perfect. Her lipstick and nail polish were the colour my friend Nathan calls "beach-slut beige," and she had a tan no one could get in Edmonton naturally. She also had an "I-take-no-prisoners" sort of smile on her face as she surveyed my low-to-mid-price-range shoe offerings. She looked me up and down, bit her cheek, and then tossed out her demand, "I need a taupe slingback. Show me what you have." I instantly went for a nice little Bandolino to which she retorted, "That's beige."

"Of course," I replied and then moved to a Gloria Vanderbilt.

"That's mushroom. I need taupe," she chortled. A taupe Franco Sarto was deemed "bone," and then I lost track as we shuffled through off-white, biscuit, cream, eggshell, and ecru.

Finally, I pulled the shoe I've mentally been calling "cat-barf beige," and she declared, "At last! A taupe shoe! 6 1/2, please." I found her size, she tried them on. She paced the store, stared at herself in the mirror for a creepy amount of time. She turned to make eye contact with me for an uncomfortable two minutes and then said, "I think they pinch. What do you think?"

"We could try the size 7s," I proffered.

She rolled her eyes and said, "I told you. I am a 6 1/2. Always have been and always will be. I do not wear size 7." She continued to stare at herself in the mirror as I scanned the store for additional cat barf–coloured shoes. I found only a pump. When I brought the shoe to her, she met my eye in the mirror, and raised a pencilled-in eyebrow.

"I believe I said it was a slingback I needed." I apologized for the insufficiency of my wares and began straightening my patent purse display. "I guess I am going to have to take my business elsewhere," she sighed, "maybe to a store where they know what colour 'taupe' is. Service isn't what it used to be. You should really work on that if you want to get anywhere in the world."

With resignation, she put her own gold strappy sandals back on, and picked through the sale-rack shoes, while I re-boxed the slingbacks, and kept my eyes down. Cordially, I thanked her for stopping by, and expressed hope she would have a wonderful day and find her taupe slingbacks. As she left the store, I swear I heard the sound of my soul being sucked from me. It was 10:25. I had ten and a half more hours left to go in my shift. I tidied my store while her cigarette-tainted, Oscar de la Renta perfume lingered in a cloud around me. I wondered if her day was brightened for reminding a shoe clerk she was hardly worth the minimum wage she earned.

Around 11:30, another woman stopped in, and said she was looking for a taupe shoe. I pointed out a few in my new display and she said, "That's a little more bone than taupe. I'm looking for something more this colour," and she pointed to a shoe I would call "moss brown." Maybe my sense of taupe really was off. She was friendly and liked the moss brown/taupe shoes and how they fit. She added a pair of sandals, some protective spray, and it was a nice sale for me. I went for lunch and returned at one o'clock. Between one o'clock and three o'clock, four more women came in asking for taupe shoes.

Having learned a few things this morning, I artfully said, "What sort of shade of taupe were you looking for?" and let them identify eggshell, beige, buff, and ecru shoes as "taupe." Each time a woman asked for taupe, I peered across the mall to the Rabid Pekingese, convinced he was finally onto my capers and exacting his revenge by hiring women to come in and torment me about the vagaries of "taupe." Every time I looked out, he seemed indifferent to the goings-on at my shop, and the women who asked for the shoes were actually purchasing them. He couldn't be that expert at setting up a prank. Or could he? If we had five returned pairs of "taupe" shoes tomorrow, I would know it was he, and I would bow to him across the mall in appreciation of his superb pranksmanship. I chalked the "taupe" day up to serendipity for the time being.

At about five o'clock, my day started to turn around. A slightly overweight, middle-aged woman with frizzy, dark hair and a very plain outfit came in. She had a nervous laugh. Her shoes suggested she had fallen for the "where style meets comfort" myth. She told me she was going to a wedding, and had just splurged on a dress at a shop down the mall a bit. She held up the bag, incredulous that she had spent so much. The girl who sold her the dress suggested she purchase a taupe shoe to go with it.

"I really have no idea what colour taupe is. Can you tell me?" I laughed a gentle laugh, nearly convinced the Rabid Pekingese had paid her to come in and ask about taupe shoes. I admitted conspiratorially that I had no idea what colour it was either. "Let's look at your dress and see what we can find," I suggested. She was very excited to show me the dress.

"My husband said to buy what I liked and not to pay attention to price. I've never spent so much money on a dress before. But I really like it." It was a lacy dress with a sweetheart neckline, cream in colour, mid-calf length. Not something I would wear, but it would look nice on my customer, and I could tell she loved it. As I admired it, she lowered her voice and said, "It makes me feel like Princess Diana." We're not supposed to let anyone other than staff in the backroom, but Maureen was on break so I suggested that she use our bathroom to change into her dress so we could find the perfect shoe. When she came out, she was transformed: her dress made her look radiant, and she was glowing with excitement.

"You look beautiful," I smiled. "Your husband is going to love it. Now, let's find you some princess shoes to go with it." We probably spent an hour trying on beige, bone, ecru, eggshell, cream, and off-white shoes. She had just about decided on a safe pair of eggshell shoes, when I suggested we try one more pair, just for fun. I selected a delicate, rosebud-pink pump with a finely shaped heel. They had just come in this morning, and I hadn't been able to put them on the floor yet. They fit her perfectly, and she stood nicely in them. There was a coordinating evening bag and I added that to her ensemble.

She turned in her shoes, smiled at herself in the mirror and said, "These are princess shoes! I love them! And this handbag!" We both stood and admired her transformed self in the shop mirror for a few minutes. As she headed back into the stockroom to change, she paused and said, "My husband told me to go treat myself and buy something pretty for the wedding. He'll never believe how pretty this all is. I couldn't have done it without you and the girl in the dress shop. I think I'm going to go get my hair done special for the wedding too. Thank you." I liked her too much to give her the polish and protective spray speech. As she was paying for her purchases, she no longer seemed like the same lady who walked in. She stood a little taller and her laugh wasn't so nervous.

Feeling as if she'd found a friend in me, she whispered, "I'm thinking I'm going to buy some pretty underwear to wear with it. What do you think? Should I?"

"Absolutely!" I suggested where she should go in the Mall, and that she should ask for Julia. As I handed her the wrapped shoes, I told her again how beautiful she looked, and that I hoped she would have a wonderful time at the wedding. She gave me a big hug, and waved as she left the store. About an hour later, she stopped by to thank me for suggesting Julia, and showed me what she'd bought.

She confessed, "I think I could become addicted to pretty things! Thank you!"

"No, thank you," I said. Although I had said thank you all day, this was the first time I really meant it. ❧

I HAVE ONE MORE HOUR UNTIL CLOSING. IT'S BEEN a nine-to-nine shift. I am exhausted, and my feet are killing me. Style and comfort, no matter what they tell you, are parallel lines that never meet: they never have and they never will. You have to pick one. When asked my opinion on this matter, I always say, "You can always recover from sore feet, but you can never recover from bad style." I should admit that, to date, no one has asked me my thoughts on style versus comfort, but my answer is ready in case someone ever does. I think Coco Chanel would appreciate that I have prepared a snappy, pithy answer.

Standing here in an empty store all night has given me time to think about how I might make the world a better place through my purveyance of middling quality footwear. Knowing how much misery the wrong shoe can bring, perhaps I could bring joy to the populace by matching each Le Petit Chou patron with the perfect shoe. Maybe I could also launch global projects to work toward the greater common good. I have been thinking about my encounter with the mean, taupe lady yesterday. Maybe I could do something to improve the lot of shoe-sales people across the country. I cannot do anything about the minimum wage or the hours, but maybe I could make a small difference in their quality of life.

To this end, I envisioned an international shoe purveyors summit commissioning a task force on the tonal parameters of taupe. I could spearhead the writing of the *International*

Shoe Colour Standards so disputes regarding the exact specifications of taupe could be easily solved. Had I such a volume in my possession yesterday, I could have opened it to the entry on taupe and been authorized to say "I'm sorry, madam, as you can see, that is not a taupe shoe, it is an eggshell shoe. If you would like a taupe shoe, kindly cast your eyes thither toward that shelf yonder. However, if it is indeed an eggshell shoe you desire, what size and heel height dost thou seeketh?"

Once the task force has completed our work on taupe, we could move on to the other pernicious variations collectively known as "that sort of beigey colour." We would scientifically analyze tones and hues so to as to make precise gradations regarding the colours commonly, yet imprecisely, known as sand, ecru, off-white, eggshell, bone, biscuit, buff, cream, café au lait, caramel, camel, oatmeal, fawn, tan, and khaki. After a stellar success with colours in the beige family, we will then proceed to colours like mauve and teal until we've reached the subtlest regions of blue-black. We would also have a small appendix section for men's shoes where we unpack the distinctions among brown, brownish, brown-black, and black. Men's shoes might just require a leaflet.

This venture could be huge. Once we can all say the word taupe, and know with certainty that others will know what we mean, peace and love should spread across the world like a sunrise. 🐝

*L*AST NIGHT'S OPTIMISM ABOUT MAKING THE world a better place through the selling of shoes has been tempered by Maureen's response to my proposed summit on taupe.

"What the hell are you on about? Taupe is taupe. And why is all this grey polish in the window?" I'd barely assembled the Stonehenge I'd created out of the overstock grey polish, and already I was commanded to dismantle it. So much for my solstice display. Granted, it would have been more impressive had I got the flashlight and dancing druids in place before she'd seen it.

This morning I was reading Henry James while waiting for my bus, and I began to wonder what kind of character I would be in one of his novels. I've come to realize that James's novels feature two different kinds of tragedy: fun and dull. Fun tragic involves torrid (*circa* 1880) love affairs, Italian vistas, and dreamy men who are all wrong for you, but who look and smell nice. Dull tragic, on the other hand, has all the miserable aspects of fun tragic, but without all the passion, Italian vistas, and dreamy, nice-smelling men. While I would like to imagine James would put me in the former category, I fear being named Molly might put me in danger of falling into the dull tragic category.

Someone named Molly in a James novel would most certainly have bad teeth, a limited wardrobe of wilted tweed ensembles, and some kind of inconvenient, non-life threatening ailment. Maybe the human equivalent of the weeping eye that afflicts our neighbor's geriatric Bichon Frise. Molly, in a James novel, would also probably have a gormless husband with a name that is difficult to say with a swoon. Something like Ronald. Try to say it with a swoon: Ronald is an entirely swoon-less name. Ronald would probably have an equally unfortunate wardrobe consisting of five pairs of mud-cultured trousers and a number of interchangeable cardigans and vests that, in spite of Molly's solemn laundering interventions, would always smell like wet dogs and kippers. Ronald would also, in spite of her gender, call Molly "Old Chap," and would say it with a gummy smile, thinking it to be a very affectionate name for a woman. However, because this is a James novel, Ronald never notices Molly fighting back the acrid bile that gathers in the back of her throat every time he calls her "Old Chap."

Further, Ronald does not know that a neighbour lad once daringly called a young Molly his "melancholy flower" behind the woodshed, and that she subsequently filled her afternoons of washing up and mending socks dreaming of swoony lovers calling her "my golden marigold," "my little love turnip," or "my sweet Empire biscuit." Ronald's use of "Old Chap" is a painful reminder that she is no one's marigold, turnip, or Empire biscuit. Although Molly has regrets, she might think, "given my bad teeth and my left eye that weeps like that of an ageing Bichon Frise, maybe being called 'Old Chap' by a man named Ronald isn't so bad after all. There could be worse fates. I am unable to conjure any, but I am certain there must be some."

And then, because she is in a James novel, Molly will spend nine pages thinking back to what could have been, had "the woodshed incident" taken a different turn (though, in reality, it was hardly an incident at all or even really a woodshed, just an awkward handshake near a pile of logs). Stirring her silt-coloured tea, she juxtaposes those girlhood dreams with her first encounters with Ronald. Because this is a James novel, Molly will recount his garrulous, yet earnest proposal, which he had outlined on crumpled paper that might have once have been wrapped around a ten-pound cod. And then, a hundred years later, an undergraduate on a crowded bus will write in the margin "Gasp! How tragic it is to be named Molly!" ❧

ONIGHT MY DAD PICKED ME UP FROM THE Mall, and we stopped at Safeway to get some groceries for my late-night supper. I was grateful for the ride home: it had been a very long day, and my feet were incredibly sore. My dad whistled a Scottish jig as I pushed a cart through the Safeway. My body said, "I am tired. Give me what I want," and I complied. I started with vegetarian hotdogs and Kraft Dinner, and then added the Peek Freans cookies with the red centres, and finished with a bottle of Cherry Coke. "Long day?" my dad asked. I could only nod. By the checkout, I noticed a display of tiny, green shamrock plants for ninety-nine cents. They were looking a bit past their prime, but nothing that couldn't be healed by a bit of real sunlight and affection. I lifted one and gave my dad a "should I?" look, and he returned with an "of course" smile. I held it carefully on my lap on the way home and named it Nora.

As I prepared my dinner, my parents sipped glasses of wine. For their amusement, I recast anecdotes about Maureen into Dickensian tales of woe, and they laughed and clapped. As I ate, they described their days: Mum gave a lengthy overview of a new Italian painter she'd started working on, and Dad was in raptures about his new book project "The Lesser-Known Eponymists." As I listened to their professorial back and forth, I tried to keep my mind from wandering back to the Mall and the second consecutive nine-to-nine shift I faced tomorrow. I would be sitting on the Mall-bound bus in less than nine hours. How do you make the most of the hours you have off when you're so tired you can hardly chew?

This morning I tried to get to the Mall early, hoping to ease myself into the long day. It's not a bad place in the mornings, before the staff rush in at the last minute, and eager shoppers peer impatiently into stores at 8:57. I like the Mall in its morning silence. I stop and say hello to the dolphins Gary, Howard, Mavis, and Maria. I watch, from a distance, the emus by Entrance Fifty. I like to give them their morning space: their days are longer and harder than mine by far. I like to watch the peacocks prepare for their day. In the mornings, they're elegant and placid, but by noon, they're screaming at shoppers with their surprisingly shrill call. Just yesterday, a shopper jumped, startled, and teetered in too-high pumps.

"What is that horrible sound?!" she asked.

"That tortured trumpet sound? It's one of the peacocks," I said.

"How can something so beautiful sound so horrifying?"

I often wonder that myself. In the open silence of the morning, the endless corridors of glass and mirrors make it seem like you can see for miles, yet all you can ever see is mall. The plants are fake, the birds caged, the waves mechanical, and the dolphins despondent. Even the sunlight shining through the skylights seems artificial as if heat, cold, sounds, and smells of the real world are things we need to be protected from. At lunch today, I wanted to see real sunlight, feel real air, and sit on real grass. By the time I walked to the edge of the parking lot and made my way across and through the backed-up mall traffic, I had to turn back or I would have been late. Maureen has already threatened to write me up for tardiness once this week, and I couldn't risk a second threat.

Every day I grow more and more convinced that the Mall is designed to wear you down: it makes you think it's easier not to leave, makes you find excuses to stay, makes you find reasons to come in on your days off. You need to pick up a paycheque, go to a movie, meet a friend for lunch, purchase that cute little handbag that just can't wait until tomorrow. First it makes you think, "All my friends are here, everything I would ever want to eat is here, everything I would want to do is here. I could live here." Then it makes you think, "I know I wanted to be a kindergarten teacher, a landscape artist, a sound engineer, a fashion designer, a hair stylist, but I have a good life here. I could stay here." One could study marine biology in the Sea Life Caverns, take a journey in a tiny submarine, skate on the NHL-size hockey rink, swim in the wave park, explore the world like Columbus on the replica *Santa Maria*, sneak away for a romantic getaway in Europa Boulevard with a special someone, network and schmooze over a round of mini golf, make your fantasies come true playing Whac-A-Mole with loved ones, or ride on the roller coaster in Fantasyland. Even better, one could meet one's soulmate at Chang's House of Egg Rolls in the Food Court and, before one's plum sauce is spilled, decide to get married at the Fantasyland Chapel, and honeymoon at the Fantasyland Hotel (perhaps selecting the "Luxury Igloo" theme room). Then, those thoughts of becoming a kindergarten teacher, a landscape artist, a sound engineer, a fashion designer, a hair stylist, and maybe even a novelist, start to fade away. I see it happening to myself and it scares me. There are times when I wonder if the screams I hear are the peacocks below or the sounds of my dreams dying.

It's 11:00 now. I should get to bed soon. I need to catch my bus in eight and a half hours. I've wished my parents a good night, and left them to their lively discussion of department politics. I gave Nora a bit of water, and placed her in our sunniest window. I wished her a sweet good night and lightly caressed one leaf. There is much delight and loveliness in this tiny plastic pot. 🐾

*T*ODAY WHEN MAUREEN GOT BACK FROM LUNCH with Rick, she was as giddy as a poodle with a new chew toy. I endured watching a goodbye that lasted eight whole minutes. Maureen was either oblivious or indifferent to the fact that she was spending my lunch hour flirting with a man in a metallic, pea-green suit. When they parted, she sashayed up to me waving a pink envelope. I knew she was dying for me to ask about it but I was curious to see how long she could last before bursting with the tantalizing news contained therein. I focused my attention on the polish rack while waiting for her to release me for my lunch break. She bounced on the spot as I moved the blue-black in front of the black in our display. She waited until I had straightened and dusted the very last black polish, and then exploded with her news: Rick had written her a poem. And not just any poem, a *love* poem. And, did I want to see it? "Absolutely not" was clearly not an option since the Polo-scented card was out of its envelope and in front of my nose before I could sneeze.

I could transcribe for you, word for word, Rick's poem, and so could you, dear reader, if you have watched MuchMusic, or turned on a radio at any time in the past four years. Rick's "poem" was nothing more than an unattributed transcription of "Never Gonna Give You Up." Somehow, Maureen had been impervious to the Rick Astley juggernaut that had taken over every stereo in the Mall for the past several years, and I hadn't the heart to burst the bubble of her elation.

"You do that reading stuff. Have you ever seen anything so beautiful?" She didn't wait for an answer, but skipped to the back room to re-do her hair, and reapply her perfume before I was allowed to go for lunch. I was livid. Not only had I missed half-an-hour of my lunch break, Rick was trying to pass off a Rick Astley song to Maureen as: (a) his own (b) poetry (c) *love* poetry.

Later in the afternoon, Rick stopped by while Maureen was helping a woman with bunions find a pair of taupe, open-toed, dressy sandals. Knowing she would be occupied in the stock room for some time, he took the liberty of sidling up to me while I tidied my new Canada Day display. I'd used red and white Keds to make a Canadian flag.

"Did Maureen show you her card?" he asked, suppressing a laugh.

"Yes, she did, Rick Astley," I said, suppressing as much scorn as I could.

"I can't believe she fell for that. I'm still laughing," he said. I stared at my asymmetrical Keds maple leaf as he waited for me to join in his laughter. I couldn't.

"You know, Rick, Maureen might not be the smartest girl you'll ever meet, but she's a good person. You can't hurt her. If you don't tell her what you did, I will." I knew standing up to a member of the management team could cost me my job but I really didn't care. Maureen wasn't my favourite person in the world, but you don't mess with hearts. Or poetry. Miss Austen taught me that. As Rick swooshed away in his metallic-pea suit, I had no idea what would happen to me or Maureen. But I knew he'd be Rick Ghastly in my mind forever. ❦

$\mathcal{T}$HIS MORNING, I WAS LATE GETTING UP. I DID not sleep well. Last night, I arrived home from work at about 10:00 p.m. and spent an hour on the phone with Susan debating who had the worse summer job. I had the whole taupe debacle, Maureen's thirst for power, Rick's excess of Polo cologne, and people's bunions. She cleaned up kiddy barf nearly every day. Le Petit Chou had its faults, but it was better than a day camp for six-year-olds. Still, I had a hard time falling asleep, since sleep only seemed to hasten another nine-to-nine shift at the Mall. I overslept, and then ended up running for the bus. As I settled into my back-bench seat and caught my breath, I realized I'd left *Sense and Sensibility* on my bedside table, and would have to endure the trip without the companionship of Miss Austen and the Dashwood sisters.

At first, I thought I would spend the forty-five minutes in quiet contemplation of the sunny morning, viewing the world as an apprentice novelist might. Within a few minutes, I was too wedged in by fellow commuters to have any sort of meditative experience. To make things worse, an umbrella became lodged under my ribs. Occasionally, I moved awkwardly in that "I'm sorry to bother you, but your umbrella is jabbing me in the ribs" kind of way. The lady next to me gave me an "Oops, I'm sorry. I see my umbrella is impaling you every time we happen upon one of the many potholes that mar the asphalt of our fair city, but alas I cannot move it" kind of look. Upon receiving this look, I reciprocated with a raised eyebrow and a look that I hoped would convey, "I am sorry. A point of clarification, if you please. Is it that you cannot move the umbrella, or will not move it?" She countered with an "I am somewhat sorry. Please, let it go." I countered with "Are you aware there is no sign of rain in the five-day forecast?" She offered the final look that said, "I have grown weary thinking of you, your ribs, and my umbrella. Let us instead solve this in the Canadian way. Let us pretend everything is fine and stare at the man eating his buttered toast, retrieved just now from his briefcase, shall we? Oh look, he has paper napkins too. What forethought." And so we stared ahead and watched a man eat buttered toast from a Ziploc bag. Sometimes I hate being a polite Canadian.

I tried to salvage the morning bus ride as best I could. I sighed and said to myself, "I will sit here and observe the world as a young Edmontonian Thackeray might. Surely riding a bus to Canada's largest shopping mall on a sunny morning is excellent training for an aspiring novelist." I waited for inspiration to come. Toast Man retrieved another course of his breakfast, and I changed his name accordingly to Peeled-and-Quartered-Orange Man. Meanwhile the serenity of the silent, morning bus ride was shattered by the arrival of two women in mid-conversation:

"Is that the brother with the girlfriend who has such terrible problems with bunions?"

"No, that's my other brother. This is the brother I hadn't talked to in thirty years."

"The one who found Jesus?"

"Well, he found him but it didn't really take."

"It's funny that you mention bunions because my brother's wife just had surgery for her bunions. [Again with the bunions....] It's quite the procedure, let me tell you...." And then she proceeded to tell not only her friend, but the entire bus the unpleasantries of bunion surgery. Why, why must I, with my non-bunioned feet, endure the tyranny of bunions in my non-working hours? (For the record, it appears that bunion surgery *is* quite the procedure.) Fending off the details, my optimistic self struggled to find some sort of artistic salvation in the morning. Finding none, I put Dire Straits'

Making Movies on my Discman, turned up the volume, and let the world fade away. There was something about this album, old as it was, that made me think of happier things. It never failed to bring me joy.

Any serenity I'd found in Dire Straits quickly dissipated. I stepped in a giant wad of pink gum in the parking lot and then Hutterites, preparing to sell eggs to merchants, stared at me for an uncomfortable amount of time. It wasn't until I looked down at the gum on my shoe that I realized my new, long, black-and-white, polka-dotted skirt was identical to the Hutterite women's. They followed me for a few minutes. Perhaps they thought me an escapee of the colony. I lost them on the escalator where I encountered the Rabid Pekingese chain smoking at the top. He greeted me with "Tsk tsk! Someone's having a bad hair day and it sure isn't me!"

When I got to Le Petit Chou, Maureen and her keys were nowhere in sight, so I waited outside for seven minutes. Having sensed her surliness from fifty feet, I thought it prudent not to remind her of the sensors in the door that reported opening and closing times to head office when she arrived. Instead I tried to lighten the mood with my new shoe joke: "Taupe o' the morning to ye!"

"What the hell are you talking about?" was not quite the response I was looking for. I'll try it out on Eugenie later. She'll laugh.

Maureen and the other managers had a meeting this morning, so after she scuttled off, I had the store to myself. Even that didn't cheer me up since Maureen left me to deal with a box of twenty-five jars of Springtime Canary Yellow polish we'd been sent instead of our requested fifteen jars of Nutty Bordeaux Brown. I was looking at the nine different forms needed to return the order when Mall Cop Kenneth arrived to hand-deliver the weekly mall crime bulletin. Normally, the latest developments in the roving shoplifting ring provide me with at least fifteen minutes of amusement but not even Kenneth could cheer me up. When I met his report with indifference, he was emphatic:

"It's getting really serious, Molly. They practically cleared out Das Leather Haus in a matter of minutes last Tuesday.

Can you imagine the kind of damage they could do here? You need to be alert. And prepared. You could be next." Kenneth then handed me a pamphlet called "How to be Alert. And Prepared." He left, pointing his finger menacingly at me: "Think about it. It could be you in next week's bulletin."

I did think about it. I started thinking about all those roving thieves with leather goods that needed protecting and polishing. I also recalled that the window displays in Das Leather Haus had recently featured many items in a hue that might be considered Springtime Canary Yellow. I then wondered how one might go about inviting a band of rogue shoplifters to Le Petit Chou to—how shall we say—take care of a certain polish problem.

Maureen arrived back from the managers' meeting fuming about mall politics ("they're way too complex for you to understand"), and declared herself in need of a "serenity break." She stomped off to find nearly an hour's worth of serenity, and that made me late for my lunch break. By the time I headed out of the store for lunch, I was inches away from quitting. How could I have forgotten the Dashwood sisters at home, especially when I needed their companionship so badly? Realizing that I could not handle another hour of mall life without a novel in my hands, I dashed to the book shop by the rink, nodded at Ray behind the desk, planted my feet firmly in the Penguin Classics section, and took a deep breath.

For the first time all day, I felt like I could breathe. I stood, poised and still, in front of the shelves of Penguins, and took it all in. There was someone else in my section, but he and the Mall faded away as I imagined losing myself in the rough, but warmly coloured pages of a brand-new Penguin Classic. I basked in that new Penguin smell. I didn't know where to start. The books seemed so perfect with their nearly identical black and red spines running the length of the shelf. Some were old friends: Miss Austen, Mrs Woolf, Mr James, Miss Brontë, Miss Burney. I touched their covers gently to say hello. Others I knew and kept my distance: a nod of respectful acknowledgement went to Mr Sterne and Mr Richardson. Mr Tobias Smollett and I pretended we did not see each other; we'd had a brief yet intense encounter last semester, and it hadn't turned out well. Others I knew by name only, and I ran my finger across spines displaying the names of Wilkie Collins, Ann Radcliffe, Anthony Trollope, Elizabeth Gaskell. I read the back covers, and each offered to take me somewhere new and, more importantly, far away from the Mall.

Standing in front of these novels, these old friends and new friends, I felt a swell of tears, and suddenly realized how tired I was. I was tired in ways that sleep would not cure. I was tired of shoes. I was tired of reading about places I would never go. I was tired of people. I was tired of the sameness of every day. I was tired of protective sprays. I was tired of feeling alone. I was tired of the endless stream of new people and the never-ending parade of the same people. I was tired of the same old thing being passed off as the next new thing. I was tired of smiling at people with smiles I did not mean. I was tired of saying "Yes, they will stretch," when I knew they would only stretch after a few painful wearings, and bridesmaids would hate me before the flower girl started down the aisle. I was tired of not being smiled at. I was tired of sad dolphins in a tank. I was tired of feeling sad for sad dolphins in a tank. I was tired of staring at people's toes. I was tired of convincing people they needed polish for shoes that would not last the season. I was tired of looking at my watch, of counting hours I would have to endure in the store. I was tired of looking at my watch, and of lamenting the countdown of minutes left on my breaks. And, finally, I was most tired of not being Marianne Dashwood reading poetry with her Willoughby.

I longed to read novels in segments longer than twenty-six minutes. I had come to the Penguin section seeking something to get me through the rest of the day, to help me escape the Mall. In spite of the lure of new Penguin authors, I kept returning to Miss Austen. I needed her friendship, her kindness, her wit. Marianne Dashwood would know exactly what I was feeling, so I slid *Sense and Sensibility* off the shelf, and headed to the checkout. It was an hour's wage, and I already owned two copies, but it was a necessity.

As I waited in line, I clung to *Sense and Sensibility*, itching to find the chapter I needed as my remaining moments of solitude ticked away. The American customer ahead of me struggled with our curious currency: "Are these Goonies worth one dollar or two?" Ray and I exchanged stoic smiles that said, "I feel your pain, fellow mall employee," while the remaining minutes of my break ran through my hands like hot sand. I expect I sighed louder than I should have. A voice behind me seemed to take this as a conversation starter.

"You seemed to know exactly what you were looking for." I turned around and saw a tall man with the same hairstyle as one of my favourite MuchMusic vjs. He looked vaguely familiar. "Back there," he added, "by the Penguins." I realized he was the man with whom I'd shared the close confines of the classic fiction section today and also, I realized, on more than one occasion. Although our conversations had never been more than "pardon me" or "excuse me," I thought from our shared fondness for Penguins that he might understand. I smiled, and said, "Yes. Jane Austen. I don't leave home without her. Well, actually, I did leave home without her this morning and I've deeply regretted it." He nodded and smiled. I added, "What are you getting?"

"Steinbeck. I always leave home without him. He's a dreadful travelling companion." I laughed and said, "I might leave him home too." He smiled, and Ray rang up my novel, giving me his discount with a wink, and placing it in a bag knowing I'd want to keep it pristine. When I left the store, I turned to wave and smile to the Penguin man. Perhaps I should have stayed to talk, but I had seven minutes left before I needed to head back to Le Petit Chou, and I needed at least five minutes of Austen to save my soul. I found a quiet bench by the rink and flipped to the page I needed to read. I breathed deeply and then began:

> The whole country about them abounded in beautiful walks. The high downs which invited them from almost every window of the cottage to seek the exquisite enjoyment of air on their summits, were an happy alternative when the dirt of the

valleys beneath shut up their superior beauties; and towards one of these hills did Marianne and Margaret one memorable morning direct their steps, attracted by the partial sunshine of a showery sky, and unable longer to bear the confinement which the settled rain of the two preceding days had occasioned.

I closed my book. I was now able to face the rest of my day. 🥀

I WILL GO OUT ON A LIMB AND PROFFER THIS: men need to read more novels by Miss Austen. If they did, I'm certain they would see that wooing women is much more than yelling "woooo!" from a moving car, or pointing duelling finger guns at them, and making an annoying "click click" sound. These two techniques have been launched at me with increased frequency ever since I started using the Body Shop's dewberry shampoo and conditioner. In fact, I've been fending off potential suitors with a stick lately. The new man, Stewart, at Monsieur Suave Suit has been buying polish from me almost daily. Eugenie is convinced he has a crush on me, but I'm certain he must buy it to condition his secret collection of Elvis leather jumpsuits at night. Both scenarios are equally creepy. Even Maureen has noticed that since I changed shampoos, men have been drawn to me like fruit flies to an overripe peach.

Last night, Susan, Genevieve, and I went to the Ritz Diner, and ended up dancing with British soldiers who were training at one of the bases out of town. In a particularly awkward romantic moment, one of them nestled into my dewberry-infused hair, and whispered, "How'd you like to learn to drive a tank next weekend?" While always keen to learn a new skill, I politely declined. He nevertheless wrote his phone number on a two-dollar bill that I used for bus fare this morning. When I told Maureen and Eugenie the tank story, Maureen said, "If this is your approach to romance, it's your own damn fault that you spend your evenings reading alone." Eugenie shrugged with compassion, and Maureen said she needed to run an errand (she returned with what appeared to be two dewberry-purple bottles in a Body Shop bag).

Maybe there is romance in my life, but just not the kind I'm looking for. None of my potential suitors has a hint of Mr Darcy, Mr Knightley, Willoughby, nor even Colonel Brandon. If the British soldier had prefaced his offer with, "My feelings will not be repressed. You must allow me to tell you how ardently I desire to teach you how to drive a tank on the weekend," I would most certainly be pondering what one might wear to drive a tank instead of reconsidering my shampoo right now. Sadly, I might have to eschew all the good things dewberries do for my hair to fend off the onslaught of what my eighteenth-century writer friends would call rakes, fops, jackanapes, and popinjays. It's sad that we do not use these words in the twentieth century. Maybe I should resolve to single-handedly bring the word "popinjay" back into modern parlance. And maybe the word "parlance." At times, I fear I've chosen a very tough row to hoe. 🪶

ONIGHT FOR DINNER, I FLED THE LAND OF mid-quality shoes, and retreated to Café Orleans. Before taxes, it's two and a half hours' wages to have soup and salad there, but the thought of eating one more stir-fry and meatless eggroll out of a Styrofoam box makes this a small price to pay for fifty-six minutes of escape. I brought Miss Austen's *Persuasion* and ate salad on a real china plate and soup from a real china bowl. I clinked the cutlery on the china a few times just because I could. Even though it cost me most of what I earned tonight, it was worth it because I was able to convince myself I was somewhere else. In many ways, the Mall should be an excellent place for me since it works tirelessly to convince its denizens they are anywhere but Edmonton. Of course, the illusion works best if you've not actually been to Paris, New Orleans, a beach, or a pirate lagoon.

As I waited for my soup, I was surprised to see the man from the bookstore seated at a table across the room. As the only two diners in the small café, it was hard not to make eye contact. I think he recognized me, too, from the Penguin shelves a few days ago. After he placed his order, he nodded at me from across the café, and raised his paperback Steinbeck as one might raise a glass of wine. I smiled, and raised my copy of *Persuasion*. He laughed a gentle laugh, and returned to his reading, while I returned to my newly arrived soup and to the Cobb at Lyme Regis where Louisa Musgrove would soon fall.

When my fifty-six minutes were up, I was no longer Molly of the Mall, tackling the nomenclature of a colour no one really likes. I was someone I liked being. Banished from my brain were words like merchandising, price-look-up codes, and regional management. I was Anne Elliot, ready to take on the Mall with cheerful determination and relentless pluck. As I passed the Penguin man, the rhythms of Austen were still dancing in my mind. I realized there was a smile on my face when the Penguin man caught my eye and smiled back. He tilted his head chivalrously and said, "I do hope, Miss Austen, that you have a very pleasant evening." His charm took me by surprise, and, before I knew what was happening, "Why thank you. I hope you have a pleasant evening too, Penguin Man," flew right out of my mouth in a Scarlett O'Hara accent that I have never used before in my life. And then, I curtsied. I have no idea why.

As I fled into the Mall's Bourbon Street, I heard his rich laugh echoing behind me. Winding through the mirrored maze of the Mall, I realized I'd just botched the one chance I had at making friends with perhaps the only other person in this mall as addicted to Penguin Classics as I.

Thankfully, for the rest of the night, I was kept busy calling every store in the district trying to round up eight pairs of the same open-toed slingbacks in peacock blue for a wedding party. Normally I would resent an evening activity like this, but I was happy to be busy and went the extra mile by securing eight jars of peacock-blue polish, too.

"Just in case," I said. "You really can never underestimate the importance of polish." I regretted Tim wasn't there to hear me quote his favourite section of the manual. When I found the final pair of 7 1/2s, the bride was so grateful she cried and invited me to the reception. As I think about it, I realize she never supplied me with the details of her reception. I smiled, nodded, and waved as she and her bridesmaids left my store and giggled down the echoing corridors.

Le Petit Chou seemed dour and silent after they had all left, and I was grateful that closing was only ten minutes away. Now, in the silence and dark of my room, I can no longer deny that I am a completely irredeemable literary heroine. Miss Austen, I know, would not have wasted a scrap of paper on me. Clearly, I am no Elizabeth Bennet, no Emma Woodhouse, no Marianne Dashwood. Maybe on my more promising days I might be a Miss Bates, a Kitty Bennet, or a forgettable character used only to make a point about the much more interesting heroine. Sometimes, I think my thwarted attempts at literary heroine status would make Anne of Green Gables recoil in horror and disappointment. I'd better go to sleep; I am a mere eight hours away from being reunited with a new shipment of ecru polish that needs to be received, priced, and restocked. 🕰

HIS AFTERNOON WE HAD AN EMERGENCY, all-staff meeting because there was a big announcement. It was decided that part-timers would oversee the stores for the duration of the meeting so that "all staff" could attend. Maureen was horrified at the prospect of leaving part-timers in charge of Le Petit Chou and articulated great detail the havoc they might wreak on our shelving systems in the hour of our absence. But we left our shop in the hands of the inadequately compensated and inaccurately name-tagged, and, according to all filed reports, nothing untoward or irreparable occurred within the hour.

The big announcement was this: July's top seller of polishes and protective sprays in all of Canada was not only in Western Canada, it was in this very mall. Yes, it was true. District 779 had the nation's top seller of polishes and protective sprays in its midst. Who could it be? Gentle Reader, it is I.

Yes. I am Canada's top Purveyor of Polishes and Protective Spray for July 1995. My achievement was met with pride by Tim, tears of joy from Diana, and smug indifference from most of my co-workers. As I opened my mouth to express my gratitude for the award and reaffirm the importance of polish and protective spray, Maureen interrupted my acceptance speech with "I taught her! I taught her everything she knows! We did it, Molly! You and I are the top sellers in Canada!" After that, I really didn't have much to say because everyone had already started to pack up and return to their stores, clearly disappointed in the big announcement. I received a photocopied certificate with "July" and my name handwritten in felt pen and a ten-dollar gift certificate for any regular-priced purchase at Le Petit Chou, Foliage, Prima Donna, or Tuesday's. Eugenie seemed genuinely happy for me, and we laughed about how it was Stewart's alleged crush on me that pushed my polish sales, as they said, "to national attention." I gave Eugenie the gift certificate, since she's a much better salesperson than I am; and she's been eyeing a cute handbag at Prima Donna for weeks. As a special treat, Tim took Diana and me to Orange You Glad, and I didn't have to use my break time.

"Anything you want, ladies!" he announced. When Diana was ordering he whispered to me, "Can you spot me? I left my wallet in the car."

In addition to earning me a certificate, the opportunity to purchase lunch for my supervisors, and the begrudging admiration of my co-workers, my polish-selling acumen won me something quite remarkable: a bit of freedom. Tim seems to think I know what I'm doing, so leaves me alone, and Maureen doesn't dare mess with me now that I'm Tim and Diana's ticket to national prominence. Today could be an important turning point for my literary career. 🦋

AUREEN HAS TAKEN HER LUNCH WITH someone else named Gordon from the Phase Two Pegasus store. She called it a "merchandising strategy lunch," and said she might be late. In her absence, I have been able to think about what I hope will be my Great Canadian Novel set in Edmonton. If suffering be the muse of great art, surely sore toes, insufferable co-workers, and peoples' ugly feet should allow me to pen something remarkable this summer, perhaps even during my shifts.

Any kind of personal activities are forbidden whilst on the floor, but I think I've hatched a solid plan in the event of a random Tim invasion or, worse still, a spot check from Diana. Using my favourite pen, I've drawn up a sketch of our polish and protective sprays display rack, on graph paper for extra effect. I have lots of arrows, measurements, and sidebars. Across the top I've written "Organizing Schemata: Polishes." My plan is to have this sketch nearby so I can quickly move it to the front of my notepad if I am happened upon. Any panic that I might exude can be explained with "I didn't want to share my new schemata until it was completely finished. Plus, I haven't even started with the protective sprays."

I know my plans will be greeted with great elation for the initiative I appear to be taking. I know this because when I took the employee manual with me on lunch one day, I happened to pass Tim, Diana, and some other HQ people as they had their power lunch at the Orange You Glad. Diana recognized the pink binder, and told Tim I had management potential. When my "going the extra mile" was raised at the staff meeting, I didn't have the heart to confess I took it because the thick binder works well as a lap desk for eating a sandwich while reading a novel. I still feel guilty about that. One of the employees from the Phase One location with management aspirations looks daggers at me every opportunity she gets. Being pegged as a "good shoe citizen" has allowed me some extra leeway, for which I am deeply grateful. I hate to misuse the system in this way, but a writer must do what she must do to pursue her craft. Miss Austen kept a door hinge unoiled to give her sufficient warning to hide her writing from family members and servants. I have a diagram of an alphabetized, shoe polish rack. We writers must all have our little tricks.

On a happier note, it appears I did not make a complete fool of myself last night at Café Orleans. I passed the bookstore on my way to eat my lunch, when I spied the Penguin Man sitting on the bench across from it. He smiled and gave me a little wave. I waved back and held up *Persuasion*. He held up his Steinbeck. For a brief moment, I wondered, "What would *Persuasion*'s Anne Elliot do now?" but then realized she would nod cordially, and proceed walking down the Mall, using her sensible millinery to prevent meaningful eye contact with a man not formally introduced to her. This might be why I so rarely summon *Persuasion* in my daily life decisions. Against her protests and hushed lectures about decorum, Anne Elliot and I accepted the Penguin Man's invitation to join him on his bench. How could anyone resist an invitation from someone who gazed at shelves of Penguin Classics like they were the Cliffs of Dover? I felt Anne Elliot bristle as I tucked *Persuasion* into its protective plastic bag, but being one of Miss Austen's more stoic heroines, she did not say much.

He drank a coffee while I ate my sandwich. He is older than I—perhaps about thirty and, considering his age, he dresses fairly well. He has warm brown eyes and hair that seems willfully askew. I am still smiling because his first question was, "How is *Persuasion*?" I told him that Louisa Musgrove had just injured herself at the Cobb and he replied, "Ah, yes, very memorable scene."

"You've read Jane Austen?"

"Of course."

"Of course?!" I said to myself, but responded, "And how are the mice and men of Steinbeck?" aloud.

"Hardly uplifting but very interesting." Before I could stop myself, I was quoting Robert Burns, "'The best-laid schemes o mice an men, gang aft agley,/ An' lea'e us nought but grief an' pain, For promis'd joy!'" As I got to "gang aft agley," I was convinced I would lose my new friend by outing myself as the complete nerd that I am, but I carried on. I had to. I was raised to never end Burns recitation in the middle of a stanza, and I would now pay the price for my questionable upbringing. Instead of the look of bewildered incredulity I was expecting, the Penguin Man smiled and said, "Burns. 'To a Mouse.'" To which I added, "'on Turning Her Up in Her Nest with the Plough. November 1785.' Sorry. I'm a bit of a Burns purist."

He laughed, and noted I knew my Burns very well. I admitted I willingly read a lot of Burns as a child, and he nodding knowingly. There was something about him that made me feel comfortable enough to make the rare confession that, on occasion, well, on most Burns Days, my family would play Burns-word Scrabble where words like "cleekit," "swarf," and "parritch" were all perfectly acceptable. I told him how my mother holds the family Scrabble record for getting "whaizle" on a Triple Word Score. Having thoroughly embarrassed myself, I turned the conversation back to Steinbeck. I had to admit to only knowing a short story or two, and mentally added Steinbeck to my list of should-reads. We talked about our favourite authors and I discovered he has read more than anyone else I know, other than my dad and, unlike most of the men I know, he reads women authors. After a short lull, he said, "I think this might be the first conversation I've had about novels in the past six months. Thank you."

"No, thank you," I replied. "I think this might be the first conversation about novels I've had with another living person in this mall." I told him I am sometimes compelled to imagine conversations with dead authors on my lunch hour to stave off the ennui and boredom. Though I didn't say loneliness, I think he knew that too.

We both smiled and sat silent for a while as we watched the scraggly crowd gather for the one o'clock dolphin show. Their presence reminded me I would need to head back to work soon. I felt emboldened to ask,

"If you don't mind me asking, I've seen you around the Mall a few times, but you don't strike me as a shopper."

To which he replied, after a brief pause, "I'm here for work." I pressed him a bit further, and he sheepishly admitted that he is a musician, and spends his time playing piano in large hotel bars across Western Canada. This weekend, he's at the Fantasyland Hotel. He met my excitement with indifference.

"It's not quite what I'd envisioned for my life when I decided to become a musician, I admit. But it pays the bills. Or enough of them."

"And you get to see the dolphin show at the Mall," I added, hoping to make him smile.

"That I do, that I do, Miss Austen." As Gary, Howard, Mavis, and Maria were being coaxed out of whatever solace they find in their tank when not performing, I knew my time with the Penguin Man was drawing to a close. I didn't know what I should say. I liked the Penguin Man. He made me smile. Anne Elliot was nervously aheming. My inner Marianne Dashwoood was shushing her. My inner Lydia Bennet was egging me on.

"Maybe I should come see your show at the hotel. What time do you play?" He laughed nervously and said, "Have you been to that hotel bar? I think too well of you to suggest you come there." Gary, Howard, Mavis, and Maria were starting to warm up—my cue to assemble my bits of lunchtime detritus and steel myself to return to Le Petit Chou. I was just starting to think that the Penguin Man's silence meant I would likely never see him again when he suddenly said, "Maybe you and *Persuasion* would like to join me and Steinbeck at Café Orleans again?" He walked me back to my shop and we made plans to meet tomorrow on my nine-to-nine shift for dinner. I saw Maureen at the counter, tapping her too-small, pointy shoes. I knew my two-minute tardiness would mean she couldn't give her hair an extra spray before she had to meet Rick. As I turned to walk into my shop, I stopped and said, "We don't even know each other's names, do we?"

"Of course we do," he replied. "You're Miss Austen and, if I recall, I am the Penguin Man."

"See you tomorrow, Mr Penguin Man."

"Have a beautiful day, Miss Austen. Sell lots of shoes."

I must have drifted off into a reverie in her absence because Maureen startled me by the cash desk, barking, "What are you smiling at?" She must have had a bad lunch with Rick. I suppose I will hear about it in due time, but I will keep my lunch adventures to myself. I will sell lots of shoes today, I can feel it.

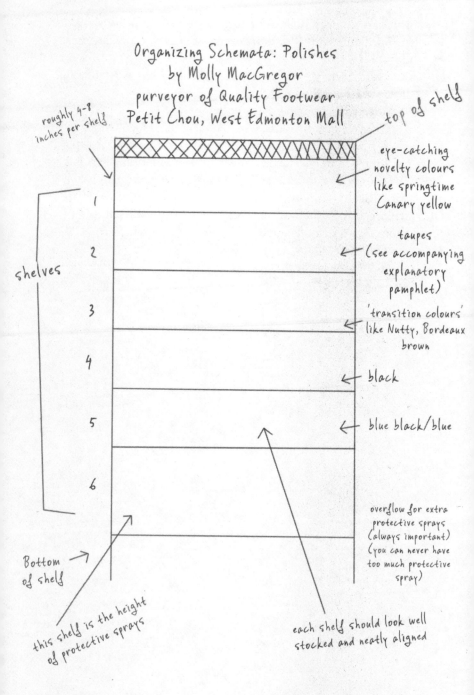

Organizing Schemata: Polishes
by Molly MacGregor
purveyor of Quality Footwear
Petit Chou, West Edmonton Mall

roughly 4-8 inches per shelf

top of shelf

eye-catching novelty colours like springtime Canary yellow

taupes (see accompanying explanatory pamphlet)

'transition colours' like Nutty, Bordeaux brown

black

blue black/blue

shelves

1
2
3
4
5
6

overflow for extra protective sprays (always important) (you can never have too much protective spray)

Bottom of shelf

this shelf is the height of protective sprays

each shelf should look well stocked and neatly aligned

ONVINCED THAT GOING OUT WITH SOMEONE I'd just met in the Mall would lead me to a horrible fate involving the trash compactor by Entrance Fifty, Genevieve wanted me to call after my dinner with the Penguin Man. She wanted all the details but all I could say was: "I had a really nice time."

"Is he cute?"

"In an old guy kind of way. He has hair like Steve Anthony."

"Hmm. What did you talk about?"

"Virginia Woolf. And how she depicts time. And her sentences. This sounds amazing, but he's the first person I've ever met who reads Virginia Woolf because he wants to. Strange, isn't it?"

"Very strange. He sounds perfect for you."

I was quiet for a moment and mulled over what she said. Genevieve interrupted my silence by asking, "Are you in love with him?"

It seemed easier to say, "No, of course not," than to have work through feelings I didn't understand myself. He was cute. But he was old. He read novels. But he didn't listen to music after 1989. I changed the subject to trumpet skirts to give me time to think. Genevieve is very smart about fashion, and clothes were a good diversion since we both tried on a really nice herringbone trumpet skirt at Le Château last week. It looked great on her, but the jury's still out on how flattering that skirt was on me, or how much attention

I wanted to draw to my behind. As Genevieve talked about trumpet skirts, my mind had time to wander. Am I in love with the Penguin Man? Can you just like being with someone and not be in love with them? Could I have fallen in love with him and not known? What does love feel like? Aren't there supposed to be sparks? Isn't your heart supposed to race? Might the shared love of an author mean you're supposed to be with someone? Would he expect me to read Steinbeck? Would I read Steinbeck for him? Would an expectation to read Faulkner be far off? Is that what love does to a person?

"You're still thinking about him, aren't you?"

"Yes. Do you think I'm in love with him?"

"I don't know. Are you going to see him again?"

"He's leaving town tomorrow so I'm not sure. He said he'll be back in town again in a while."

"Did he kiss you?"

"No."

"Did you want him to kiss you?"

I lied. "I didn't really think about it."

"Well, then, I think you're probably safe. Want to check out the sale rack at Ralph Lauren tomorrow? I heard they're going to reduce those sweaters we liked this week." Genevieve is so well informed. And such a good friend.

After I got off the phone, I needed to re-read chapter four of *Sense and Sensibility* where Elinor and Marianne discuss the nature of love. My inner-Elinor and inner-Marianne duked it out over my thoughts of the Penguin Man. My inner-Elinor said, "Molly does not attempt to deny that she thinks very highly of him—that she greatly esteems, that she likes him." Marianne retorted, "Esteem him! Like him! Cold-hearted Elinor! Oh! worse than cold-hearted! Ashamed of being otherwise. Use those words again about Molly and I will leave the room this moment." Oh, Miss Austen, I come to you for answers, but so often you just give me more questions. 🐧

I KNOW I ONLY TECHNICALLY WORK FORTY-FOUR hours a week, but if you add an hour and a half for bus rides to and from work, the mandatory unpaid lunch, coffee, and dinner breaks, plus the time it takes to close up and drop off the deposit, this job really takes up more like sixty hours a week. I suppose this is fine, but it doesn't really allow for much time to drink coffee with friends, do laundry, sit on a park bench, read in increments of longer than twenty minutes, or think lingering thoughts without watching the clock. I'm glad classes will be starting again in a month. Knowing I will be out of here soon keeps me going and makes taupe and the peacocks a little more tolerable. Every once in a while though, I get a chance to escape the Mall and be myself again. Tonight was one of those nights.

The Princess Theatre shows *A Room with a View* in their rotation every six months, and Genevieve and I go every time. Ever since we saw the summer movie schedule, we have been planning to go and then meet Glenda and Susan for coffee after. We never watch *A Room with a View* with anyone else: it's too sacred, and we cannot abide anyone else talking about our movie. The first time we saw it, we were in high school and we went to the $2.50 Tuesday matinée. As we left the theatre, we squinted against the startling afternoon sun and neither of us said a word for about five minutes. Finally, Genevieve grabbed my hand and whispered, "I think that movie changed my life" and I nodded in hasty agreement.

We went to see it again at seven o'clock, and then again the next day, at full price.

We never talked with each other about how this movie has changed our lives; it's just understood. Maybe we don't want to pull too hard on its magic in case it crumbles before our eyes. If pressed, I think I would say this movie reminds me of beauty. And sunshine. And hope. And places other than Edmonton. Tonight, as the theatre darkened and I sunk into my red, crushed-velvet seat, Kiri Te Kanawa sang the first notes of "O mio babbino caro." Everything but Italy, truth, and beauty ceased to exist. When Puccini's aria returned at the end of the movie, and the camera retreated from the room with the view of the Arno, we were pulled back into our lives and, as always, we didn't know whom we were crying for or what we were crying over. We watched until the final credit had rolled, wiped our tears, and descended the stairs into the lily-pink lobby and the din of the crowd gathering below for the nine o'clock show. We sighed, remade our pact to learn Italian, visit Florence together, and wondered aloud if we'd ever find our George Emersons in a world full of Cecil Vyses. We made our way through the crowded lobby and onto Whyte Avenue, which was pulsing with conversations and laughter. Streetlights and store signs glowed, music from car stereos filled the street. It was the kind of night I cling to and summon in the depths of winter when I wonder why I continue to live in this city. As Genevieve and I scanned the street looking for Glenda and Susan, I heard someone call my name.

I turned to find Mark Forster, Tess's old boyfriend. He gave me a big hug, and introduced me to some of his polit-ical-science, grad-school classmates. Genevieve cast me a knowing glance and went to grab Glenda and Susan. Mark and his friends were at the back of a long line to see the late showing of *Eraserhead*. I issued my condolences, and they laughed only as people would if they had not actually seen *Eraserhead*. They would understand my gesture soon enough. Mark and I said the usual things:

"It's been too long."

"We should get together soon."

When his line started moving, he stepped out of it and said, "Are you free for coffee now? I'll skip the movie." I pointed to my group of friends grinning like Cheshire Cats and said I really couldn't. He took my hand and said, "It was great to see you. And I'll see you soon."

"Soon!" I said.

"Soon!" he replied as a smart-looking girl in the group pulled him into *Eraserhead*. I hugged my much-missed friends and we walked arm in arm toward the café. As we were waiting for a walk light to cross the street, Genevieve whispered, "Speaking of finding our George Emersons…."

I shushed her with, "Nonsense." And it was nonsense. When the light changed, I looked back to see if I could see Mark and his grad school friends through the glass on the theatre doors. I thought I could see the smart girl hanging on Mark's every word. Genevieve saw me looking and raised an eyebrow. "Nonsense," I repeated and we crossed the street.

In high school, Glenda and Genevieve used to bug me about being secretly in love with Mark, but it was never like that. My biggest regret about Tess's tumultuous love life was that she broke up with Mark. I think I took their break-up harder than either of them. I liked him, and I liked having him around. He taught me things and made me laugh. We all liked Mark. My dad was also deeply disappointed in their break-up and I overheard him ask my mum if they could still invite Mark around to dinner. When she said no, he said, "*We* didn't break up with Mark. Nobody consulted us about the break-up." One night, when our family was lamenting the absence of Mark's dinnertime conversation, Tess said, "I'm starting to think you like Mark more than you like me." We all drifted into silent contemplation wondering if one of us would be brave enough to say "Sometimes we do." Instead someone said, "Dessert?" and we all changed the subject to cake. As much as we liked Mark, we had a hard time wishing for them to stay together, since they were so clearly mismatched and not, unfortunately, in any interesting way that would yield a riveting novel worthy of Masterpiece Theatre dramatization.

What I liked about having Mark around was that he always had interesting things to say, and always made me feel like my life was way more interesting than it was. I liked that he asked how things were going for me, and that he waited for an answer. When I was in high school, we'd often take the same bus in the afternoons. He'd be coming home from the university, and I loved hearing about his classes and his life on campus. Sometimes, we'd get off at an earlier stop to walk the long way to our houses, stopping on nice days at the park bench that overlooks the river valley. Unlike my own family and friends, he always seemed genuinely interested in what I was reading, thinking, and doing. He asked the kinds of questions I wished my friends and I would talk about. Being older and in university, his life was clearly more interesting than mine but he never made it seem that way. I listened to him greedily as he talked about his classes, assignments, professors, and readings. Reluctantly I'd reciprocate with a tale about the tapeworm we'd dissected in biology, an anecdote about a prank someone had orchestrated on the substitute in English, or a detailed depiction about why precisely I hated gym as much as I did. I envied the lectures Mark went to and the friends he had. I admit I listened carefully for the repeated mention of a girl's name. I thought it might be my sisterly duty to keep Tess informed.

It was at that park bench where he'd loan me books, and then later quiz me on them. Often he'd laugh at what I had to say, but he'd always call me out on shortcuts I was taking in school, or when I'd take the easy way out of situations or ideas. He would chide me gently for my ignorance of, and ambivalence toward, politics and current events and occasionally his chiding could be harsh. Once I told him I'd napped and re-read *Mansfield Park* instead of watching the coverage of Margaret Thatcher's third re-election:

"It's got nothing to do with me," I soon regretted saying.

"Nothing to do with you? We're on the brink of nuclear annihilation, and you think Margaret Thatcher has nothing to do with you? And Jane Austen does? Really, Molly, you're one of the smartest people I know, but you've got to start using your brain for something other than novels." I can't recall all that followed, but I remember the shame in realizing that the re-election of Margaret Thatcher actually did have a lot to do with me. He stopped by our house the next day to apologize:

"I'm glad you read novels. I just want you to know how important all of this is." I promised I would pay better attention to British and American politics.

"What about Canadian politics?" I asked and he laughed.

"You can pay attention to Canadian politics, and still have lots of time to read those thick novels you love." We left on good terms, better perhaps than ever before. While some might have ended the friendship there, I liked that Mark told me things I needed to know. I'd always been told I was clever, but only Mark told me that it was never enough just to be smart—you needed to do something with whatever you had. He reminded me that there is a world outside of fiction. I forget that. I forget that a lot.

As we walked to the café, I decided to forget about Mark seeing *Eraserhead* with a smart girl who, in all likelihood, willingly watched election coverage and never read novels. Instead, I could concentrate on how much I loved nights out with my friends. I had been spending almost all of my waking hours either at the Mall or alone at home reading novels. Tonight reminded me I am alive, and that there's a whole other world around me. Glenda, Susan, Genevieve, and I sat at our favourite table at the Coffee Factory and teased our favourite waiter. We laughed at everything and nothing. We drank cappuccino, and shared espresso cheesecake. And then we drank more coffee. And had more cake. I'd forgotten what it was like to laugh, and to be around people who know me and understand me. I'd also almost forgotten about Mark.

It was an early night because we all had to work in the morning. Not thinking about the Mall for just a few hours has made me feel more like myself again. I want to cling to tonight and not let tomorrow arrive. I cannot bring myself to think about my place of employ and cannot taint a perfect evening by mentioning it by name. It can't be as bad as I'm making it out to be. Can it?

I WAS LATE GETTING UP AND STILL TIRED. I had such a nice night last night and dreaded going into work. Seeing Mark last night reminded me of exactly the CD I needed for my day: Oasis's *Definitely Maybe*. I dashed out the door with the Gallagher brothers, and, by the time my bus arrived, Noel's guitar had already worked its magic on me. As my bus edged westward, I imagined Liam singing a special version of "Rock 'n' Roll Star" called "Polish and Protective Spray Star." I made a mental note to tell Mark about how, yet again, this Oasis album had made me blissfully happy. One of the things I love about Mark is that he can put his encyclopædic knowledge of music to uses greater than winning bets in bars. He can tell you which Kinks track was on what album (and usually what track of what side) and name all Four Tops. Perhaps Mark's greatest gift is being able to recommend exactly the album or song you need to hear. The better he knows you, the better the recommendations.

When he was dating Tess, I was obsessed with The Jam and listened to them almost exclusively. He said I needed to broaden my horizons. One day he brought over a stack of records for me to explore and I listened to them studiously. I liked all of them but Dire Straits' 1980 album *Making Movies* stood out. Perhaps an odd choice for a junior-high-school girl, but I loved the music and the stories the songs told. Mark has a way of finding me the music I wouldn't find on my own. Last year, I happened to see him on the bus and as we chatted, he stopped midsentence and said, "You need to listen to this." He pulled *Definitely Maybe* out of his bag, and put it on his Discman to play for me. From the first bars, I was hooked. I knew I had to get my own copy, if only for all the pictures of Noel and Liam in the booklet. I've listened to this CD so often, it's starting to skip and sound a little garbled. I think "Rock 'n' Roll Star" is my favourite track, but it might be "Live Forever." Mark and I have debated the merits of both quite often. I tend not to discuss my other Oasis conundrum with him or anyone else for that matter. It's a little too embarrassing: which Gallagher brother would I date?

On the one hand, Noel writes the songs so he's sort of the brains behind the band. On the other hand, it's Liam who really brings the songs to life. Most days I think Liam has better hair because it reminds me of Paul Weller's hair, but sometimes I like Noel's more George Harrison-y hair. Noel has the furrowed brow of a thoughtful man, while Liam has the look often seen in sheepdog puppies—sort of vacant, yet also fully prepared to hunt down a squirrel. Noel writes lyrics so that makes him sort of a poet, which is entirely sexy. But, then again, he rhymes "supersonic" with "gin and tonic." Liam, on the other hand, can take lyrics with sketchy rhymes and make them blossom like a Shakespeare sonnet. Liam or Noel? It's a tough call.

As I enumerate their merits and limitations, there is a small part of me that wonders what I see in the Gallagher brothers. Is it just their great hair? Or is it that they're so un-Canadian with their tantrums, their haircuts, their glasses, and their cans of beer that we can't get here? Staring at the CD booklet and listening to their loud guitars makes me want to be anywhere but here. Maybe if I imagine Liam singing about me being a "Polish and Protective Spray Star" long enough, I'll feel better. 🎸

*F*OR THE PAST THREE WEEKS, I'VE BEEN DEALING with the Mall by immersing myself in the world of George Eliot's *Middlemarch*. I don't think there's anything better for my mall ennui than 613 pages of tiny-fonted, novelistic beauty. I have savoured every complicated, compound, clause-y sentence—sentences with lots of commas and dashes, and ones that use the negative to tell you about things that are really important. Like, "Reader, you should not doubt that Will Ladislaw is not, by far, the man who does not make Dorothea tremble in her not-quite-sensible shoes—although her shoes are hidden by what is not an inconsiderable amount of clothing—she is, in short, not un-in love with Will Ladislaw." I have been smitten with Will Ladislaw ever since chapter twenty-one when he resented that "dried-up pedant" Mr Casaubon for "having first got this adorable young creature to marry him, and then passing his honeymoon away from her, groping after his mouldy futilities." True, "Will was given to hyperbole," but I loved him for it. It's been agonizing reading about the perfectly kissable Will Ladislaw, while Dorothea has been burdened with Mr Casaubon and his *The Key to All Mythologies*. But then today, about halfway through my sandwich, I turned page 593 and Will kissed Dorothea. I couldn't believe my eyes. He kissed her. And it only took 593 pages.

I knew I had to tell someone, anyone, everyone about literature's finest kiss. With "Will kissed Dorothea! Will kissed Dorothea!" running through my head I ran to Julia's shop to tell her, but she wasn't there. I went to the bookstore to tell Ray but he had a huge line of customers. I passed by the Ottoman Empire to tell Kevin, but he was on the phone. I darted and dashed around Phase Three hoping I would find someone, anyone, who would listen to me. I passed the Rabid Pekingese lounging and smoking by the ice rink, thought about it for just a second, and kept running.

Passing Mall Security, I imagined bursting, breathlessly, into their inner sanctum, declaring, "This is urgent! I must address the shoppers! No time to explain." I imagine they'd scratch their matching shaved heads and then hand over the PA system mic. "Attention shoppers," I would start, "I have been reading George Eliot's *Middlemarch* non-stop for the past three weeks, and I must tell you this. After 593 pages, Will Ladislaw has just kissed Dorothea. What does this have to do with you? It has everything to do with you. This is literature's finest kiss. Here, let me read it to you." Mall Security would exchange glances that say, "Stop her!" but the effort required to dislodge their endomorphic forms from their reclining chairs would give them ample time to reconsider. The burlier one would see the earnest look of desperation on my face and say, "Well, maybe this is an emergency." The one with hockey hair would then say, "As a culture we are somewhat remiss in our reading of Victorian fiction, aren't we?" "I am fond of literary kisses," a supervisor might say, "and it's been a while since I've read a good one. Let her go. I'm curious how this all turns out." "Thank you," I would say, "you won't regret this." And then I would take a breath, pause, and read page 593 for all mall shoppers: "'While he was speaking there came a vivid flash of lightning which lit each of them up for the other—and the light seemed to be the terror of a hopeless love.... Her lips trembled, and so did his. It was never known which lips were the first to move towards the other lips; but they kissed *tremblingly*, and then they moved apart. The rain was dashing against the window-panes as if an angry spirit were within it, and behind it was the great swoop of the wind; it was one of those moments in which both the busy and the idle pause with a certain awe.' That is all. Copies of *Middlemarch* are available at the bookstore on the upper level by the ice rink and, of course, at your closest branch of the Edmonton Public Library. Carry on with your shopping and enjoy your day." Even though I know the world would be a better place if more people read this kiss, I wasn't sure Mall Security would see it that way so, prudently, I carried on.

Having found no one to tell in Phase Three, I decided Maureen was a captive audience and I ran back to Le Petit Chou to read it to her. My thoughts were so full of rain dashing against window-panes and great swoops of wind that I did not see the person exiting Le Petit Chou as I rounded the corner. I ran into him with a force that threw me quite off balance. He caught me and steadied me back to my kitten-heeled feet. It took me a moment or two to realize I had just been caught by the one person who would fully understand why I would want to read this page over the mall PA system. It was my Penguin Man.

"Miss Austen, what's wrong?" I was so flustered that all I could say was, "*Middlemarch*. Will kissed Dorothea. Will kissed Dorothea. Page 593." I handed him the book, my finger still marking the page. He walked over to read the paragraph under the skylights that shone on the peacocks below. Closing the book, he said, "I think that might be literature's finest kiss. Thank you for sharing it with me." Still shocked and out of breath, I started to ramble on about Mall Security, vivid flashes of lightning, and the word "tremblingly." I am sure I made no sense at all but he put his hands on my shoulders and said, "Miss Austen, I have missed you. And so, I believe, has your co-worker. She tells me you are seven minutes late." He turned me around so I could see Maureen simmering by the door's edge. Her gaze burned all the way through whatever happiness Will and Dorothea's kiss had brought me. I ran into the store while the Penguin Man remained outside the shop presciently. He had encountered the fury of Maureen in my absence and rightly feared to set foot in the store again. After I punched my timecard and assumed my position on the floor, she stormed out of the stockroom, swinging her new studded leather handbag like a Viking cudgel. The Penguin Man nervously peered into the store, and I gave him the all clear. Because I was seven minutes late, Maureen would take an extra half hour on her break or maybe even forty-five minutes. That's how it worked with us. She was full-time full-time and I was merely summer full-time. As she often pointed out, there was a hierarchy, and she wanted it to stay that way. As my penance for being late and for being seasonal, she left an hour's worth of shoes for me to re-box and re-shelve. Normally I would have been in a horrible Le Petit Chou mood, but I wasn't. My Penguin Man was there to see me, and the sun was shining brightly through the skylights. He surveyed the pink walls and soft lighting of my shop and sighed,

"Ah, the scenic confines of Le Petit Chou." We chatted about things I can't recall because I was still processing Will and Dorothea and my gratitude to have run into my Penguin Man when I needed to share that scene with someone. I'm not sure anyone else would have understood how momentous that paragraph was to me. Post-lunch hour customers were starting to shuffle in to peruse my well-displayed wares, and it was getting hard to talk. We made plans to meet tomorrow. On the way out, he paused like he was about to say something and then thought better of it. All he said was, "I will see you tomorrow." In the boredom of the afternoon, I summoned Elizabeth Bennet, Marianne and Elinor Dashwood, and Emma Woodhouse to help me think through what his look meant. Of all Miss Austen's heroines, I trusted their judgment the best. I tend to leave the more stoic Fanny Price and Anne Elliot out of these matters. Catherine Morland, while charming, has her head in too many novels. I have enough of that myself. I spent the rest of the afternoon imagining conversations I might have had with my Penguin Man if Le Petit Chou had not interfered. ❧

THE MALL WAS SLOW TODAY, AND THE CALL of the peacocks below continues to haunt me. Eugenie and I were on our own for most of the afternoon. Maureen was at the Prima Donna store getting some extra tutorials on "re-shelving techniques" from Rick. Eugenie and I just rolled our eyes and enjoyed the silence. As we were assembling pink and peach shoes into a new display, another shoe employee from a rival shop stopped in asking for Maureen.

"Tell her Gordon stopped by," he said with a wink. Eugenie and I managed to hold our laughter until he left the store.

"What's weirder," Eugenie asked, "that Maureen has so many shoe-store guys after her or that they're all named Gordon?"

"Being surrounded by Gordons does seem to be a distinctly Canadian occurrence," I observed. "The weirdest part is how she keeps her job." I thought it best not to ask too many questions or think too deeply on that subject. When Eugenie went on her break, I used the time alone to plot out the Great Canadian Novel set in Edmonton I aspire to write.

Immersed in jotting down thoughts related to fur traders, Mounties, and rogue elk, I was mortified to look up and to see Maureen and Tim right in front of me staring at my page. I'm not sure how they managed to sneak up on me since Maureen is covered in noisy jewellery and Tim had on his new metallic, salmon-pink suit that makes a squeaky, swishing sound when he walks. "What are you doing?" Tim asked with a hearty chuckle, "Writing a novel?" Maureen guffawed as if nothing could be more ridiculous. I couldn't bear to confess that I was indeed plotting out a novel nor did I want to say I was attempting to stave off the soul-rotting ennui I faced daily working in this particular store. I knew that I had to come up with something quickly to explain what I was doing writing on company time. In a panic I blurted out, "I'm writing a fan letter to Roy Orbison. I really like his song 'Only the Lonely.'" Monsieur Suave Suit had been playing that song loudly as I'd walked by on my break and it stuck in my head. Blank looks were exchanged. After an awkward silence, Tim looked at me and said, "You know he's dead, right?" I looked at the floor and nodded. I whispered, "It's still too soon. I don't want to talk about it."

Tim shook his head and the skylight sun glinted off the metallic threads in his salmon suit as he shuffled down the mall. The peacocks below sounded their desperate yawp. I felt uncomfortable all afternoon and I wasn't sure if it was because I had lied to Tim and Maureen, or that I had concocted a story with so little creative merit. I felt bad for lying but at the Mall, we all create stories. Whether it's about the importance of protective sprays, about fan letters to Roy Orbison, about how nice your aging butt looks in those jeans, or about the existence of "tutorials on advanced shelving techniques," we all need to find a way to make another day in the Mall seem tolerable. 🐗

*W*HEN I WANDERED OUT ONTO THE FLOOR to start my noon-to-nine shift at 11:57, Maureen was angry I had forgotten it was Dollar-Off Tuesday at the Teriyaki Grill, and because of my tardiness she would be tangled up in the noon rush. Storming out into the mall to meet one of the indistinguishable Gordons, she yelled over her shoulder,

"Some guy dropped something off for you. At least I think it's you. He didn't know your name. It's under the till. Call Mall Security if he's a stalker." Curious, I thought. Could the Rabid Pekingese have left me a letter bomb? Might Stewart have returned all the polishes I sold him? Might one of the Hutterite men who stared at my long, polka-dotted black skirt have dropped off some corn and cucumbers?

Under the cash desk I found a book-sized package, wrapped carefully in brown kraft paper and tied with a cream-coloured satin ribbon. There was a card. "Miss Austen" was written in nice ink on the front in surprisingly elegant handwriting. My heart raced and a lump formed in my throat. My Penguin Man.

I opened the card gingerly and smiled to see penguins on the front. He'd written: "My dear Miss Austen, best wishes for your semester. I hope to see you again very soon. Your Penguin Man." I paused before opening the package. I knew it was a book, but what one? It couldn't be a Miss Austen since he knew I had two copies of each. Was it something he thought I would like? Something he thinks I should like?

What if it's poetry? It would be so Marianne and Willoughby if it were poetry. But were we at a poetry-giving level in our relationship? Are we in a relationship? What if it's something he thinks I should like and I really dislike? What if it's Tobias Smollett? Would I read it, and pretend to like it when I next saw him? Maybe I would read it, realize I was completely wrong about Tobias, and see my true calling is to be a Smollett scholar. What if I really hated it? Or, worse still, what if it's Steinbeck? What if it's *Of Mice and Men*, the book he bought the day we met? I would definitely have to read it then, and pretend to like how Steinbeck's sentences sound like clods of earth falling heavily to the ground from a rusty shovel. Why did he have to get me a book? When someone gives you flowers, at least you know what they are thinking: red roses, they love you. Pink roses, they like you. Yellow roses, they think you're nice. Daisies, they think you're cute. Carnations. Well, either they don't realize you shouldn't send carnations to a girl you like, or they've given you the floral brush-off. Either way, you'd best start looking for love elsewhere. But a book? I let the book remain wrapped in mystery while I tended to a "just looking" shopper for a few minutes. When the store was empty, I summoned my courage, untied the ribbon and eased the tape open. It wasn't Steinbeck.

It was the *Collected Works of Oscar Wilde*. A novella, some tales, and several plays. A Penguin Classic. Mixed genres. I laughed to myself: he'd given me the literary equivalent of a bouquet of red roses, yellow roses, daisies, and carnations. I opened it up, and saw he'd inscribed it: "To Miss Austen, A charming book for an equally charming girl. Your Penguin Man." I visualized Marianne and Elinor standing in front of me—their hands on their hips, their eyebrows raised. "Well?" they asked. I ignored them and went to the back room to tuck my new Wilde book and its card carefully into my bag. They followed me back. "Do you love him? Esteem him? Like him?" I continued to ignore them.

I walked through my customer-less store, needlessly adjusting shoes on the sale rack, and restoring order to the already well-ordered store. Standing at the entrance of my store, I stared into the Mall for a few minutes. If this were a John Hughes movie, my Penguin Man would be standing outside the store waiting for me, and everything would make sense. But my life is never like a John Hughes film. I wasn't sure when I would see the Penguin Man again. Or if I would ever see him again. Was this a parting gift? If so, what did he mean in the card by "I hope to see you very soon" instead of "I will see you again very soon." The giving of books was, in my mind, a serious gesture, but did he see it that way too? Tess first knew Mark liked her when he gave her a book. They broke up, in part, if I recall, because she never read the book and couldn't remember the title. The gift of a book doesn't mean the same thing for everyone, it seems. Was I reading too much into what was simply a nice gesture by the Penguin Man?

The corridors were quiet, and sunshine poured in from the skylights above as if to mock me. Even the peacocks were sedate below. The only movement I saw was the Rabid Pekingese dusting and talking on the phone; the feather duster punctuated his sentences. He was mad at someone, and those shelves would be sparkling in no time. The new Aloysius & Flint guy walked by, turned his fingers into guns, and did that weird "wink and shoot you twice" thing he does when he sees me. I smiled at him and at men in general. What does a wink and a finger pistol mean? What does Oscar Wilde mean? What does charming mean? Three American, senior ladies to whom I'd sold shoes yesterday walked by basking in the Mall's retail glory. They waved excitedly, and I waved back. Gary, Howard, Mavis, and Maria would be starting to get ready for their one o'clock show about now. My eyes wandered toward the lagoon, and I pretended not to look at my bench. I wasn't sure if I wanted to see my Penguin Man there or not. I pretended not to be disappointed when I didn't see him waiting for me. I couldn't let my thoughts wander in that direction so I focused on having only half-a-week of shifts left until I go back to school.

I am excited about it, but also pretty exhausted. I thought about how maybe I should just stay here at the Mall. I'm feeling sort of comfortable here. And ... I can't even say it. If

I stay here, I might see him again. If I leave, it's unlikely I will ever see him again. I imagined Elinor sighing, and Marianne rolling her eyes. "He got you a mixed-genre book, Molly," Marianne said. Even Elinor had to admit that a mixed-genre book was the equivalent of a bouquet where carnations outnumbered the red roses.

When the twelve-thirty announcement for the next dolphin show was broadcast, I went back into my store, and pulled my hair into a ponytail. I tied it with the cream-coloured ribbon I still held in my hand. There was nothing else to do in the quiet of the store, so I busied myself making a new window display. A shipment of spectator pumps had just arrived, and they looked like nice shoes. My display turned out well, especially mixed with the patent pumps and fall handbags. As I admired my shoe-artistry, I realized I could propose a new two-for-one polish promotion with the purchase of two-tone shoes. After a summer here, I had come a long way in understanding the purveyance of footwear. I understood the power of a well-crafted display, the allure of the polish and protective spray mythology, what people were actually shopping for when they looked for shoes. Maybe I was meant for this business. Perhaps I'm not meant for an English degree and writing books. And maybe I'm not meant for the Penguin Man. I felt Marianne and Elinor looking away. The peacocks were waking from their noon naps, and their cries echoed off the glass and mirrors. The sunshine, diffused, filled one small corner of my shop. 🌸

ONIGHT WAS MY FINAL NIGHT OF WORKING at Le Petit Chou for the summer. Trust Maureen to have filled my last, half-week with four nine-to-nine shifts. Before he left for the weekend, Tim stopped by to wish me luck. He offered, and I agreed, that I would come back for the Christmas rush and also next summer. He let me keep my name tag so Maureen wouldn't give it to the transitory part-timers. I thanked him.

"We might put you in Prima Donna, if you're interested," he noted. "It's busier and a bit of a promotion." When I said I thought I might not be Rick's first choice of employee, he looked around nervously and said, "I'm not sure you'll need to worry about Rick. He might be heading to Tuesday's, if you know what I mean. I think Eugenie might be getting a promotion too. We have our eye on a guy named Gordon for a management spot. Do you know him?"

"One of them," I replied.

"He would be quite the catch for us," he noted. He paused for a minute and then said, "You have management potential, you know. If this English degree doesn't work out for you, we'd be happy to consider you for one of the stores. I think you'd do very well here. Your displays are top-notch and your polish sales? What can I say? You're a legend." I thanked him for the kind words and said I would definitely keep his offer in mind.

I spent the rest of the evening alone. It was a quiet evening in the shop. I dusted, tidied, wiped the mirrors, and vacuumed very carefully. When it was quiet, it was a nice little store, and it had been good to me. Eugenie would be opening up tomorrow, and when I hid the cash float in the backroom, I left her a drawing of me waving goodbye. I would miss her. After cashing out and gathering all my things, I turned the lights out. I stood in my dark store for a moment trying not to hope the Penguin Man would be outside waiting to say goodbye. I listened to the silent store until a peacock cry pulled me out of my reverie. I pulled the doors closed and double-checked the lock. I walked over to my bench to say goodbye to the dolphins and wished them well. I passed the peacocks with a wave, dropped the deposit and keys off at Prima Donna, tapped gently on the emus' glass enclosure to say goodbye. They returned my gaze with their usual look of shocked bewilderment.

Walking out of Entrance Fifty toward my bus, I couldn't help but remember all the summer nights I had imagined walking out of my very last shift of work in Le Petit Chou. I didn't feel like I thought I would. I rounded a corner, and saw my bus pulling out. I ran for it and thanked the driver for waiting. As we pulled into traffic, my fingers wandered to the ribbon around my ponytail. "Goodbye, Penguin Man," I whispered to no one, as I found a seat and headed home. I rummaged in my bag for a cherry Life Saver, and realized I still had the Oscar Wilde book in my bag. I took it out of the wrapping again, skipped over the inscription, and started to read the "Preface to *Dorian Gray*" as the bus streamed through dusk-darkened Edmonton: "The artist is the creator of beautiful things. To reveal art and conceal the artist is art's aim." I continued reading and found that the Penguin Man had softly underlined something for me: "All art is at once surface and symbol./ Those who go beneath the surface do so at their peril./ Those who read the symbol do so at their peril./ It is the spectator, and not life, that art really mirrors."

I smiled at my reflection in the bus window: he's warning me not to read anything into this gesture. I closed the book and lost myself in *Making Movies* for the rest of the bus ride.

When I got home tonight, I engaged in some small, familial chatter with my parents and Heathcliff, but I wanted to be alone. I am ready for my new semester and whatever it will bring. My framed portrait of Miss Austen smirks down at me knowingly. I think she thinks I'll be okay too. 🙟

September 1995:
Third Year, Semester One
University of Alberta, Edmonton

'M SITTING IN MY ROOM, PUTTING OFF GOING to sleep. It's one of those late summer nights that are so warm and silent that you think winter won't come. I noticed one or two leaves turning yellow this afternoon, but I'm blocking that from my mind now. I have my window open, to enjoy the sound of wind in the aspens while I can.

I spent the day on campus completing my registration, getting my new ID card, buying my textbooks, reconnecting with various friends and acquaintances, drinking a Java Jive coffee, and having some soup at Patria. When I got home, my dad was keen to look at my new books. We laid them out on the table, and he gently held each book in his hands, as one might hold a bird's nest dislodged from a tree in a storm. I smiled when I realized my fondness for sniffing the pages of new books must be genetic. I've now arranged the new books in my room alphabetically, and by course, and am both excited and nervous about this semester. Almost all of my courses are 300-level and three of them are seminars. I hope I can keep up with what is expected of me. It will be harder to hide behind the chatty students in smaller classes. I am excited about taking "Gender and Courtship in the Long-Nineteenth Century" with Professor St. Hubbins. I really like her shoes and the reading list is fantastic. We're starting with *Pride and Prejudice*. It's been at least a year since I read it, and I am excited to read it again. I am also taking nineteenth-century poetry with Professor Widgett-Jones (who inspires me to purchase a tweed suit at some point in my life). The course has a very thick anthology, and I am looking forward to reading it cover to cover. I also have my third-year Honours seminar with the aging and adorable Professor Wilbert K. Throckmorton (readings TBA, he says) and first-year psychology (ick, last requirement).

I am particularly worried about my "Hegemony, Hermeneutics, and the Humours" seminar with Professor Byron Keats. I looked up each of those words in the dictionary, but I'm still not sure what they mean, individually or collectively. Hegemony: "leadership, predominance, preponderance; esp. the leadership or predominant authority of one state of a confederacy or union over the others." Hermeneutics: "the art or science of interpretation, esp. of Scripture. Commonly distinguished from *exegesis* or practical exposition." The humours: "in ancient and mediæval physiology, one of the four chief fluids (cardinal humours) of the body (blood, phlegm, choler, and melancholy or black choler), by the relative proportions of which a person's physical and mental qualities and disposition were held to be determined." I am struggling to see how these things fit together, but I trust by the end of the term, all will be clear as day.

As we drank our after-dinner tea, I asked my dad to explain how hegemony, hermeneutics, and the humours connect, and he zoned out into a reverie. Finally, he said to my mum, "Byron Keats' course" and she said, "Ah" in that loaded noncommittal way she has. They both stared at me for a moment before leaving the table. Passing me, my dad smoothed my hair and said, "You'll be okay, sweetie." My mum patted me on the shoulder and kissed my head. She said, "The semester will be gone before you know it. And we'll be proud of you no matter what." Tomorrow the semester begins anew and I'd best start it with a good night's sleep. Welcome back, English Major Molly. I've missed you. ❀

HAVE SURVIVED THE FIRST WEEK OF MY THIRD year, and all appears promising. My classes look interesting, and I don't believe there are many people in my classes who use words like sardonic, *Festschrift*, and *Schadenfreude* without having to look them up first (which, for the record, I always have to do). Unfortunately, the guy who calls us "ignorant churls" when we say things he thinks are stupid is in my Honours seminar. And Jason Richards is, once again, in almost all of my classes. With the exception of grade three, I believe I have always been in class with Jason. Now and again, he'll remind me of the day in kindergarten when I agreed to marry him. He always says, "I think you said yes so I would give you my juice." We laugh but I think we both know it is true. I always did want more apple juice than I was allotted.

This afternoon, I was ensconced in a desk on the fourth floor of Rutherford Library North looking out over the sunny campus. It was filled with people equally excited to be back on campus. I'd originally thought to get an early start on my psychology reading but instead I went for a stroll through the shelves. I have missed this library.

First, I climbed to the fifth floor using the wide, main stairs. The weight of the heavy door into the stacks, the smell of books that hung heavily in the air, and the sound of my shoes on that carpet made me feel like I was home after a long journey. Usually I go and work with the literature books on the fifth floor, where I am surrounded by the hefty wisdom of novelists, the laconic advice of poets, or the furrowed admonishments of critics. The shelves on the fifth floor are filled with old friends, best friends, and potential new friends. I know where all my favourites are without looking up a call number. I know exactly where to find Hopkins if I need reminding of why I am grieving over Goldengrove unleaving (It is *Molly* you mourn for). Or if I need to see Virginia Woolf to confirm the wording of that passage from *Mrs Dalloway* I want on my tombstone ("and no one in the whole world would know how she had loved it all"). Or if I needed Miss Austen to confirm the exact wording of Elizabeth's rebuke to Mr Darcy ("I have every reason in the world to think ill of you").

After greeting the fifth floor, I found myself in my childhood haunt, the fourth floor where the art history books are. Wandering the stacks, I touched the spines of old Italian friends. I feel like this library has been mine since before I was born. Soon after starting her master's thesis on Botticelli, my mum was expecting me, and much of her work was done here. I was born two days after she defended. She even dedicated it to me: "To baby Molly who came to life alongside this work and who is more beautiful than a Botticelli Venus." While Tess and my mother have the kind of battling mother-daughter relationships I read about in the angsty teen books I took out of the library when I was twelve, my mum and I have always been "collegial." She began her doctorate when I was three, and she seemed to treat me more as an academic partner than a child. I learned early on that the best way to get attention with a demanding older sister and a brilliant older brother was to be agreeable and amenable; it would have been a full-time job to have more huffy tantrums than Tess, and, frankly, I knew from a very young age that I had better things to do with my time. And there was no way I could compete with Heathcliff. Having trained myself to be silent in libraries, I could go with my mum, and not have to stay at the campus daycare, where the older kids would cough on me and take my toys, while the younger ones would stare at me and touch me with inexplicably wet fingers. I learned to love the silence of libraries, and the endless hours during which I could roam the adult world, colour, read, draw, and craft stories in my head.

On library days, she'd pack each of our satchels: hers loaded with books and paper and mine with crayons, paper, colouring books, a contraband snack, dolls, and my pink blanket. I still find the library a fine place for a nap and am tempted some mornings to sneak what's left of my pink blanket into my backpack. Each day she would pick art books for me, and I would flip the pages slowly looking for something to draw. Eventually, I worked my way through the Renaissance to the Impressionists. I loved the watery Monet and sunny Renoir paintings especially. Many of the books my mum used to pull down for me are still here. "How about you spend the afternoon with Fra' Filippo Lippi" or "Today seems like a good day for some Raphael, don't you think?" In my perusing and drawings, I would attempt, in my own artistic endeavors, to emulate my mother's intensity as she poured over huge picture books of Italian art. It's funny to walk through these stacks working on my own schoolwork, having spent so much of my childhood in this library plying my trade as a miniature scholar and artist.

When I look at these drawings now (carefully archived by my father), I see people in my versions were usually smiling and waving (even in *Lamentation over the Dead Christ*). I also added a lot of kittens, a few bunnies, and, on occasion, a couple of cupcakes. If Tess or Heathcliff had made me mad, they would appear as the bad characters. Sometimes on weekends, Heathcliff would come with us. I would draw pictures, and then he and I would whisper and write stories based on my pictures. My father has a file called "Heathcliff and Moll(y): Juvenilia," and in it you could find great tales like "St. Francis of Assisi Goes to the Zoo," or "Venus and Her Magick Shell Bote" (Venus zooms about on her shell shopping for a new dress) and a rather embarrassing misinterpretation of "The Scream" called "The Surprise Party" where I added a cake, presents, and smiling, waving kittens wearing party hats to Munch's menacing orange sky.

As I got older, she would tell me more about her work. I used to say, "Botticelli and his contemporaries and their depiction of light," when people asked me what my mother did. I slowly grew to understand that not everyone's mother had a dissertation to write and eventually added "for her PhD." Although I didn't fully understand what she studied until fairly recently, all I knew was she looked at pictures of sunshine. Sometimes I'd watch her as she looked up from her sunny, Venetian paintings, and gazed out across the icy quad toward the frozen North Saskatchewan River, or through the grey, spring rain looking for hints of green. Sometimes I worried she was sad so I'd crawl up on her lap with my latest creation, and she'd discuss my picture with me in great detail in a hushed library voice. Other times, books of sunny gold angels in far-away places would lie open on her desk, and she'd just hold me in my pink blanket as the snow fell or the leaves scuttled across campus. When she took me out for a snack, she'd tell me stories of Donatello, Giotto, Michelangelo, and Brunelleschi with such affection, I thought they were much-loved and much-missed friends of hers whom I would someday meet.

Once, when I was in grade five, I went with her to her office on a cold Sunday in February to work on a very detailed shoebox diorama of Samuel de Champlain travelling through Quebec. I'd made miniature canoes out of birch bark from our yard and filled them with explorers and coureurs de bois made of modelling clay. I'd sent them on their voyage with a crate of oranges. I knew I would be docked points for historical inaccuracy, but, like many children my age, I was particularly affected by the curious emphasis our school curriculum placed on the perils of scurvy in the Age of Exploration. After a time, my mother dimmed the lights in her office, and filled one wall with a slide of Botticelli's *The Allegory of Spring*. I could hear angry winter winds shaking the windows but the room was filled with sunshine and gold.

She stared at it for what seemed like hours, walking back and forth across the room. After a while she sat down and looked like she'd just woken up. She said, "I saw this painting when I was in Florence. I was never the same again." Although I was almost too old to do so, I crawled onto her lap to get a better look. We stared at it together and I wondered if it would change me also if I got too close. My mum was silent, and I didn't want to move.

"I bet you're hungry. We should get you home." She packed up her slides and books, and I returned my crayons, scissors, and glue to the section of bookshelf she had set aside for me long ago. Even though I was old enough to dress myself in my winter clothes, she bundled me up against the cold, and we walked hand-in-hand carefully over the ice to our car. I remember how as she pulled out of the parking lot, she stopped at the stop sign longer than usual. Both of us looked back as if we'd left something behind.

I've always wondered where she goes when she looks at Italian art. I may never know, but I do find comfort in being surrounded once more by my old Italian friends, Botticelli, Donatello, Giotto, Michelangelo, and Brunelleschi. I whispered, "I've missed you," as I passed their shelves and touched their dusty spines. I like to imagine they said, "Welcome back, Molly. We've missed you too."

IVEN MY FULL COURSE LOAD THIS SEMESTER, I am not sure I can squeeze in writing of a "remarkable watershed Canadian coming-of-age novel" in my spare time as I had originally planned. I can, however, draft notes for what I imagine will be my second novel: a historically accurate, gothic bodice-ripper set in Saskatchewan, the most gothic of all the Canadian prairie provinces. To this end, I've started assembling a chart, which, when completed, will mean my second novel should basically write itself. Here's what I have so far:

Gothic	Saskatchewan
Romance	Ruminants
Castle	Cattle
Terror	Terriers
Caves	Calves
Captured virgins	Grain-eating vermin
Fear of confined spaces	Fear of wide-open spaces
Harrowing	Harrows
Heroine	Heifer
Skeletons in closets	Cow skulls in hay racks
Sublime	Subsoil with lime carbonate

Monks	Mounties
Traitors	Tractors
Beefy Byronic heroes	Tommy Douglas with a side of beef
Bravado	Buffalo
Passions	Pastures
Nightmares	Mares at night
Ancient manor upon the craggy vista	Aging granary upon the semi-arid steppe
Madness	Seasonal Affective Disorder
Decay	Drought
Hereditary curses	Curséd Herefords
Persecuted maidens	Persevering milkmaids
Haunted houses	Bat-filled barns
Madwoman in the attic	Rabid badger in the woodshed
Dastardly villains	Corrupt private grain trade system representatives
Perambulating maniacs	Ruminating herbivores

I believe the combination of madness, rabid wildlife, and inhospitable landscapes could help me secure a major Canadian literary prize.

UMBERS AND I DO NOT GET ALONG, BUT THERE are a few numbers I know: my home phone number, my student ID, my grandfather's phone number, and the Library of Congress call number for *Sense and Sensibility*. A librarian once told me that you could go to almost any library in the world and use PR4034 to find *Sense and Sensibility*. That seemed like a magical power to me, so I set out to memorize it. It comes in handy since I so often pick up a Miss Austen book to keep me company. Today Elinor and Marianne are sitting with me on the shelf of my carrel as I try to summon the energy to study for psychology. I need to summon Elinor's stoicism to balance the excessive sensibility and fondness for dead leaves I share with Marianne so I can pass this multiple-choice exam.

Jane Austen, unlike Burns and Botticelli, is entirely mine: no one in my family much cares for her, which is fine by me. I first met Miss Austen when I was ten, and my Uncle Tom sent me, out of the blue, a tiny, tidy copy of *Emma* from England. I remember unwrapping it from the waxy, foreign-feeling, brown paper with its magical stamps. It came with a note that simply said, "Your Granny loved this novel and I hope you will too." The book fit perfectly in my small hands and it had a mint-green dust jacket and blue cloth binding. Austen, *Emma*, and Everyman were embossed on the blue cloth spine in gold. On the first page of the book, it said, "Everyman, I will go with thee, and be thy guide,/ In thy most need to go by thy side." I now know that every novel Everyman publishes contains this inscription, but, at age ten, I took the inscription as a directive: this tiny novel would go with me and be my guide, and in my most need be by my side. My parents told me that I might have to wait until I was older to understand *Emma*, but I was intrigued with my uncle's gift, and began reading it stealthily after my allotted bedtime reading. After my light was turned out, I reclaimed my confiscated flashlight from its hiding place in the linen closet, and started to read.

The first line told me that Emma Woodhouse was handsome, clever, and rich, with a comfortable home and happy disposition. Like me, she was the youngest daughter. But unlike me, Emma could do just about anything she liked. I was intrigued and envious. I remember feeling like the author—this Jane Austen—was talking just to me, whispering her story so that no one in my family would be awakened and so that I could keep reading. My parents found me the next morning with my finger marking the place in the book where I'd fallen asleep, and my about-to-be-re-confiscated flashlight giving off the faintest of glows. My mother woke me by saying, "Molly, what did I tell you about reading?" and I replied, "You told me I would have to be older to like this book. But I love it so much."

I read *Emma* non-stop and by late Sunday afternoon, I had not only finished *Emma* but I had convinced my parents to rush me to Greenwoods' Bookshoppe before it closed to get me another Miss Austen novel. I touched each and every cover, and lingered over each title as long as I could. My parents were impatiently indulgent and the clerks antsy. The store was closing, and I needed to decide. I eventually picked *Sense and Sensibility*; it was the one where my finger rested most often, and I finished it too in a matter of days. By the end of the week, I would only refer to her as Miss Austen, and my parents decided they needed to purchase copies of the rest of Miss Austen's novels for me. For Christmas, I received her juvenilia, and for my birthday, the collected letters. I wrote a letter to my uncle thanking him effusively for *Emma*, and outlining how much I loved Miss Austen and all of her novels. A few months later, he sent me a one-line reply on a postcard from the National Portrait Gallery in London writing, "I'm so pleased you love Miss Austen, Molly." The postcard featured the only known portrait of Miss Austen, drawn by her sister Cassandra. My parents bought me a little frame and I hung it over my bed. It remains there still.

In the year or two that followed, I read and re-read each of the six novels. I ranked and re-ranked them, struggling to decide which was my favourite. I made stickers for their covers out of gold tinfoil candy wrappers to designate their elevated status in my bookcase. My family listened as I talked through my rankings in what I now think was probably an agonizing amount of detail. Soon Tess and Heathcliff would successfully lobby for a house rule that made it impossible to talk about Jane Austen during meal times, but my parents still listened when they drove me to piano or ballet. Around this time, I began feeding neighbourhood cats, and was meticulous in selecting the most suitable Austen character to name each one after. I was quite successful, I think, except for the whiney, whinging cat I named Mr Collins. When he delivered a litter of kittens one spring in our marigold planter, I renamed him Charlotte Lucas. I knew it wasn't fair to Charlotte Lucas, but life was never fair to Charlotte Lucas, was it?

Over the years, I learned to keep my passion for Miss Austen to myself. In part, I didn't want to expose myself to the tortuous scorn my classmates heaped on the boy who talked about Gandalf as if he were his dad's best friend, or the girl who was convinced she would not only own a unicorn one day, but would ride it to school and not let any of us pet it, ever. Miss Austen was too special for me to expose her to taunts at recess and mean notes passed among the popular girls. While I kept Elizabeth Bennet, Mr Darcy, Willoughby, and Marianne to myself, Miss Austen was, as my first copy of *Emma* had predicted, someone who would go with me and be my guide and in my most need, be by my side. And so, here she sits by my side as I make helpful psychology study notes like, "B.F. Skinner is the mean guy." I imagine her nodding with approval. "You've got this, Molly." 🎴

OR THE MOST PART, MY PARENTS' RECORD collection is something I wish were hidden behind closed doors, not publicly visible in our living room for the open mocking by our visiting friends and neighbours. Although Mark calls their collection "eclectic," I find the assemblage of albums by Carole King, the Bee Gees, the Irish Rovers, Bob Seger, and Boney M itemizes all the things that are totally uncool about my parents. Tess taught me that every time my dad got out the soundtrack to *Hair: The American Tribal Love-Rock Musical*, we needed to "secure the perimeter," and make sure none of its noxious notes could escape open windows in our living room, and contaminate whatever amounts of coolness we might have at school. Every time Mum and Dad sang along to "Age of Aquarius," I heard the sound of my future dying. Could I ever be cool with parents like these?

The one redeeming item in their collection, however, is the four-album box set *The Greatest 64 Motown Original Hits*. I love all sixty-four hits. On Saturday nights when we were small, my parents would put on one of the four increasingly scratchy records, and turn the volume up high. We'd do puzzles, play board games, and dance in our pyjamas until bedtime. When, on rare occasions, I had the house to myself in junior high, I'd be running for the box set the minute my parents closed the garage door. By the time their car was at the end of our block, I'd have slid one of the carefully selected albums out of its white paper sleeve, picked the side

I most wanted to hear, and placed it gently on the turntable. I'd spend whatever time I had home alone lying on the floor, listening to those bass lines, that famous echo, those horn sections. Even now, there's not a bad mood that can't be soothed or a boy problem that can't be solved by a Motown record. Smokey Robinson tells me I'd better shop around. The Supremes caution me that I can't hurry love. The Four Tops give me hope that maybe, one day, someone will be there to love and shelter me, be there, and always see me through. I like to think Miss Austen would have liked Motown. I do wonder, however, if all the Miss Austen novels I've read and all the Motown songs I've sung have given me a messed-up sense of what love is.

It is an odd thing, love. I read about it in Norton Anthologies. I argue about it in pubs and cafés. I underline passages about it. I can deconstruct, reconstruct, new historicize, and postmodernize any form of literature about it in five to ten pages in MLA format. I can roll my eyes when people sigh about it. I can nod compassionately about it. I memorize passages about it when I am lonely. But, really, what is this thing called love? Love is not love which alters when it alteration finds? Nay, love is tainted. Love is a battlefield. Love is all we need. Love hurts. And love will tear us apart again. Maybe it's because I don't think I've ever actually fallen in love with a real person that makes love such a mystery. Although I'm often sought out for advice on matters of the heart because I read novels, the only serious relationships I've had have been purely imaginary. Particularly formative have been my imaginary relationships with Willoughby (until chapter fifteen of the first volume of *Sense and Sensibility*; after that, he's a cad), Mr Darcy, Paul Weller, John Cusack, Noel (or Liam) Gallagher, and Liam Neeson (in that order). My imaginary self has broken their hearts many, many more times than they would want you to know. Sometimes they break my heart too. But not irreparably, because I have Motown and Miss Austen on my side, and they know what becomes of the broken-hearted better than I do.

SOMETIMES, WHEN I SHOULD BE PAYING ATTENTION in my Gender and Courtship in the Long-Nineteenth Century class, I work my way across each row of students and ponder each male classmate. I wonder, could I love him? Could he be the Mr Darcy to my Elizabeth Bennet? The Will Ladislaw to my Dorothea? More often than not, it's a no or a maybe. Every once in a while there is a hint of a perhaps. But then I worry. What if he likes classic rock? Or is a member of the Young Progressive Conservatives? Or, worse still, what if he eats veal without guilt? Or doesn't use a refillable travel mug? And then my worrying makes me worry. Am I too hard on mankind? And then, every once in a while, I see someone and think "could he be the one?" More often than not, the person I think this about is Cute Angus. Until he did something quite despicable.

All semester, Cute Angus and I have been flirting with each other, and I was just, this week, starting to think things might go somewhere with him, but then this happened. We had our short response papers on *Pride and Prejudice* returned today. I received a B+ which, I admit, stung a bit, especially since I consider Miss Austen and the Bennet sisters close personal friends; how could I *not* understand that novel? Be that as it may, I do realize that sometimes that kind of emotional closeness to a text does not allow one critical distance, so I accepted my B+ as fair. As I was leaving class, Cute Angus started to walk with me, and we compared grades. He got an A. My first thought was "He *gets* Miss Austen! He *is* perfect!" I was just about to ask him out for coffee when he made a confession: he had not actually read Miss Austen's novel. He had only read the Coles Notes version.

"Isn't that hysterical? I did a whole paper about how Austen's white Anglo, upper-middle-class, heteronormative perspective offered a limited view of marriage and courtship and she loved it." I hardly felt able to laugh, smile, or breathe. The ground I stood upon felt like it was about to crumble. How could he not read Jane Austen? And *Pride and Prejudice*? Not reading Tobias Smollett or Samuel Richardson, I could accept, and maybe even applaud. But Jane Austen?

"She said my reading was concise and insightful. Funny, huh? Want to go for a coffee?" He gave me a smile that I would have found irresistible a mere hour ago. I made an excuse about needing to go to the library to study for psychology. Instead of drinking coffee with Cute Angus, I fled to the fifth floor to sit among the panicked, the unbathed, and the sleep-deprived, and to feel my world implode with questions.

Is reading the Coles Notes summary of *Pride and Prejudice* in lieu of Miss Austen's novel really the mortal sin I think it is? Would it have been as egregious to me if he hadn't read, say, Wordsworth? Am I just miffed that someone who didn't actually read *Pride and Prejudice* got a better grade on a paper about *Pride and Prejudice*? Or am I just devastated that I was so wrong about someone so cute?

I grabbed a biography of Miss Austen off the shelf to stare at her portrait. Was it easier in her day when there weren't ever more than one or two men who would be appropriate for you to consider? It seems to take Miss Austen's characters the length of a quadrille to decide whom they love, and a quadrille cannot be much longer than, say, a bus ride home in rush hour. And there couldn't be more than a dozen eligible men at a ball. How did they decide? How would I decide? What if someone on my rush-hour bus said, "Before you get to your stop, you must choose a husband from this dozen, randomly assembled eligible men or be alone for life. Who will it be?" I'm not sure why someone might run onto the bus and force someone like me to choose a total stranger to marry, but it's fun to play along. How would I decide? Maybe there would be, as it seems in most Miss Austen novels, only two or three real contenders in that dozen. Would I find myself saying, "Is that veal parmesan in your lunch bag? For real? Next. What's that on your Walkman, kind sir? Journey? I don't think so. Sir? Yes, you in the sweater vest. What are you reading? Ken Follett? Yikes. Well, at least he reads. And Ken Follett is fiction so there will be hope. I think I'll have to take that man in the second row. Yes, the one in the brown sweater vest. He may not be Mr Right but, because I must, I will settle for Mr Not-So-Bad."

But this isn't about a man on a bus or a man at the Netherfield Ball. It's about Cute Angus. Oh Angus. Why couldn't you have read and loved *Pride and Prejudice*? You were so perfect. 🌿

*L*AST NIGHT I STAYED UP LATE READING Thomas Hardy poetry for fun. The mere act of reading Hardy for fun has made me realize two things about myself: one, how truly pathetic I am and two, how many things about my life I would never admit to anyone. Bored in my psychology class, I assembled a list of all my pathetic attributes and arranged them into what could qualify as the worst personal ad ever.

Twenty-year-old, female, Honours English
student seeks dreamy artistic male with poetic
soul, persistent yet subdued joie de vivre, and
hints of melancholia that are properly channelled
into quality artistic ventures, not wasted on
inartistic moping. On a good day, I can repress
my low self-image to assemble enough external
affirmation to believe myself to be sufficiently
attractive, and in possession of what I hope are
nascent glimmers of Miss Austen's sparkling
wit. Hobbies include: walking through fallen
leaves on bleak fall days and thinking about
Gerard Manley Hopkins, listening to Oasis,
not writing about the excess of black bile,
imagining self to be descendent of plucky
historic Scotswomen like Flora MacDonald,
having crushes on men who are fictitious or
know naught of my existence, and concealing

from friends and family the amount of Victorian poetry I read. Seeking like-minded soul with good fashion sense and thoughtful haircut for: sipping coffee in cozy cafés, debating merits of classic novels, comparing notes on shoes and clothing, strolling in romantic foreign locales, debating merits of current trends in pop music, and kissing "tremblingly" like Dorothea and Will in *Middlemarch*. Ability to speak Italian a bonus. Must not be currently registered in an Honours English programme. Performance artists, philosophy majors, and children of faculty members need not apply. Men who list "The Road Not Taken" as their favourite poem should not apply either; instead, please use the time you would have spent responding to my ad to read a few more poems. Really, I think you owe it to yourself to branch out a bit. Must like kittens, sheepdogs, horses, coffee, Giorgio Armani, Virginia Woolf, Art Nouveau, Mars bars, and really nice soap. Non-vegetarians will be considered, but not veal eaters (shame on you). Oh, and no mimes. No P.O. Box will be provided for your response since I am sure you do not exist. Nevertheless, I thank you for your consideration and, if applicable, your sympathy.

The fact that I am currently single shouldn't be a mystery to anyone after reading this. ❧

Y NOTES FOR PROFESSOR WIDGETT-JONES's lecture consist of today's date, the month, and the year. That's the extent of what I've understood today. We were talking about the socio-political, poetic economies of the sonnet, and I am entirely lost. Everyone else was laughing knowingly and nodding at key points, but it all flew over my head. I double-checked that I read everything that was assigned, and that there aren't missing pages in my anthology. Clearly, I am missing something huge about iambic pentameter. I like Professor Widgett-Jones: she's very nice and her suits are the best in the department. Sometimes, however, it seems like she just makes stuff up so she can use funny lecture titles. For example, today's lecture is called "'Iamb what I am': Poetic Metre and the Creation of the Self in Romantic Sonnets" and last class' "(I)ambiguity and the Narrative Poem: Browning's Use of Metre in the Creation of Unreliable Narrators." If these are my father's colleagues, it's no wonder he is so weird. He's actually starting to emerge as one of the sane ones. Surely, there must be more important things to ponder than poetic metre and the "wailful choir the small gnats mourn."

While my classmates clapped the rhythm of Keats' "Ode to Autumn," my mind wandered to the topic for my courtship paper. I'm not sure what it's about, but I have a great title: "Better Homes and Gargoyles: Gothic Edifices and Courtship." I'm not sure what I'm trying to argue, but I think if I come up with a great title, and then invent enough stuff to fill out a semi-logical argument, I should be okay.

From there, my mind wandered to my first Gothic novel with Canadian content, and I began making notes for *Cattle Shed of Otranto*. This is what I've got so far:

Saskatchewan. 1934. Contentious amalgamation of pasture land. Menacing indigenous fauna. Underground tunnels disguised as Richardson's ground squirrel warrens. Tempestuous dustbowl storms. A few more details and I think I have the foundations of the Saskatchewan Gothic.

I got so involved in my Gothic musings that I forgot to fake participation in class. I failed to punctuate the last twenty minutes of class with deeply ponderous nods and thoughtful, furrowed brow gazes out the small window in the corner of the room. If I had the guts, next class I'd attempt one of my black-bile classmate's "sardonic chortles" to express my fake delight at discovering a particularly poignant nuance to Keats' use of stressed and unstressed syllables. But I can't. Maybe if I wore a turtleneck, I could pull it off. I think Widgett-Jones is onto me. I hope she doesn't notice the only thing I scribbled in my anthology is "iamb confused" beside "Ode to Autumn."

ODAY I SAT IN RUTHERFORD LIBRARY SOUTH, not doing my Gender and Courtship readings. I love this space and how, in those rare moments where everyone in the room happens not to be shifting, shuffling, and shushing, there's a sudden moment of silence reminding me of how noisy the work of thinking actually is. I love how the stairs are gently worn on the left-hand side, like small smile shapes on the edge of each step. I love wondering how much my own mid-term and final-exam footsteps have contributed to its gentle erosion. Maybe years from now I will return to see the steps even more worn, and know that in my own small way I have made my mark on this building.

I love the height of the ceilings; the impress of some-one else's notes in the wood of the long tabletops; I love the rigidity of my chair; I love imagining the millions of words being read, thought, and written throughout the room; I love imagining what that man over there is thinking as he squints into his newspaper. I love imagining how many boys and girls fell in love over these very tables. I love imagining both of my parents studying here, not knowing each other, or maybe, unknowingly, sitting next to each other, or pass-ing each other, maybe exchanging a polite smile as they pass through that narrow doorway. Sometimes my mind wanders and I imagine that somewhere in here is a man whom some-day I might be unable to imagine a time without.

I looked along the tables and wondered if today might be the day I meet that very man. How would our conversation start? What would we talk about? Across the room today, for example, was a man of Rupert Brooke–like beauty who was working his way through a stack of bound periodicals. His brow was furrowed, his eyes intense, but kind. I imagined he was thinking really hard about something good and important—like saving endangered penguins, not deconstructing a hegemonic metaphor as I had been. He had the beauty of a bygone era, and I imagined falling truly, madly, deeply in love with him. He seemed like the kind of man who would have—and consult—his own personal reference collection. He seemed like someone who couldn't imagine spelling encyclopædia any other way.

Having the powers of imagination at my disposal, I imagined myself having the beauty of a bookish Helen of Troy—the kind of beauty that might launch a thousand, well-written sonnets. I imagined he of the Rupert Brooke–like beauty looked up from his yellowed volumes, caught my eye, and smiled. He did this two or three times before standing up, stretching, and walking to return a bound volume to the re-shelving cart. He gave me a glance that said, "I pay attention to posted signs and placards that tell me not to re-shelve library books," and I reciprocated with a look that says, "I find your adherence to library etiquette very alluring." Immediately, we understood we were both good library citizens, and that added to the mutual attraction. On his way back to his table, he stopped by mine to whisper something superlatively romantic. Something like, "Excuse me, you wouldn't happen to have a copy of *Sense and Sensibility* with you, by chance? I know there are nineteen copies of it in the PR4000 section in Rutherford North, but I'd like to get the line Elinor says to Marianne about dead leaves just right without interrupting my train of thought too drastically." Of course, since I was not actually myself in my reverie, but someone prettier, more sophisticated, and articulate, I said, "Would you prefer the Oxford or Penguin edition?" in sexy, hushed library tones. We agreed the Penguin edition was superior, and I retrieved it from the very stylish book bag I currently covet, but do not yet own. We both noticed how nicely the book bag matched his sweater, and shared the unspoken belief this was a sign we were meant to be. I skimmed the well-worn pages and whispered, "Are you talking about the passage on page 114 of the Penguin edition where Elinor says, 'It is not every-one who has your passion for dead leaves'?" And he responded, "Yes, that's precisely it. Thank you. By the way, you wouldn't be interested in accompanying me for a cup of hot almond milk and a raisin scone, would you? You would? That's absolutely splendid! I just need to add that Miss Austen line into the nearly completed draft of my article, and then I'm ready to go. My article? I am writing about how the birth weights of a particular breed of newly hatched, endangered penguins are higher if they are read Jane Austen while in the incubator. Yes, it is remarkable, isn't it? We'd tried it with James Joyce but the results were catastrophic; *Ulysses* sends the penguin eggs into a frenzied, angry state. One nearly rolled himself off the table. It was if he were trying to escape the "Nausicaa" episode at any cost. Anyway, shall we go for that hot almond milk? Or shall I simply retreat into your imagination, and take my place beside leprechauns, unicorns, and Fluevog boots you can safely wear in ice and snow?" I sighed, stretched, and returned to this week's hegemonic metaphor, but my mind kept returning to a Miss Austen–reading man of Rupert Brooke–like beauty. 🕸

*I*F I DIDN'T KNOW BETTER, I'D SWEAR THE ENGLISH faculty lounge had one of those machines that they show on televised lottery draws. Instead of numbers, however, the ping-pong balls have critical and literary terms on them. At various points in the semester, professors would line up and use this machine to create paper topics and mid-term exam questions. I imagine them chortling in their joy as Professor Byron Keats draws Hermeneutics, then Hyperbole, and finally Black Bile. "Ho ho! Imagine the poor kid who gets that one!" "Oh! Oh! Give that one to Moll(y)," my dad laughs. "Brilliant, Hamish, brilliant!" and they cackle conspiratorially like plaid-wearing, sweater-vested Weird Sisters as they visualize me fretting and typing away in the intellectual version of a Hieronymus Bosch painting in which I currently exist.

I have spent the past nine hours working on my paper, and have nothing to show for it. I do confess that the word "working" might be an exaggeration. I went to the library at about one o'clock, and started reading page one of Robert Burton's *The Anatomy of Melancholy*. I read one paragraph, and then noticed there was a woodcut picture of Burton on the frontispiece. I knew Susan would find his haircut amusing, so I wandered around the fourth and fifth floors looking for her. Unable to find her, I returned to Burton, read a page, and then wondered if anyone has ever brought a Renaissance-era woodcut into a hair salon, saying, "I would like a new haircut. Can you make me look like Robert Burton?" I giggled to myself, and knew Susan would also find this funny. I went out again to look for her, expanding my search to the third floor. As I wandered, I wondered if the library had any books on Renaissance haircuts. It would be good to know if they actually used bowls in the Renaissance to cut hair in that style. Maybe some sort of wooden bowl. What sort of bowl technology existed in the Renaissance? Where might I find this information? It might be exactly the kind of information I might need for my paper. After checking out the second floor as well, I re-searched the third, fourth, and fifth floors, then gave up my search for Susan and returned to my desk.

I opened my book, but every time I started to read, I'd see Burton with a giant wooden bowl on his head. Slowly I began to wonder if his bad hair were the cause of his melancholia. I made myself read. I finished the first paragraph when Susan stopped by my desk to see if I wanted to go get a coffee. I had Burton reading to do but I also had to ask her about possible connections between bad haircuts and melancholia. I tapped woodcut Burton on the head and told him I would return shortly and commence my research on what would undoubt-edly prove to be a well-wrought piece of cutting-edge Burton scholarship. I like to think he nodded approvingly.

As we were standing in line at Java Jive talking about bad haircuts, Susan spied Prufrock Van Beekveld going into Dewey's Pub and I knew I was sunk. I had grown up with Prufrock and his younger brother Pellinore and never liked them. Prufrock and I were the same age, and it was initially assumed by our professorial parents that he and I would be great friends. Pellinore is two years younger and carried a plastic Arthurian sword everywhere he went until he was about twelve. Since birth, Pellinore has been smelly, doughy, and allergic to everything. His parents hovered over him as if he were made of glass, leaving Prufrock to wreak havoc wherever he went. On what was to be their last visit to our home, Prufrock decapitated all of my dolls and left his teeth marks on my arms. Visits with the Van Beekveld family ceased.

You can imagine, then, my nausea at seeing Prufrock Van Beekveld in my first-year English class, and my disgust at having Susan fall so hopelessly in love with him. It disturbs me that Prufrock's nastiness gets overlooked because, as hard as it is for me to admit this, he is smart and very good looking. It horrifies me that Susan is one of those people. When Susan said, "Oh, come on! Just one teeny beer. I'll buy," Future Burton Scholar Molly's rhetoric didn't stand a chance against Best Friend Molly's need to save Susan from Prufrock. Susan seemed to think that if I were around whenever she "ran into" Prufrock it wouldn't seem like she was stalking him, which, of course, she was. She carried his class schedule around with her along with a schedule for his bus route. She doesn't know that I know this, but in her wallet she carries a note he left in her notebook in the library: "Pseusan, can I borrow $20? On third floor. PvB." Lest you think "Pseusan" is a transcription error on my part or a spelling error on PvB's part, rest assured, gentle reader, that it's his calculated gesture of precociousness. Or, an inadvertent indicator of pretentiousness. Take your pick. Such were my thoughts as we drank our half pints of Big Rock porter.

Prufrock pontificated on all manner of subjects related to himself for over an hour and Susan hung on every word. After I ate my muffin and chatted with anyone who wasn't Prufrock for an hour, I realized it was almost dinnertime so I ordered a small vegetarian pizza and chatted with others who also weren't Prufrock. Meanwhile Susan laughed at everything Prufrock said and Prufrock just kept smiling at me; he winked at me three times. When I finally left Dewey's at 6:30, my unwritten paper was percolating feebly in the recesses of my mind, and I was upset with Susan. In the bathroom, I reminded her of the doll-head episode and she said, "He was seven." She dismissed my, "Can't you see, the dolls were foreshadowing!" argument as the result of me reading too many novels. I left her swooning and giggling over his spurious wit and went back to the library.

By the time I got back to my desk, it was seven o'clock and full panic set in. I opened Burton, put a yellow sticky note over his bad haircut, and set my mind toward the more pressing matter of black bile, hermeneutics, and hyperbole. I read as much as I could, and, at nine o'clock, I realized if I caught the next bus, I could be home in time to watch *The Simpsons*. Even if I don't finish Burton, I feel I am learning a lot about melancholy and black bile experientially. ◌

*I*N AN ATTEMPT TO MAKE MYSELF FEEL ON top of my semester's assignments, I have given each course a different colour of sticky note, and assembled all assignments chronologically on my bedroom wall: it's like a time-management Seurat painting. I actually feel worse now that my workload is visualized. I had all the best intentions of starting a draft of my Gender Constructions of Courtship project tonight, but realized I needed some new music to finish this paper, which is still a mess. I decided to call Mark for some suggestions. I hesitated—would he be too busy? Would he find me annoying? Would he be with someone? I steeled myself and dialled his number. He answered quickly and seemed happy to talk with me. He said he'd been hoping to run into me on campus. We talked about everything but music—catching up on our semesters and his plans to go to Europe next semester. After forty-five minutes, I remembered why I'd called. I assuaged my procrastinator's guilt by asking for music that would be conducive to writing a paper on Jane Austen and courtship. We debated where Miss Austen would fall on the music spectrum. Mark thought we should be scientific so we started at A: "Would she like Adam and the Ants or a-ha?" Adam and the Ants. "Bauhaus or Bananarama?" Bauhaus. "The Cure or the Cult?" The Cure. "Duran Duran or Depeche Mode" Neither. By the time we got to "X or XTC" (which we debated for another ten minutes and finally decided on XTC), I was no closer to finding the perfect music to accompany writing a paper about Jane

Austen than I was before my nearly two-hour phone call.

When I finally got off the phone at about eleven o'clock, I picked up *Pride and Prejudice*, and hugged it tightly. It occurred to me that if I were Elizabeth, and I had a Mr Darcy, he and I would have expressed our feelings for each other in the only possible way: we'd make each other mixed tapes. After a long night, here is the beginning of my Gender and Courtship project:

"*Pride and Prejudice*: The Mixtape Paper"

Introduction: It is a truth universally acknowledged that a young man wooing a young woman must be compelled to show his affection through the creation of a mixtape. Similarly, a young woman shows her reciprocal affection for a young man through her creation of a response mixtape. While the mixtape was not a mode of courtship available in Miss Austen's time, if Elizabeth and Darcy lived in our time, their wooing would most certainly have involved the creation and exchange of mixtapes. The cassette tape I have included with this paper attempts on Side A to tell the story of *Pride and Prejudice* from Elizabeth's perspective, and, on Side B, from Mr Darcy's. In my selection of music, and the accompanying explanatory liner notes, I attempt to show how gender informs how both Mr Darcy and Elizabeth might have conceived of their relationship, had they lived in 1990s, and had access to records, a turntable, and a tape recorder. Footnote: In this assignment, I do not wish to imply anything about the musical tastes of either Elizabeth Bennet or Mr Darcy. Undoubtedly, both would be fond of Motown, but it would be highly unlikely Elizabeth would listen to Cher. Similarly, I predict Mr Darcy would have balked at listening to the Ramones until Elizabeth gently realigned his limited musical horizons. Unfortunately, I think it highly plausible that Mr Darcy would have both Foreigner and Chicago on his turntable at frequent intervals. Elizabeth would learn to tolerate this, because it might be one of his few failings as one of the dreamiest literary heroes in the British literary tradition.

I have handed in my tape paper—taper, if you will—and have my fingers crossed. I think I'll drop off a copy of the tape for Mark as a thank you for his help. 🎵

AGFA CRX 60

 60 Pride and Prejudice: The Mix Tape

 AGFA CRX 60

1 Elizabeth to Darcy

- "You're so vain" - Carly Simon
- "Don't you Want Me?" - Human League
- "What's Love Got to Do With It?" - Tina Turner
- "Sweet Talkin' Guy" - The Chiffons
- "Tell Him" - The Exciters
- "Material Girl" - Madonna
- "If I Could Turn Back Time" - Cher
- "How Sweet It Is (to Be Loved By You)" - Marvin Gaye

Darcy to Elizabeth 2

- "Money for Nothing" - Dire Straits
- "Do You Wanna Dance" - The Ramones
- "Is She Really Going Out With Him?" - Joe Jackson
- "Do You Really Want to Hurt Me?" - Culture Club
- "Heaven knows I'm Miserable Now" - The Smiths
- "Ain't Too Proud to Beg" - The Temptations
- "Hard to Say I'm Sorry" - Chicago
- "Waiting for a Girl like You" - Foreigner

ODAY, I LISTENED TO A CLASS PRESENTATION on phlegm. Thankfully, Professor Keats, after wincing through the first five minutes, interrupted to inform the presenters that the g in "phlegm" is silent. I fear I may be partially responsible for the calm and unemotional presentation put on by the phlegm group. Two weeks ago, my group did our presentation on black bile, and Professor Keats publicly applauded our attempts to "corporealize our humour." When he said that, we all looked at each other and repressed shrugs. True, we all dressed in black and used The Smiths' "How Soon Is Now?" to open and close our presentation, but all four of us usually wear all black and The Smiths clip was a moment of last-minute, serendipitous brilliance: our presentation was a few minutes short, and my group mate Simon noticed The Smiths poster in Keats' office last week. We tossed it in to get up to our required twenty minutes. In our written feedback, he called our presentation "smartly yet irreverently self-referential," and gave us a grade of B+. It isn't hard to corporealize sleepless melancholia in this class.

Last week, the group doing yellow bile wasn't so lucky. They tried to capitalize on our accidental brilliance by "becoming one" with their humour. Unfortunately their attempts to embody "easily angered" got out of control, and Professor Keats had to intervene after one of the girls started crying and another started pelting her group members with tiny pieces of chalk. Despite their protests of "No! We're just choleric and easily angered!" he called the presentation to a close. Judging by their sullen looks when they received their grades today, I don't think he saw the self-referential quality of the yellow bile group as terribly smart. I suspect he also failed to comment on the performative brilliance of the Juicy-Fruit-wrapper, yellow shirts they bought and had to endure wearing all day. Our B+ seems a little tawdry now; I tried to smile sympathetically at one of them, but they're avoiding eye contact and muttering things about melancholia.

In preparing for the mid-term that I know I am going to fail, I assembled a little chart about the four humours and, as a bit of a heuristic, added myself, my siblings, and our cat, Hodge the Younger, to round things out.

Humour	Blood	Black bile	Yellow bile	Phlegm
Hippocrates	Spring	Autumn	Summer	Winter
	Air	Earth	Fire	Water
	Courageous, amourous	Despondent, sleepless	Easily angered	Calm, un-emotional
Galen's four temperaments	Sanguine	Melancholic	Choleric	Phlegmatic
Paracelsus's four totem spirits	Changeable salamander	Industrious gnomes	Inspired nymphs	Curious sylphs
MacGregor Children	Hodge the Younger	Me	Tess	Heathcliff

For a long time, I assumed my family is the way it is because we are descended from people whose history is replete with generations of inter-clan feuding and a lot of porridge. Now I am starting to think that it's less about the porridge and more about the humours.

For the most part, my family is a fairly typical, mild-mannered Canadian family. There is, however, on both sides, Scottish blood sufficient to make us all placid, yet mercurial, quick to ire, yet patient enough to incubate a grudge, and then release it like an angry raptor at the perfect moment. We may have an excess of yellow bile. I wonder if there is a supplement we could take. If I weren't so despondent and sleepless, I would be galled that Tess gets to be an "inspired nymph," and Healthcliff a "curious sylph," while I am relegated to being an "industrious gnome." It's always this way, isn't it? But Hodge, dear Hodge, is the picture of the courageous, amourous, sanguine, and changeable salamander. It's sad that none of my experiential knowledge of black bile and phlegm could be used for the mid-term. 🐝

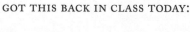

I GOT THIS BACK IN CLASS TODAY:

Response to "*Pride and Prejudice*:
The Mix-tape"

Miss MacGregor, I have never received a
mixtape and liner notes in lieu of a paper
before, and I am, quite frankly, uncertain how
to mark this assignment. On the one hand, you
undoubtedly deserve an F for not submitting a
formal paper. On the other hand, you've not only
demonstrated keen insights into Austen's work
and world, but made valuable connections with
the way gender constructions inform courtship
rituals today and in Austen's time and could
deserve an A. I was going to go halfway, and
give you a grade of a C, however your masterful
use of MLA format on your liner notes is truly
commendable and groundbreaking. I applaud
your pioneering efforts on this front. And I agree,
Darcy would have liked Foreigner. So, a B it is.

I SPENT MUCH OF TODAY'S BLACK BILE CLASS trying not to think about Cute Angus and, instead, concentrate on the critical triangulation of humours, hermeneutics, and hegemony.

After nearly half-a-semester, the only connection I can see among those three things is that they all start with the letter H. Can I stretch that intellectual gem into an in-class essay for the mid-term? Today's class droned on, and on, and on, and I appear to be the only one who does not understand anything about hermeneutics. Marvin Gaye sings "What's Going On?" non-stop in my head, while everyone else leaps up to proffer comments that don't even sound like real sentences, laughing at things that don't seem like jokes. Is dehegemonification even a word? Can one's subjectivity really be deconstructed by a consideration of black bilification? Is that the joke? What am I missing? I also think I have failed my paper for Professor Keats because I now see I completely misread the assignment; it was not black bile AND hyperbole, AND hermeneutics, but black bile OR hyperbole, OR hermeneutics.

It is taking all I can muster to stay awake in class. Last week, I tried to waylay my boredom by drawing a cartoon character I invented: "Hegemony Cricket." I tried to stifle my laughter when I gave him a Byron Keats turtleneck. Tea came sputtering out my nose, making me laugh even more and I had to dash from class to regain my composure. Even kind-hearted Jason gave me a "really, Molly!" sort of look and Professor Keats has been darting me an evil eye ever since.

Last night, knowing Keats would pounce on me the minute my attention wandered, I prepared what I believed to be a foolproof plan for today's class. On an index card, I wrote a response that can answer anything he might lob at me. Toward the end of class, my attention wandered and Professor Keats leapt on me with a pointed question. As I'd practiced last night, I tilted my head, pretended to think for a moment and then tossed out my well-crafted answer:

"I can see both sides of this issue, and I feel really conflicted once I consider the ambiguities inherent in this question. So, it's not that I don't have an answer, it's just that if postmodernism has taught us anything, it's that we can never definitively say yes or no. Rather, the best we can do is offer a highly qualified 'maybe' or 'perhaps.'"

When I stopped speaking, I discerned a most agonizing silence working its way through the room. The whole class turned to stare at me. They didn't just turn their heads. They turned their whole bodies so they could all get a really good look at me. My body knew I was in trouble long before my mind caught on. My wool sweater became naggingly itchy as I started to sweat. The silence was finally broken by a few ahems and stifled giggles. I sat, waiting, hoping for some indication of the exact nature of the monstrous act I had inadvertently committed.

Finally Professor Keats broke his icy, hate-filled stare and said, "So. I will write a note to myself that the instructions for the mid-term next class are perfectly clear to all members of the class, except for Miss MacGregor by whose name I shall write, 'unable to commit to a yes or a no due to a questionable reading of postmodernism.' If there are no further questions, I shall see you all next class. I trust all of you, especially Miss Molly MacGregor, will have a very pleasant afternoon. Good day." I sat paralyzed, while those around me gathered their books, and avoided making eye contact with me, the class's look-alike Madge Wildfire.

Before Professor Keats left the room, he paused at the door, and shot me a look that said "pretentious professorial spawn." His turtleneck entourage shot me their own versions of those looks, as they greedily scuttled after him with their questions about Heidegger, bile, and who knows what else.

As I looked at my index card, I realized I'd hate me too for saying what I'd just said. I'd become my own worst nightmare. My classmates all slouched away and, in the silence of the now empty room, the carrot muffin I had just eaten was raging in my stomach and every coffee I'd ever consumed had returned with a vengeance to pump angrily through my veins.

I left the Humanities Building and walked quickly, yet aimlessly around campus hoping the shock of what I had done would wear off. After an hour, I snuck up to my dad's office hoping for a ride home, taking the lesser-used stairwell, lest I run into the turtlenecks. In some small way, I think I was hoping that letting myself be driven home by him would somehow atone for the "professorial spawn" faux pas he would soon hear about. I knew I'd not only embarrassed myself, but my parents too. In any other professor's class, it could be laughed off after the initial sting of embarrassment wore off. But things with Professor Keats were different.

Last week, I overheard my dad telling my mum about the recent department meeting where the faculty debated how to spend the proceeds of the coffee fund. Apparently, my father had formed a splinter group supporting a toaster oven over a new microwave. Professor Keats interpreted this gesture as hegemonic. When the microwave had been overruled by the groundswell of support for the toaster oven, Professor Keats had rolled his eyes and muttered "Leavisites."

"What," my father demanded, as he overzealously scoured a pie plate, "do small kitchen appliances have to do with F.R. Leavis? Besides, when one actually reads Leavis, one can see that his ideas are more complex than people give him credit for. And what's so New Critical or hegemonic about wanting to toast an English muffin now and then? Is an English muffin really an icon of colonialism? Are they even English?"

"Let it go, Hamish," my ever-sensible mother advised, "let it go." It wasn't clear if she was talking about the toaster oven or the rigorously clean pie plate.

Clearly, my faux pas would add fuel to the fire of the toaster-oven coup, and I couldn't face imagining what I had just contributed to my father's intra-departmental woes. I slid my book bag to the floor outside my dad's office and slouched down beside it, waiting for him to return from class. Eventually, I heard him whistling down the hall, and I knew he was in a great mood. When he came around the corner and saw me, he sang, "Good Golly, Miss Moll(y)," dancing as I would imagine Kingsley Amis's Lucky Jim might dance. The more embarrassed I grew, the more energetic his dancing became. The ridiculousness of him trying to sing and dance like Little Richard, while wearing a MacGregor tartan tie, and toting a hardcover edition of Boswell's *Life of Samuel Johnson*, finally made me laugh. Later, while he fluttered papers around and rearranged stacks of books from one side of his desk to the other and back again, he asked how my classes had been. I was too embarrassed to tell him what had happened, but when I was finally able to muster "Fine," he stopped what he was doing, met my eye, and held it for a minute. He knew.

I continued: "Professor Keats thinks I'm a complete freak and loser. And he's right. I am a complete freak and loser." My dad put down his papers and walked over to me. He leaned over, kissed the top of my head, and sat down beside me.

"Moll(y), Byron Keats doesn't know a poem from a pothole. Take it as a compliment." I couldn't say anything as I feared my tears would escape.

As we walked out the building to our car, my dad treated me gently, just like when he picked me up from elementary school when I was sick. We drove home in silence, but it was nice to still feel small enough to be looked after by my dad. I remembered how when I was small, my dad's students seemed so old and so grown-up. Now that I was that age myself, I didn't feel very old or very grown-up at all. When we turned into our driveway, my dad did not open the door when the old Volvo shuddered to a stop. He was silent a moment, and then said, "Your mother and I are very proud of you, Molly." I felt a giant lump forming in my throat and sputtered something about how if he knew what I'd said in class, he wouldn't be so proud. He then said the most amazing thing, "No, I do know. Alice Widgett-Jones saw a dozen of your classmates whispering and laughing in the hall. She asked Jason Richards what was happening, and he told her that you kicked Keats' pompous ass well into the next millennium. Alice's words, not Jason's, of course. She ran to my classroom to tell me. I have to say, you became a bit of a hero in the faculty lounge today. Professor de Bere even asked if you could chair next month's departmental meeting." I started to laugh. Unbeknownst to me, I'd gone from freak to folk hero to the faculty in a few hours.

"You're certainly your mother's daughter, and she'd be the first to applaud your bravery and convictions. But she'd also be the first to tell you to be careful. Okay?" He tugged on my ponytail until I smiled and nodded. We headed into the house like nothing had happened.

At dinner, we did not talk about the incident, but I noticed my parents seemed more relaxed, and we all laughed more than we usually do at this time of year. Now, in my room, I think about my dad's talk about bravery and convictions, and I feel like a fraud. My equivalent of Jane Eyre's defiant foot stomp was, in fact, entirely accidental and hardly worthy of the parental pride my father now has for my apparently willful stance against pretension and the decontextualized use of literary theory.

I pondered whether I should confess my spurious claims to folk-hero status. To rebut my folk-hero status, I'd have to distance myself from my statement or the emotions behind it. Even though I didn't plan it, I still said it, and I can't claim that I didn't mean it. Had it been someone else in that class who did this, I would have applauded. Would retracting my stance be like Jane Eyre saying, "Oops, I take that back; I was just stomping on a bug on the floor not stamping my tiny foot in defiance"? Or Flora MacDonald saying, "Really? That was Bonnie Prince Charlie? Now that you mention it, that Irish spinning maid did look a little manly"? Defiance is defiance, however it manifests itself. And it feels pretty nice.

I must admit that I'm a little disappointed that I'll never

be able to use that line again: it was gold. My penance for my behaviour will be that I now have to pay attention in class. It's harsh, but I probably deserve it. 🐉

THIS MORNING, I WAS BEING PUSHED ALONG HUB Mall toward the Tory Building among the throng of those soon to be late for their nine o'clock classes. I was mentally preparing for an hour of psychology by filling my eardrums with The Jam's "In the City," when someone grabbed my arm. I turned around to see Mark laughing at me.

"You're in your own little world, aren't you?" I laughed back, "I often am," and snuggled in for the hug he offered. He was heading to one of his seminars and shuddered compassionately when I told him I had psych. We didn't have a lot of time to talk, but he had exciting news: the new Oasis album came out on Tuesday and Southside Sound had copies. I was ashamed I did not know about this.

"I've been looking for you all week," he said. "I didn't think I could buy it without you. Want to go this afternoon?" I explained that I had my black bile class and we were getting our papers back.

"I should go to class," I sighed. I then visualized myself, confused amongst the nodding turtlenecks, and then visualized myself walking down Whyte Avenue with Mark on a glorious fall day. I hastily retracted my commitment to black bile, and made plans to meet him outside Dewey's at two o'clock. Psych suddenly seemed more tolerable. I put my headphones back on, and started "In the City" from the beginning. As Paul Weller's guitar ripped through the morning, he sang that there were a thousand things he wanted to say to me (assuming, as I liked to do, that he was singing to me). I realized I had a thousand things I wanted to say to Mark.

Time crept along and when my Love and Courtship class got out, it felt decadent to flee the Humanities Building. I passed my mopey, black bile compadres, and tried not to meet their jealous eyes as I dashed off in the opposite direction to meet Mark. He was waiting for me when I got to Dewey's, and it seemed as if we both had a thousand things we wanted to say to each other. We talked non-stop in the fall sunshine as we walked down 109th Street and turned onto Whyte Avenue. Mark amused me with stories about his version of the turtlenecks (policy wonks) in his graduate seminars, and I reciprocated with some exaggerated tales of phlegm and the literary tradition. When I described my idea for a band of English majors called Herman and the Neutics, he didn't look at me quizzically as my classmates had, but laughed so hard he almost fell off the curb. As I pulled him back to the sidewalk, I wished I had people like Mark in my classes: he could have made even black bile seem tolerable.

Mark opened the door to Southside Sound, and I stepped into that particular record-store smell, a cross between musty cardboard boxes, junior-high boys, and stale Glade air fresheners. We were both drawn to the new arrivals rack, where two copies of the beautiful new Oasis album sat. We each picked up a copy, and suddenly I was really nervous. What if it isn't as good as *Definitely Maybe*? What if Noel disappoints me? What if it's amazing? What if this album changes my life? Why are there parentheses around "(What's the Story)" and not "Morning Glory"? What if I love it, and Mark thinks it inferior? Or Mark loves it and I hate it? Could I ever hate the Gallagher brothers without dating one first? Finally, I whispered, "Is it weird that I'm really nervous about listening to this CD?" and he shook his head.

"I'm nervous too."

We paid for our CDs, and then stood for a moment outside the shop looking up and down Whyte Avenue. Our mission was complete. I stared across to the Princess Theatre and then to the Bagel Tree. Mark also looked up and down the street. I hesitated and then asked, "Do you want to get a to-go coffee and walk to the bus?"

"Only if you let me buy," he said. It was an easy deal to make.

Coffees in hand, we walked toward 109th Street, stopping now and then to look in shop windows, and comparing childhood memories of the street: this is where Auracle Records was; this was the bakery where my mum bought Eccles cakes and brown bread dusted with cornmeal on Saturday mornings after my ballet classes. This is where Mark took guitar lessons. Stopping outside Scottish Imports, we sipped what was left of our coffees and perused their window display of sun-faded Scottish shortbread tins, kilts, sporrans, and clan-themed plaques.

"Is this where your dad gets his ties?" Mark asked timidly.

I nodded and then added, "And his T-shirts. And our Robbie Burns tea towels. And most of my mother's Christmas gifts. And, see the Robbie Burns figurines? My birthday presents." He laughed knowingly and when our eyes met in the reflection of the window he said, "I love the MacGregors." I chewed on the lid of my coffee for a moment and then replied, "They miss you." When I turned to look at him, I saw our bus home rush by. There was something in the fall air that told me days like this were about to become very scarce. I started to say, "It's a long way but...." and Mark finished my sentence, "Do you want to walk home?"

We talked about his plans to travel in Europe for six months next year and I told him I was deeply envious, but excited for him. My mind wandered to what my next six months would look like: more of the same, plus a return to Le Petit Chou in the summer. No more chances of randomly running into Mark. Or late-night phone calls about music. Maybe it was the new Oasis album weighing heavily on us, or a reminder of the assignments we needed to complete for tomorrow, but we didn't talk as freely as we did on the way there. We were almost silent by the time we arrived at the street where he goes south to his house and I go north. We'd stopped at this corner many times before, and I tried not to look in the direction of the bench where we often sat.

Mark was busy. He had seminar papers to write and grown up amounts of reading to do. Out of the corner of my eye, I noticed him staring toward our bench.

"Do you have your Discman with you?" he asked. I did. "Do you have half an hour to listen to the new Oasis?" I looked at my watch before I nodded so I wouldn't appear too eager. Sitting on our bench, shoulder to shoulder, with my headphones between us, the river folded through the golden aspens and dark evergreens below.

We clicked through the first two tracks, listening for a few seconds as a way to preview the whole album. But then we heard the opening bars of "Wonderwall" and everything stopped. There are events and moments that you know, before they're even over, that you will cling to and yearn for in weeks, months, and years to come. I knew instantly that I would never be able to hear the acoustic guitar that opens "Wonderwall" without conjuring up that fall Edmonton day with Mark, feeling the press of our shoulders as we shared my headphones, and watched the river below us. When the final bars faded out, Mark turned off my Discman and handed it back to me. "This was amazing," he said and I silently agreed. We sat quietly for a few moments and then picked up our book bags and headed back to the corner where he goes south and I go north. Dusk started to settle in. He gave me the kind of hug he used to give me when he was dating Tess and wished me a good night.

"See you soon, I hope."

"Yeah, see you."

My parents were cooking when I got home, and I said nothing about skipping black bile or hanging out with Mark as I set the table. After we ate, my mum felt my forehead. "You don't seem like yourself. Are you coming down with something?" I replied I thought I had an excess of black bile and had lots of homework to do. I spent the rest of the evening in my room trying to do my Gender and Courtship reading, but becoming distracted by Oasis. I listened to the album five or six times, but skipped over "Wonderwall" each time.

I FOUND THIS IN MY MAILBOX IN THE HONOURS Lounge this morning. My paper and comments from Professor Byron Keats:

"Miss MacGregor: I am impressed by your initiative. While other students had taken on hyperbole, OR hermeneutics, OR black bile (as was the assignment, if you recall), you have ambitiously and courageously taken on all three. Initially, I had thought your paper hovered precariously on the edge of inanity. After prolonged and deliberate reflection, I have determined that your paper exhibits a modicum of creative, critical fluidity and near-admirable interpretive insight. I have a few quibbles about your reading of hermeneutic hyperbole; see my recently published article on the subject for clarification and elucidation. A perusal of chapters three, four, and nine of my monograph on black bile would also be worth your while in illuminating some of the dark corners of your argument. In short, your paper falls into the "nearly-almost-astute" category, and I am thus rewarding your keen efforts with a generous B. With a few qualifications, this is, for the most part, almost, excellent work. Your contributions in class, however are, at times, less admirable: please refocus your attention and efforts."

$\mathcal{L}$ AST NIGHT, I FOUND MYSELF PERUSING THE shelves in our family library the way one might gaze reflectively into the refrigerator looking for that perfect bedtime snack. My literary needs, I realized, are not unlike Canada's Food Guide Pyramid. On any given day, I need the equivalent of six to eleven servings of fiction, three to five servings of late-eighteenth-century novels by women, and at least two to four servings of Jane Austen just to feel healthy. It's good to round out my day with two to three servings of poetry from across the centuries and two to three servings of early-twentieth-century British literature. At the top of my pyramid, I have writers like Milton, Robert Burton, Samuel Richardson, and most of the American naturalists. Like fats and oils, it's best to use them sparingly: they're good for maintaining a stalwart constitution but not much else.

My literary cravings took me to the PR section (yes, my father uses the Library of Congress classification system to organize our own family library), where I found myself looking at our holdings of George Eliot. As I was trying to determine which of her tomes would offer more sustenance, a black-and-white photograph fluttered to the floor from the pages of *Daniel Deronda*. It was a photograph of a young woman with an Audrey Hepburn haircut and an impish smile. She is sitting on the back of a Vespa, with her arms around a laughing man. But not just any laughing man, a beautiful, laughing man. There is a sidewalk café in the background where people are drinking and smoking.

It took me less time to identify the setting as Italy, than to identify the young woman in the photograph as my mother, and the laughing, smiling, beautiful man as someone who was not my father. I tucked the photograph back into *Daniel Deronda*, and crept back to my room, wishing my parents a good night as I scurried by. They were watching television— *Fawlty Towers*, again—unaware of what I had found. And I wanted to keep it that way.

My siblings and I had long known the lore of our parents' meeting. Both of them were from Edmonton, and both studying for the summer in Europe; my father doing research at the British Library, and my mother taking a summer art history course in Italy and travelling around. They both grew up on the same side of the river, attended the same university, and studied at the same library. It wasn't in Edmonton that they met, but on the other side of the world at the British Museum, both seeking respite from the rain on the same afternoon, both wandering independently among the Elgin Marbles and coming, miraculously, it always seems to me, to stand silent and still at the same moment, both enraptured with the same Grecian urn for very different reasons. After their eyes met across the urn, my father, sensing a kindred spirit, said, "'Beauty is truth, truth beauty,—that is all/ Ye know on earth, and all ye need to know.'"

"That's beautiful," my mum sighed.

"John Keats," my dad responded.

"Oh," she laughed, "I thought you just made that up. It's beautiful anyway."

"'Ode on a Grecian Urn.' 1819. And my favourite chiasmus too."

"Technically," my mum added, "we were looking at a hydria not an urn." They started talking of Keats and chiasmuses, odes, and red-figured water jars, and then talked for the rest of the afternoon and evening about everything else. They made plans to meet the next morning to visit the Keats memorial at Poets' Corner in Westminster Abbey. I can't recall if they were actually able to find the memorial before their giggling was deemed so disruptive that they were asked to leave. I have the blue guidebook my mum bought that day on my bookshelf, hoping to visit there myself one day. The story of their meeting was almost identical when they both told it. Only the endings varied somewhat.

"She was smarter than anyone I had ever met before," my dad would say when he told the story and then, looking around to make sure my mum could hear, he'd add, "And beautiful. So very beautiful. And you still are, Elizabeth." When my mum told the story, she always laughed at herself:

"I was so impressed he could come up with something so beautiful right there. Even when I learned it was Keats, I still thought it was pretty impressive that a poem would mean so much to him." They'd smile at each other like they were still twenty years old.

She finished the summer in Italy, and he stayed in London. In the weeks that followed, they exchanged addresses, and made plans to meet for coffee in Edmonton in September at a place on campus that is no longer there. Those weeks in the summer were the longest they've been apart ever since. At the end of the story, they touch hands. He always smiles, and she always laughs as if it could have turned out no other way. Listening to them talk made it seem as if waiting for the love of your life to arrive was as certain as waiting for the morning sun. Tess usually rolled her eyes at the whole narrative, and Heathcliff usually humoured them. But I loved hearing this story, and asked to hear it again and again. I always asked my mum, "How did you know he was the one for you?" She always answered, annoyingly, "I just did."

"But *how* do you know that?"

"I just did. And so will you."

Perhaps it's because I heard this story over and over again that I grew up thinking this is how you find the love of your life: you would meet in a way that made it seem as if was always meant to happen this way, and you would know instantly that this was the person who had been sent to you. And, most importantly, you would meet the person you would most love while doing something that mattered to you both. I asked to hear the story again and again to be reminded of love, chance, truth and beauty, beauty and truth.

And, so it was that beauty and truth, truth and beauty

were running through my head last night as I stared into the eyes of a young woman who was not yet my mother. I peered into her eyes looking for clues that she somehow knew in a few short weeks she would meet my dad in a London museum, that she would leave Italy for good, that she would return to Edmonton, and that, within a few years, she would have Tess, then Heathcliff, then me. As much as I want to see all of that, I cannot: there is nothing of my dad, my siblings, or me in this photograph. I look even closer hoping for a glimmer of knowledge that she knew that decades later, her own daughter would stare into her eyes trying to imagine the warmth of the Italian sun, the press of the Italian boy's arms around her, the smell of coffee, petrol, and cigarettes, the sounds of summer life on a crowded sidewalk. And that her daughter would wonder how she left it all behind to live in Edmonton of all places. But I didn't see any of that as I looked into the young eyes of my mother: I only saw how she embraced the Italian boy, and clung to the perfect happiness of a moment, captured in time by chance in the square snapshot, pressed in the pages of the novel I held in my hand.

I had always known that it was chance, truth, and beauty that had brought my parents together. But I also knew it was a strange confluence of chance, truth, and beauty that put this photograph in my hands, and had me staring into the eyes of the stunningly beautiful Italian boy on a Vespa with my mother. There's part of me that thinks if an Italian boy as beautiful as this ever said to me, "Come live with me and be my love,/ And we will all the pleasures prove," I would say "Yes!" before he could even finish the stanza.

I am sure if I asked my mother about the Italian boy and life in Italy, she would smile and answer me in clichés. I am more than willing to accept that this Italian boy—no matter how beautiful—was not the man for her. I am also willing to accept that life in Italy—no matter how beautiful—was not the life for her. What I really want to know are the things my mother would never answer truthfully: do you ever think about him now? Do you ever wonder if he— not dad—was the man? Do you ever wonder if Italy was the place? And, perhaps more than anything, I want to know: are you thinking about him when you look at Italian art and get that far away look? Do you ever worry you chose wrongly?

As I climbed into my cold bedsheets, Edmonton seemed particularly frigid, dark, and desolate after thinking of warm, sunny Italy. I took the photograph out of the book, and propped it up beside my bed hoping to dream of warm, sunny streets, cafés, and beautiful, Italian boys. I awoke this morning disappointed: I dreamt I was trapped on a city bus with Geoffrey Chaucer, who would not stop talking about his Prologue until I gave him my carrot muffin. 🌣

ESPITE MY BEST INTENTIONS, MY FULL COURSE load this semester has made it impossible to write a great Canadian novel set in Edmonton. However, it has also occurred to me that I might be able to increase my understanding of nineteenth-century poetry and hone my nascent literary prowess by writing nineteenth-century-style poems about Edmonton. Here is my first attempt.

"Ye Banks and Malls o'Bonnie Doon"

Based on Robert Burns'ss "Ye Banks and Braes o'Bonnie Doon"

by Molly MacGregor

Ye banks and malls o' Bonnie Doon
Why don't you bloom so fair
Why can't we have some bonnie braes
Instead o' concrete squares.
Thou breakest my heart, thou Bonnie Doon
That sits atop the plain
So diff'rent from the fairer lands
With glens and gloomy rain.
Thou breakest my heart, thou Bonnie Doon
Thou miles of donut shops
For I so yearn for fairer lands
Where birds and bunnies hop.

Aft hae I roved through Bonnie Doon
To have some fresh poutine
I pined for lands with rocky cliffs
And craggy landscapes green.
With downcast heart, I caught a bus
The noble Forty-Three
Begone ye concrete malls and banks,
Petro-Cans and CIBCs.

$\mathcal{O}$N OUR HONOURS SEMINAR TODAY, WE WERE assigned William Carlos Williams' poem "The Red Wheelbarrow." It's the time of year when all we can muster is something that resembles a dour, plodding, academic version of "Button, button, who's got the button?" Idea, idea, who's got an idea? Professor Throckmorton began with his never-successful conversation starter, "So. Thoughts. Anyone." Silence. It was raining hard, and I counted nine drops of water as they hit the window. If someone didn't say something by drop fifteen, I decided I would take one for the team. Around drop thirteen, Stephanie tentatively offered, "I like that there's a chicken in the poem. You don't get many poems about chickens." We all tilted our heads while mentally flipping through our inner Norton Anthologies trying to recall any other poems about chickens. I, myself, could come up with none. We all nodded appreciatively: Stephanie made a good point. Well done, Stephanie.

I began a small sketch of a white chicken in the margin of my notebook. I counted nine more drops. Jason, sensing someone should say something to support Stephanie, offered, "I like chickens. In general. But in poetry especially." We smiled, nodding cattle-like before our eyes collectively moved to the ceiling, as if it were somehow a repository of poems about chickens. I counted forty-eight raindrops in all, while we passed awkward glances and avoided eye contact with Professor Throckmorton. I drew my chicken a wheelbarrow. She looked bored, so I drew her a book to read. I titled it

Norton Anthology of American Poultry and laughed to myself. Whether we admitted it or not, we all knew what was coming. It happened every week. Any minute now, Derrick would emerge from his recumbent position in his chair to unleash his wrath at our critical inadequacies. I could tell Derrick's wrath was building like a swarm of frenzied bees. I didn't even need to look up to know that Derrick was leaning forward, ready to slam both of his hands flat on the table. He would assume what I've come to call his Honours-English-Alpha-Male posture. I knew a guttural sigh would be forthcoming and that he'd start rubbing his temples as if to alleviate the sheer agony of the superior insights building inside his square skull. I knew too that a pronouncement would be forthcoming, and when the words burst forth, he'd probably use at least one word that would shock our grandmothers. We waited. Derrick waited. Finally, Professor Throckmorton gave him his cue:

"Derrick." We shifted in our seats and waited for the performance to begin. I sat up a little straighter as one might when the lights dim in a movie theatre. There was a pause. Derrick made eye contact with each one of us before he began. He straightened out his sleeves, tapped his lower lip three times with his thumbnail, and then began.

"This poem is bullshit." Thirteen sets of eyebrows went up around the table. Suppressing a yawn, Professor Throckmorton replied, "Would you care to elaborate, Derrick." I noted the absence of a question mark.

"Yes, I would. This poem is bullshit. Williams knows that a wheelbarrow is, as Beckett has proved repeatedly, essentially meaningless. By arguing that everything depends upon a red wheelbarrow, Williams is begging us to declare 'bullshit' at the end of this poem. The chicken is just smoke and mirrors. The red is a self-reflective, red herring. Nothing depends on a red wheelbarrow. End of poem. End of discussion." He clasped his hands behind his head and returned to his recumbent pose.

Nothing depends on a red wheelbarrow? That's all he had? That's all he could muster? Stephanie and Jason looked at each other nervously. How could the heretofore much-loved chicken be meaningless in this poem? I saw them scrambling to find contradicting evidence in the poem. I just stared at him, incredulous that all he had was a re-working of the first line. At the beginning of term, I noticed Derrick shut us all down every week with what appeared to be a more sophisticated logic than we all possessed. But today, it was finally undeniable that it was he—not the chicken—who was all smoke and mirrors. I felt my inner Jane Eyre stir, and I felt compelled to defend the chicken. Suddenly, a lot of things were depending on that red wheelbarrow.

I started squirming in my chair. Jason caught my eye and looked nervous. I shot him a look that said, "Watch this." Jason returned with a look that said, "Abort! Abort!" I leaned forward and planted my elbows on the table. I bit the inside of my cheek for a moment, and then said, as sweetly as I could, "That's really interesting, Derrick. You're saying that Williams is consciously trying to mislead us. If, as you argue, 'nothing' depends on the red wheelbarrow, even though he says that everything does, you're arguing that Williams is actually part of the absurdist notion drawing attention to the meaninglessness of American poetry and poetic expression in the twentieth century. In short, you're suggesting that all attempts to make meaning—including your own, just now—are also essentially meaningless."

Derrick leaned into the table again and looked at me. I met his eye and I didn't flinch. There was silence again, and furtive glances were shuffled between my classmates. Derrick smiled at me, laughed, and then threw his hands in the air. He clapped a thuddy, mitten-y clap in my direction and shouted, "Finally! Someone finally gets what I'm talking about. It's about time." I did a small ironic curtsy in my chair and hazarded a look at Jason who was staring very intently at the coil on his notebook. Professor Throckmorton stood up and walked over to the window. He sat on the ledge and stared at me for a moment.

"I think, Miss MacGregor, you've raised a very good point here. Things are not always as they seem. Sometimes people place meaning and importance in meaningless and unimport-ant places. If you really look at things, you'll see that they're never quite what they appear to be. And everything depends on that. This poem is really about looking at things we see every day, but never really see. Tonight, when you go home, I'd like you to look at something you see every day, but never look at. When you look at the world in this way, I think you'll see that everything does depend on how one sees a red wheel-barrow. Or a chicken, as the case may be. Let's call it a day." I packed up my books and as I passed Professor Throckmorton in the doorway he whispered, "Well done," from behind his textbook. Jason and I left the classroom, and dashed down the hall where it would be safe to laugh. We had just turned a cor-ner when we heard Derrick's voice boom down the hall:

"MacGregor. Wait up. I need to talk to you. Alone." I nodded to Jason who stood back a few steps. I realized, stand-ing next to Derrick, that he was much, much larger than he seemed sitting in our seminar room. I'd never realized how tall he was. Jason must have realized this too since he stood poised and prepared to protect me. I was suddenly finding myself more nervous than I wanted to admit or him to know. Again, I summoned my inner Jane Eyre, and reminded myself why Derrick was the bane of my Honours English existence. If he wanted to debate existentialism, absurdism, poetics, and poultry, bring it on. I was ready for a fight. I had Elizabeth's line to Mr Darcy ready to launch at a moment's notice: "I have every reason in the world to think ill of you." But I wasn't ready for what he would say next:

"I find women who agree with me really sexy. We should go out." I was inexplicably speechless. "I just wanted to let you know I'll call you. We'll go out." My inner Jane Eyre had failed me. I stood speechless and stunned as Derrick lum-bered off.

Jason made the mistake of saying, "Wow, you really showed him." The words I could not find for Derrick flew out of my mouth, and I raged at Jason. "When are you going to realize I will never, ever be in love with you, Jason?" I instantly saw how deeply those words wounded him. Jason walked deep into the end-of-class crowd and was gone before I could catch him. He wasn't on our usual bus home, and he's not answering his phone. I'll have to find him tomorrow. I'll bring him some juice, but I fear he'll never forgive me.

$\mathcal{E}$VERYONE ELSE IS OUT TONIGHT, AND I AM GRATEFUL to have the house to myself. After wandering from room to room, lonely as a cloud, I found myself standing in front of the fridge eating a whole bowl of chocolate pudding. It should have been an incredible day, and now I should be basking in my triumph against the Honours English bully. But I had yelled at Jason, who was just trying to be helpful and comforting. In my bedroom, Miss Austen's books stared down at me, and I felt her judgment upon me. None of her heroines, even Emma, came close to being as nasty as I had been. And none would have eaten so much pudding. I felt them all turn their heads from me in shame.

I have escaped Miss Austen's downward glance and am now lying on the cool, hardwood floor on my parents' bedroom, hoping all of these feelings will subside. In addition to inflicting the biggest stomach ache ever on myself, I've managed to get asked out by one of the more repulsive specimens of mankind—Derrick, a man with "ick" right in his name—and offended Jason, one of the nicest. Maybe Professor Throckmorton is right; maybe nothing is as it seems. And maybe everything depends on that. On the coolness of my parents' floor, I remember our homework: "Tonight when you go home, I'd like you to look at something you see every day." I stare up at the collection of baby pictures on the wall and look for glimmers of the fiasco I would turn out to be.

In all our family photos, Tess seems to be stopping mid-performance, the way bejewelled celebrities stop on the red carpet on Oscars night for obligatory interviews with the peons, on their way to something bigger, better, and infinitely more glamorous. Even in her baby pictures, she seems to have a flair for the dramatic. Her demeanour makes her look like a nascent Gloria Swanson, but without the turban. Here's Tess in ballet, or skating, or gymnastics, always unquestioningly aware of how pretty and perfect she is. She smiles as if knowing the world will rush to open doors for her.

Heathcliff, on the other hand, seems content and patient, smiling at the camera in every single photograph. Nothing like Brontë's dark, wild, and brooding tragic hero, our Heathcliff is blond, ethereal, and placid. According to almost everyone, it was evident from his first few minutes of life that Heathcliff was no Heathcliff. Friends and teachers over the years have tried various names. "Heath" and "Cliff" never fit. Neither did nicknames like "Skip" (Mr Richardson next door) or "Sparky" (Grandfather MacGregor). However ill-fitting a name, Heathcliff was the name he was given and the name my brother stoically took and carried, like a large, docile, St. Bernard puppy entrusted to his care. In almost every photograph of him, he is holding something gently in his hands—a feather, a kitten, a leaf, a jar of bugs. He's looking directly at the camera and always seems to be mid-sentence, sharing his encyclopædic wonder at anything and everything that could be found in our backyard.

My father, too, is always smiling, but always engaged in conversation with someone outside the frame. My mother, pixie-ish and pert, smiles winningly at the camera in all the photographs. At least until I come along. After I arrive on the scene, she seems mostly concerned with keeping me inside the frame and still.

In almost every photo we have of me when I'm a baby, I appear to be trying to escape. In the photographs where I'm older, I hover close to the edge of the frame, my mother's arm always around me. I know the look on my face: it's not that I want to escape, I just have things I want to do. As the youngest child, there are the fewest photos of me. I used to think it was because I was far less interesting than my siblings. But when I look at the photos my parents have of me,

I see that they're rarely posed and they were usually taken without my knowledge. As I look at these photographs with fresh eyes, it might be, as my mother insists, I had things that I wanted to do instead of sitting for a photograph. In every photo of me, there is always something else—a book, a pencil, some crayons, or my dolls and bears on their way to, or from, a theatrical performance I had written and directed for them. There's one photograph though that I particularly like: I am colouring and painting at the kitchen table. My mother must have taken it from the dining room, because I seem entirely unaware of her presence. There are crayons and paints all over the table, and my pink plastic scissors are conveniently nearby. My head is tilted and I hold a crayon thoughtfully above my picture. On the back, I see my mother has written, "Molly, aged four and a half. My tiny Monet." As my pudding-inspired cramps subside, I begin to wonder if William Carlos Williams is right after all: maybe so much does depend upon a red wheelbarrow, glazed with rainwater, beside the white chickens. 🪶

I FOUND JASON STUDYING ON THE THIRD FLOOR of the Humanities Building. I quietly snuck up beside him and placed a bottle of apple juice on the bookshelf over his desk. I had attached a sticky note that said "Sorry." He managed a small smile and whispered, "It's okay. Derrick can bring out the worst in people." I nodded and whispered back, "Even so, I'm sorry." I sat down in the desk next to him and took out Christina Rossetti's "Goblin Market" to read for my nineteenth-century poetry class. Jason continued to read, and he left the juice on the shelf above him. I read the first lines of "Goblin Market" over and over, but my "sorry" sticky note seemed to taunt me with all the things I should apologize to Jason for: I'm not only sorry I yelled at you when I should have yelled at Derrick, I am also sorry I stole your juice in kindergarten; sorry I said yes so reluctantly when you asked me to the grade-eight dance; sorry I hardly talked to you in high school; sorry I ignore you in the classes I have with Cute Angus; sorry I don't invite you to Dewey's more; sorry that you're so nice, and that I do not like you the way you want me to like you; sorry that you don't notice that Stephanie really likes you, and that, because I've read *Emma*, I refuse to try and set you two up even though I really should because you two would be really good together. I read "Morning and evening/ Maids heard the goblins cry: 'Come buy our orchard fruits,/ Come buy, come buy,'" five more times before giving up. I convinced myself buying a new pencil at the drugstore, maybe some fruit, would help with my concentration. I packed up my books, patted Jason on the shoulder, and left him with Milton and my sticky-note apology.

The new pencil did not help with reading "Goblin Market," nor did an over-priced orange that I purchased, fearing I might be coming down with scurvy. Nor did a walk around a cold campus. Around 4:00, I decided I would try and catch a ride home with my mum who had office hours until 4:30. When I arrived at her office, I heard muffled voices behind her door, so I sat down in the hallway and recommended reading "Goblin Market," new pencil in hand. Although I wasn't listening, I did hear my mum say the words "plagiarism," "dean's office," "failure," and a student's voice mumbling. I shook my head, and wondered what kind of person cheats in art history. I returned my attentions back to Laura and Lizzie and their run-ins with the vile goblin men. I was making good progress until I heard my mum's door squeak open. I looked up. Cute Angus was the mumbling student dispatched to the dean's office. Our eyes met and he seemed surprised to see me. I saw the precise moment where he put two MacGregors together and understood what I was doing in the Fine Arts Building.

"Hey Molly."

"Hi Angus." And that was that. When I sat down in her slouchy chair, my mum seemed frazzled and despondent:

"I hate when they make me fail them."

I nodded, paused for a moment, and then said, "I guess he's not going to ask me out now."

She looked over her glasses at me: "Angus?"

"He is pretty cute," I offered. She thought about it for a minute and nodded non-committedly. She shuffled papers around, made new stacks of old stacks, and gathered up exam booklets, and crammed them into an already stuffed book bag. She sighed when she turned her light off and closed her door. Outside, the weather was turning cold, and we did not say a word until we got in the car and stopped at the first red light.

"I didn't know you're going out with Angus." I explained I wasn't, but I thought maybe he might ask me out. I withheld the information about his Coles Notes crime against Jane Austen.

"That is, until you nailed him for plagiarism," I added. Still distracted, she nodded.

"Cute is as cute does, Molly." That's one of those sayings my mum has that make perfect sense until you really think about them. When we pulled into our driveway, neither of us seemed to have the energy to get out of the car. We sat for a few moments as dusk settled into the aspen trees above. My dad had a night class and Heathcliff was out on a research field trip. Neither of us felt like cooking. I started to ask, "Want to go out for dinner?" and she restarted the car before I'd finished the sentence. We went back up to Whyte Avenue for Chinese food at The Mandarin. We ordered a litre of wine, and a few sips into it, our days faded away in the din of the crowd. We told each other stories only the two of us seem to find funny. Partway through dinner, my mum refilled our glasses with the remaining wine and looked at me in a way that convinced me she wanted to ask me something I might not want to answer. I knew what it was but I let her speak it anyway:

"So. Angus." I shrugged and ate a few more Szechuan green beans.

"He's cute," was all I could come up with. I saw her fighting back the mum lecture she really wanted to give.

"I know he's cute. But, do you like him?" I thought about his charms: the way he held doors open for me, the time he called me a melancholy flower, and the ways he flirted with me in class. I also thought about his Jane Austen paper. How I know he never does the reading, because he asks me for summaries at the beginning of class every day. And how he dominates class discussing poems he hasn't read. And, occasionally, like yesterday, how he raises the points I gave him before class and everyone thinks he's brilliant. I knew my mum was right, but I still didn't want to give in. I turned her question on her own past.

"So. In your old copy of *Daniel Deronda*, I found a picture of you and a boy on a Vespa in Italy. A cute Italian boy. Did you like him?" My mum seemed very surprised and then flashed the very smile captured in the picture.

"Carlos," she said. "Yes, I did like him."

"And yet," I leaned into the table, "you married Dad." She sat back in her chair and laughed. I continued my line of inquiry, "You could have been married to Cute Carlos and living in Italy. But you're in Edmonton, and it's cold and dark. And you would never have to tell Carlos he shouldn't wear tartan pants to work. Or to turn down the bagpipe music?" Still laughing, my mum said, "Carlos was very cute. And he was a lot of fun. But he wasn't the one for me. I knew at the Grecian urn—the hydria, technically—that your dad was the one I would love." I raised an incredulous eyebrow.

"He made me feel smart. And funny. And pretty. He made me feel like I do when I'm happiest. And Carlos? He was cute. That was it." She raised an eyebrow back. I thought about Cute Angus and felt a lump in my throat.

"Of course, he made you feel that way. You are smart, and funny, and pretty." She took my hand and said, "So are you. You just can't see it yet. And don't let any man ever make you feel otherwise." She gave her mum nod, the one that means the discussion is over. "Now, finish your wine, and tell me more about those turtlenecks." The wine let me exaggerate a few turtleneck anecdotes to ridiculous levels. She particularly liked my story about Hegemony Cricket and his Professor Keats hair. On the car ride home, we were still laughing and, when we pulled into the driveway again, she said, "You know that it's all going to turn out brilliantly, right?" And though I wasn't fully convinced, I nodded.

I went to my room, tucked the picture of Mum and Carlos back into *Daniel Deronda*, and returned it to its shelf. I made it most of the way through "Goblin Market" before nodding off. ❦

I REMEMBER HEARING ABOUT THE ROMANTIC poets and having such hope that they would be exactly what I needed and wanted in poetry. When I bought my Romantics anthology, claret-coloured and embossed with gold, I thought it would be like being with Marianne Dashwood, and talking about fallen leaves and dead lovers, but I must admit it has been anything but romantic. Today is the kind of Sunday I dislike: the promise of leisure undermined by guilt for not attending to the work that needs to be done for the week. I was restless all morning, and when I finally sat down with my anthology, my mind wandered and resisted. I tried more coffee. I tried a cinnamon bun. I thought maybe I needed Willoughby to read Wordsworth to me as he did in chapter ten of *Sense and Sensibility*. I started imagining him reading "Kubla Khan" to me and then I realized he really is a cad and would break my heart soon enough.

I tried to summon Marianne as a reading partner, but I imagined when she saw the portrait of Wordsworth, she'd likely point out that he was probably wearing a flannel waistcoat, and then remind me that, "a flannel waistcoat is invariably connected with aches, cramps, rheumatisms, and every species of ailment that can afflict the old and the feeble." I read and re-read "Influence of Natural Objects in Calling Forth and Strengthening the Imagination in Boyhood and Early Youth" and paused on these lines each time: "In November days,/ When vapours rolling down the valleys made/ A lonely scene more lonesome; among woods/ At noon." Noon in November in Edmonton looked nothing like what Wordsworth was describing. Looking out the window, I noticed it was a rare sunny day, and I thought of the snow that would soon fill our backyard. I imagined Wordsworth telling me that the best way to study Romantic poetry was not sitting at one's desk, but wandering outside amidst the grasses, hopping bunnies, and wandering clouds. A walk, albeit in Edmonton, really didn't seem like procrastination did it? "Think of it as studying *en plein air*," he said. I was easily convinced. As I shut my anthology, he urged me to dress warmly: "perchance wear a flannel waistcoat."

I made my way over to the University Farm where I walked on fallen leaves, surrounded by tall grasses. The wind in the treed trail in the far edge of the farm blocked out all sounds of traffic, and all the houses disappeared from view. I found myself in a little Romantic oasis. True, there were no vapours, gloomy hills, or icy crags, but there was magic in the tall golden fescues and Saskatoon berry bushes that surrounded me. Everything was preparing for winter. Birds scattered above me, and I heard a rustle in the leaves, and caught a glimpse of an auburn fox tail. I was grateful for Wordsworth's nudge, and breathed in the remnants of autumn. After a long walk around the edge of the farm, I was still not ready to go back and read.

I extended my walk through the part of the University Farm where the cattle were kept. I admit I knew the path would eventually lead to the Balmoral Curling Club, where Mark worked most Sundays. I walked into the familiar confines of the curling club, and saw many of my grandfather's old friends in patterned curling sweaters knit by their wives in the 1970s. I chatted briefly with some of them and then made my way to the window to look out onto the ice. As I hoped, Mark was working today. I watched him and another man pebble the ice and noticed Mark had a style and elegance his co-worker lacked. When he was done, I knocked on the glass and waved. He smiled and gestured that I should wait: his shift would be over soon. He brought us out large paper cups of hot chocolate, and we sat laughing as we eavesdropped on the old Scottish men in the lounge and listened to normally mild-mannered, retired women shouting, "Hard! Harrrd! Hurry hard!" on the ice. When our cups were emptied, we left the building and started walking toward home.

By now the sun was beginning to set, and the grasses on the University Farm fields were glowing golden. The wind rustled in the aspen trees as birds settled into their branches for the night. Above us, a hundred starlings swooped over the field. We stopped and marvelled at the shapes they made overhead. As they shifted direction, they looked like ballet dancers in the sky, and we both said at the exact same moment, "Murmuration!" I talked about my exams and papers and my resistance to reading the Romantics. He talked of revisions to his MA thesis and, briefly, about his trip to Europe in January. When we approached the corner where we could go home or to our bench, we moved with silent assent to the bench. We both had Sunday ennui—that feeling of sadness that the weekend is almost over, mixed with a vague nervousness about the week to come. As dusk started to settle into the river valley, we both said we should head home, but we sat there until it was almost entirely dark. Streetlights spread a warm glow over the river and the din of birds calmed.

"Have any of your Romantic poets described anything like this?" Mark asked. I shook my head. Once it was fully dark, we walked quietly back to our houses in the new cold of evening. Slowing down at my house, I found myself unusually wordless. I'm not sure who started it, but as we parted, our fingers caught and lingered and we whispered goodbye with a smile. I've been staring at a Coleridge poem in my poetry anthology for longer than I care to admit. Having flipped through the entire anthology, I see there is nothing any of these poets can say that comes close to what I'm feeling right now. ❧

$\mathcal{S}$INCE I WAS A CHILD, EVEN BEFORE I KNEW what a mid-term was, I disliked this time of year. Now, as a student, I dislike it even more. Before class, I overheard some students refer to my dad as "The Nutty Professor." They were laughing at him because he'd forgotten the term papers he was handing back, and so had to run to his office. While there, he left the day's novel behind, and had to run up again. The story they told didn't surprise me: he does those things. I think it comes from spending your days thinking about the importance of the eponymous tradition. What surprised me, however, was that they didn't see this behaviour as what makes my dad funny, nice, and wonderful: they saw this behaviour as what makes my dad laughable. For the first time, I had to see my dad as they see him. I know the students talking did not know that I was his child. Only Jason stared at me kindly and apologetically. I smiled back with gratitude, and continued last week's drawing of Liam Gallagher as Mr Darcy. As I pencilled in his velvet waistcoat, however, I was thinking about my dad and what students were saying about him.

Just as woodland creatures become attuned to the subtle changes in the elements to survive, my entire family has learned to adapt to seasonal shifts of the academic year. Just as squirrels understand that the slightest decrease in daylight means it's time to start gathering and hiding nuts, children of academics understand that finding bags of frozen peas under the kitchen sink, or boxes of garbage bags in the freezer, means that we'd best establish a secret cache of granola bars in our rooms and ensure that a stockpile of frozen pizzas finds its way into our parents' grocery cart. True to Darwin's theories, adapting to the university rhythms was essential to our survival.

Tess and Heathcliff were much more attuned to these rhythms, and they passed along their hard-won wisdom to me. Shelter generally wasn't an issue, but food and clothing usually were. When he was in grade one, Heathcliff showed up to school at the end of the spring semester dressed in his cowboy pyjamas and Batman cape. In my father's defense, I should point out that it's not that my dad didn't notice that Heathcliff was wearing pyjamas, a Batman cape, and rubber boots. It's just that he didn't have the mental energy to come up with a good enough reason why Heathcliff shouldn't wear his pyjamas and cape to school. When he tells the story, my father always says, "What choice did I have? Heathcliff made a rhetorically sound argument with sufficient supporting evidence. Insisting that he change his clothes would go against all I'd taught him about the importance of a good argument." Unfortunately, when he got to school, my brother failed to find a sufficiently convincing argument to make his classmates stop laughing at him. As a result, Heathcliff always ensured that my clothes were appropriate, seasonal, and coordinated and Tess redid my hair when my father attempted my ponytail.

At the end of the fall semester one year, my parents got a phone call from the principal wondering why Tess's lunch consisted of a kitchen sponge wrapped neatly in waxed paper, and our garage door opener folded into a crisp, Robbie Burns tea towel. Had the principal visited our home that day, she would have found Tess's sandwich in the ceramic frog by the sink, and my parents accusing each other of losing the garage door opener. The principal took Tess to Dairy Queen for lunch, and sent the bill to my parents. From then on, Tess insisted she be in charge of not only our lunches, but my parents' as well. Maybe this experience is what inspired her to leave for France to study to become a chef. And stay bossy. And dramatic. We ate well when she cooked, and no one complained.

I too have a story about being the child of an academic. It involves the day my dad had to take me to his class, because he'd forgotten to drop me off at school. My parents tell this story as an example of my dad's forgetfulness, but my version—which I've never told—is about me and how much I loved my dad. It is true that he could not hear me say "Daddy?" from the backseat because the CBC morning news was playing loudly, and he was singing one of his Scottish songs. But nobody knows that I whispered "Daddy?" because I didn't want to go to my school. My mum made me wear the thick white tights with the argyle pattern that I hated. It was a Tuesday, and on Tuesdays we had gym. The only thing I hated more than gym itself was running around the gym while being hounded by a bruise-coloured utility ball thrown by my more agile classmates, who were not forced to wear too-big, thick, white tights. I did want to miss gym for the day, but I also wanted to go to my dad's big kids' school and be with him.

I remember the details of the day precisely: I remember how everyone loved my dad, and how happy they were to see him, and to meet me. I remember how his students smiled at me as I drew and coloured in the front row. To this day, my dad still has one of the pictures I drew that day hanging in his office. The edges of the picture are worn, the once brilliant colours have yellowed, and the brittle bits of scotch tape he'd used to tape it to his filing cabinet many years ago are still affixed, though it's framed now. In the picture, his arms are held over his head in a celebratory manner, and he has a book in his hand. He is standing in front of a chalkboard, surrounded by dozens of smiling, waving students. I added a springy line underneath him, like I'd seen under Tigger in my Winnie the Pooh books. The students were excited too, so I added springs under them as well. I remember how much fun the students had, how they and my dad laughed as they talked. I remember thinking that my dad was the best dad in the world. I could hardly wait until I was grown-up, and could come to my dad's school where I would never have to run wearing tights that were too big for me, or be chased by a ball. I finished my picture by drawing a big red heart over the classroom.

After he was done teaching, he held my hand, walked me across campus to my mum's office, waving to all he knew, and introducing me to his friends. My mother was surprised to see me, but she thought the story too funny to be angry. She gave me her sandwich to eat while she finished up some work, then she took me home. We played cards and ate cake in the unfamiliar silence of our house in the afternoon. I thought it was the best day I'd ever had. The next day, they sent me to school with a note that my teacher read with one eyebrow raised. She sighed and said, "Ah, the MacGregors. Is it mid-term time again?" handing me the worksheets I'd missed. I returned to my spot in the pod of desks, where we spent most of a morning making decimetres out of white centimetre cubes. I put my centimetre cubes in the shape of a heart, and thought about the kind of day I could be having if I were a university student. From that day forward, I told everyone I wanted to be a student when I grew up. People laughed, and said, "But you're already a student." I always thought, but never said out loud, "I want to be a student like dad's students."

Sitting in the very same classroom today, I realized my grade-two wish has come true: I am a student at my dad's school. I was right that I would never be chased by a ball in these corridors, or be forced to run in ill-fitting tights, unless I'm late, and then it's my own fault. But I thought university would be about talking, laughing, and getting excited. Looking around at my classmates, I saw one folding an empty Java Jive cup into a complex Styrofoam flower, two others sharing flirty notes, while people in the rows behind were trying to read these notes over their shoulders. More than a few were sleeping off hangovers. Drawing a Liam Gallagher as Mr Darcy was not much better, I admit. If I were to draw this particular class, I think Professor Keats would look like the Grim Reaper, and my fellow students would resemble wilted houseplants in desks.

On the day when I drew the picture of my dad teaching, I thought my dad was the most wonderful man in the world. I could see how much his students loved him. Today, I see that students still love him, but they love him because he's kind of quirky, almost anachronistic, demanding but fair. And you never know what he'll come up with. To them, he's a professor—a performer even. I wanted to point out that what made him forget the papers in the first place, was his excitement over today's novel. True, Professor Keats never forgets a stack of papers, but he also never explodes with excitement over the glorious placement of a word in a perfectly crafted sentence. It has taken me a long time to realize that the things that embarrass me the most about my dad are also the best things about him.

When my family tells stories about Heathcliff's cape, or Tess's lunch, or my day on campus, we narrate them with a happy pride. Events like these made us different from the other kids at school, and, in this way, they also defined us as a family. We survived the seasonal journey of mid-terms, finals, and the processes of academic tenure and promotion (which to this day I still don't understand since both Tess and Heathcliff told me to never ask about it). I guess one spends the early part of life thinking one's parents are the coolest, most wonderful people in the world. And then there's a good chunk of one's life when they embarrass you, and you want to hide from their existence, and deny your genetic connection to them. And then, finally, there's a time when you realize that they are people, too, that they're more than what you see or have ever seen of them. ❧

*T*HERE ARE TIMES, LIKE PERFECT MAY DAYS when lilacs are in bloom, when I wonder why there are no lovely poems about Edmonton. Why, I have wondered on more than one occasion, has no one waxed poetic about the cold winds that shake *our* darling buds of May? Why, I wondered earlier this week, as I sashayed across campus on the first brisk day of winter, has no one captured the romantic elegance of the urban tundra? My long red hair, my flowing black skirt, and my scarlet scarf billowed so romantically I bethought myself Meryl Streep in *The French Lieutenant's Woman*. Surely, I thought to myself, if Thomas Hardy or Henry James had seen me in such a setting, they would have thought:

"Oh, there's a lovely girl blooming with hope and romantic visions. I am inspired to fashion a nebulous plot, and concoct a beautiful man-villain who will take her to a warm climate and, because of his jackanapish behaviours, make her yearn for her former romantic self and the barren frozen landscape of her stolen youth. 'Alas,' this novelized version of me laments in the final pages between consumptive coughs, 'that I fell for Armando, the beguiling bullfighter, instead of Ernest, the faithful, beagle-like, prairie accountant.'"

And then there are times, like today, when I know perfectly well why there are no poems about Edmonton, and also why, if Thomas Hardy did see me, he'd not make me the romantic heroine in his tragic pages, but instead the sturdy, snuff-snorting charwoman who shuffles in and out of chapter twelve and then never returns. I've just arrived at my desk in the library after quite the ordeal. My morning began by waiting forty minutes for a bus that allegedly comes every fifteen minutes. I then stood, sardine-style, wedged between two, tall engineering students' backpacks for half-an-hour as the bus inched toward campus. I swear I still have an impress of a carabiner on my forehead. At my stop, I was desperate to extricate myself from the press of polar fleece and Mountain Equipment Co-op attire and decided to lunge toward the open back doors. I'd over-estimated my lunge and under-estimated the peril. I slipped down each of the four snow-filled stairs of the bus into a pile of snowy muck, arriving with a gushy, slushy thud on the sidewalk. There was a moment of silence as my fellow bus riders peered out the windows to gawk at my fallen form. As the bus drove away, it spun its great tires in the pools of melting muck, covering me in something that resembled a mud and gravel Slurpee. As I stared at the sky in shock and wonderment, a betoqued man leaned over me and said, "That was spectacular!" As he helped me to my feet, I attempted to summon an Audrey Hepburn-esque "Oh, la! I've just fallen down the stairs of a city bus into a pile of greasy snow in front of a hundred people. La la!" but all I could summon with my bruised knees and scraped hands was a tiny whimper. He tried to dust me off as best he could, and sent me on my awkward way. My Meryl Streep elegance of a few days ago was nothing but a dim memory.

Once upright, I attempted to dash across campus to my just-started class. Instead of sashaying with the melancholy elegance I've been practicing, I found myself lurching, like Frankenstein's monster in a dress. My long, now-soggy skirt was freezing to my legs, shortening each step. Meanwhile, my hair and scarf flapped about in opposite directions in an entirely unflattering way, my bruises and cuts stung in rhythm with every frozen step I took. My nose was running in ways too gross to describe. If Susanna Moodie had seen me, she would have included a chapter about me in *Roughing it in the Bush* as an exemplar of all that is horrifying and soul-destroying about Canadian winters.

Despite my best intentions, I was half-an-hour late for my class, and as I stood frozen, sore, and soggy outside the door, I realized I couldn't walk past everybody like a half-drowned Madge Wildfire. Instead, I headed straight to the library where I now sit reading the first lines of "Frost at Midnight" over, and over, and over: "The Frost performs its secret ministry,/ Unhelped by any wind." For tomorrow, I am supposed to write a two-page response to "Frost at Midnight." So far I have, "You want to talk about frost, Coleridge? Do you? Well, let me tell you about frost. Walk a mile in my seasonally inappropriate footwear in twenty-below-zero, and then we can talk about frost, my friend. Secret ministry? Silent icicles? Bah!" I need a carrot muffin before I can deal with Coleridge. I'm in no mood for him. I am grateful the semester is about to end. ❧

*I*T'S THE LAST WEEK OF THE SEMESTER, AND tonight I sat in a crowded bus shelter waiting for my bus home in the snowy dark. My fingers were cold, but I assumed all the best novelists tolerated cold inky fingers so I embraced mine as a gesture of kinship. I overlooked the fact that Frances Burney, George Eliot, Jane Austen, and Emily Brontë wrote their enviable masterpieces by sunlight and candlelight, with quill pens in rustic homes surrounded by inspiring landscapes, not scribbling with a drugstore fountain pen, beneath the crackling, orange glow of a ceiling-mounted heater in a crowded, barn-like transit stop. My fellow commuters shuffled like cold cattle in a corral, and stared at me with suspicious bovine glowers. I was tempted to put away my notebook, but I carried on, knowing Christina Rossetti would not have let the stares of grumpy, toque-wearing people deter her from plying her poetic craft, nor would Miss Austen have put a scene at Pemberley on hold because a large man in a camouflage parka was trying to read over her shoulder (even after I wrote, "Just because you're wearing camouflage doesn't mean I can't see you reading over my shoulder. Please desist."). In the spirit of Christina Rossetti and Jane Austen, my fountain pen and I carried forth and wrote in defiance of nay-saying, glowering toque-wearers.

After I determined to defy the glowers with my trusty pen, I found myself at a loss for words. What does one write about in a bus shelter in Edmonton? True, Miss Austen insists that three or four families in a country village is "the very thing to work on" but that didn't work very well for me at the Mall, and I'm not sure three or four families in south Edmonton would work any better. What is "the very thing to work on" in Edmonton? Could *Pride and Prejudice* ever have been written in a place like this? Could Miss Austen have written *Emma* if, rather than strolling around Chawton with her sister, she took the bus every morning? Can I live in Edmonton and write novels like hers? Can one create art and become an esteemed authoress when one spends half of one's life listening to Professor Byron Keats theorize about phlegm, and the other half in transit shelters waiting for buses that never come? Where is the romance in that? Where is the beauty? Thinking about that made me want to run through the darkened, icy Southgate parking lot yelling "Truth! Beauty! Beauty! Truth!" But instead, tired of sitting still, I braved the elements, and went for a brisk walk amidst the swirling snow in the parking lot to revitalize my soul.

Unfortunately, what I hoped would be an enlivening, Marianne Dashwood–esque walk amidst the elements did not turn out as I had hoped. Whereas Marianne faced "animating gales of a high-southwesterly wind," I dodged parents herding snow-suited kids into minivans, navigated massive snow drifts, and patches of black ice, all the while being followed by a predatory, maroon station wagon hoping I would lead him to my car, where I would then liberate a parking spot for him. Even though it was cold and miserable, Marianne, I knew, would tough it out, and see the beauty of frozen asphalt and tundra-like conditions and so, I thought, should I. Finally, after a few minutes of my well-intentioned, but foolish constitutional, I spied my bus edging around the corner. I started to run, but because I was wearing stylish, but seasonally inappropriate Fluevogs, I flew through the air and landed on my back like Charlie Brown when Lucy grabs the football. Stunned in the snowy silence, I lay on the ice, and gazed up into the hazy parking-lot lights, as the snow gently fell on my face. "If this were *Sense and Sensibility*," I thought, "Willoughby would arrive just about now with his 'manly beauty and more than common gracefulness' and carry me home." I fell into a reverie about Willoughby until I felt something nudging me. I blinked and noticed, remarkably, a betoqued man standing over me, prodding me with his snow boot. "That was awesome!" I winced and attempted a curtsy as he helped me up. Bruised, stunned, and shamed, I made my way back to the shelter where I waited for the next bus. Fighting tears, I realized I could never be Marianne Dashwood. I would never be an authoress. I would never find truth or beauty in a parking lot. I put my pen away and took my place among my fellow bus riders, quietly shuffling my feet like cold livestock, and, worst of all, wishing I had a toque to keep my ears warm. 🎭

*S*ITTING IN PROFESSOR WIDGETT-JONES'S CLASS today, I was thinking about my parking lot fiasco at the bus stop last night. Because I could no longer ponder "the politics of the pyrrhic," I made a list of the sad realities I should just succumb to and accept. Here it is:

- I will never write a novel that will be respectfully misunderstood in my lifetime, but rediscovered and revered several generations hence.
- My life is doomed to be unromantic. I will never be Marianne Dashwood. I will never be rescued by a Willoughby after tumbling down a picturesque hill. I will only wipe out on ice and get bruises no proper Regency woman could ever show to her Willoughby, even if he asked.
- Even were I Marianne Dashwood, it would not be Willoughby at the bottom of the hill, but Wordsworth looking down at my twisted ankle and responding to my pleas for help with, "Why ever are you walking about in inclement weather without a flannel waistcoat?"
- Maybe I should start wearing a toque now as a signal to the world that "I am doomed to a life that is antithetical to romance and beauty."

Surveying the list, I realized, as good Honours English students should, that one cannot simply make claims like, "I am doomed to a life that is antithetical to romance and beauty," without providing sufficient supporting evidence. One must examine the text—or, in my case, life—closely, assess the findings, find support for one's argument with evidence from the text, and then boldly state one's claim. To this end, I offer the following chart:

Person	Lead Beautiful, Romantic Life	Temporarily misunderstood, but eventually deemed great	Wore Toque	Lived among toque-wearers	Lived in Edmonton	Cool
Jane Austen	Yes (final illness excluded)	Yes	No	No	No	Yes
Emily Brontë	Yes (though there's that nasty consumption episode)	Yes	No	No	No	Yes
Virginia Woolf	Yes (though tragic, it was beautifully tragic so it's a wash)	Yes	No	No	No	Yes
Me	No, not yet. But I am still young	No	Was forced to as a child	Yes	Yes. Whole life	Hardly

I know enough from Psych 105 to know that this random sample is not sufficiently scientific to be statistically significant. However, it is sufficiently convincing to me that I might as well just admit defeat, don a Petro-Canada toque, and wear sandals and socks year-round. Oh, my aching ennui and excess of black bile. This semester cannot end soon enough. 🦋

I HAVE JUST FINISHED WRITING MY LAST EXAM, and I know not what to do. They were all pretty predictable: my Honours seminar exam was a close reading of e e cummings. Professor Throckmorton brought liquor-filled chocolates that helped numb my annoyance with Derrick's agonizing habit of groaning under the burden of thinking his terribly important thoughts. I managed to write an essay called "Em-pyrric: Two Short or Unaccented Syllables and the Politics of Colonialism" for nineteenth-century poetry (think I nailed it). The question "Would you date Wickham?" was not on the Gender and Courtship exam, which is unfortunate as that's the question I'd prepared for in the final hours of cramming. Similarly, my psych exam did not ask the only question I was well-prepared to answer: "Who is the mean guy?" (Skinner). My last final was my black bile exam, the one I dreaded most. There was one essay question, and it was steeped in arty minimalism: "Hegemony. Hermeneutics. Humours. They are connected. Discuss." Initially I wrote, "'I would prefer not to.' Melville, 'Bartleby the Scrivener.'" I stared at it for five minutes debating if such an answer would get me an A+ and shortlisted for the Third-Year Honours English Book Prize or a failing grade. Professor Keats could go either way. I decided to cross out the answer, and write strings of jargon that I hoped would, to a superior mind like Professor Keats, appear like well-crafted thoughts. I have little sense whether my Plan B was the smart move or not.

I am, I hope, now free to never think of phlegm or black bile again. I know I should feel happier to be done than I am. Perhaps it's because Tim called me last night, asked if I could work some long shifts over the holidays, and I agreed. I would like the time off, but I also thought I could maybe put some money away in my dormant, and somewhat depleted, Europe fund. 🙚

A FEW DAYS AGO, MY DAD PASSED ALONG A PHONE message from Mark inviting me to the Grad Pub to celebrate his MA defense today. I was excited to go, even though it meant I would have to miss the usual Fin-de-Semester Fest at Dewey's. I was very tired, and the press of people in the Grad Pub made me question whether I should just turn around and go home. I looked around and spotted Mark at a big table with his friends. The party seemed pretty well underway, and even from a distance I could see that Mark had been the recipient of quite a number of congratulatory pints and shots. Just as I was thinking about turning back and going home, Mark saw me across the room and yelled, "Molly!" over the din. Seeing me trapped in the crowd, he leapt over a table, and crawled across some grad students, and I laughed at the sight of it all. I gave him a congratulatory hug and told him I was tired and couldn't stay. He wouldn't hear of it, and said he had a pint of porter waiting for me. He took my hand and led me through the crowd to the pint of porter he really did have waiting for me. There was also a chair reserved for me. When I sat down, he interrupted a drunken debate about Peter Lougheed and the National Energy Program to introduce me to his friends. They smiled, nodded, and then quickly resumed their anti-Trudeau diatribes. They were so loud, and the pub was so full, that talking was impossible. Mark and I just smiled at each other as we sipped our pints. I recognized the smart girl from the *Eraserhead* lineup, and it was clear she was attached to another classmate. More friends came to congratulate Mark, and I nodded hello to people whose names I couldn't hear. I watched him describing his defense to this new group of arrivals, making them laugh at his imitation of the fight that broke out between the chair of his committee and the external examiner. I had never seen Mark in his element before, and I realized I had never just watched him. His classmates loved him and his occasional interjections about Lougheed silenced even the most belligerent of his cohort. I was fading into a reverie, but snapped out of it when one of his classmates pulled heavily on my sleeve. He leaned in to whisper drunkenly in my ear:

"Are you the girl with the sister?" Shuddering from his gin breath, I nodded.

"I do have a sister."

"And Mark dated her?"

"He did."

"Hmm," he said, looking me up and down before returning to the never-ending, never-progressing discussion of Alberta politics. There was one sip left in my porter and I downed it quickly. I got up to leave. I gave Mark a quick hug, told him I had to work in the morning, and that I would catch up with him later. He tried to convince me to stay, but I pretended I could not hear what he was saying. Serendipitously, members of the Golden Bears hockey team passed between us, and I was able to make a quick escape through the crowd by following them. I turned to wave goodbye, and saw him talking to the gin-breathed friend.

Once outside, my lungs were shocked by how cold it had suddenly turned, and my ears rang in the dark silence of the nearly abandoned campus. I tied my scarf tightly around my neck, and headed toward the bus stop. Snow swirled around my feet, and I concentrated on the sound my pointy boots made on the pavement. It wasn't until I was safely on my bus home that I reprimanded myself for even thinking Mark could like me as anything but Tess's little sister. It was clear that Mark is still talking to his friends about Tess, and that I shouldn't waste any more time thinking about him. Tess is beautiful and leads an exciting life in Paris. I could see how it would be hard to get over her. I need to stop thinking about him, because I have to be up early in the morning to be at the Mall. I am happy for them and happy for me too. Tim told me that if my sales of polish and protective sprays are strong this holiday season, I could still qualify for western Canada's top seller for 1995. At least I have something to which I might look forward. Welcome back, Molly of the Mall. 🐾

*W*HEN TIM SAW ME BACK AT LE PETIT CHOU, he nodded with approval, and said, "Those Le Petit Chou name tags never go out of style, do they?" I waited a moment for some sort of ironic chuckle from my co-workers, but none emerged.

"Absolutely," I concurred. Tim's errand this afternoon was to drop off the head office-approved Christmas CDs that we are supposed to play on a loop starting today.

"Why two copies of Boney M's Christmas album?" I queried with innocence.

"In case one wears out, stupid," was Maureen's rejoinder, "You're going to be playing these for twelve hours a day until New Year's Eve. It will wear out." Eugenie and Tim nodded.

"But Boney M?"

"It's the official soundtrack of Christmas, Molly." Eugenie and Tim nodded again.

For the most part, little has changed at the Mall: Maureen is still chasing one of the Gordons; the recently promoted Eugenie has proven that one can be in management and also be a nice person; Rick has retained his docile joie de vivre, in spite of his recent demotion to Phase One; and the Rabid Pekingese is still a chain-smoking, coffee-swilling bundle of nerves. There are a few changes: there are new employees and management at Monsieur Suave Suit, and none of them seems remotely interested in me; Orange You Glad has been supplanted by YögenBurger as "the" place to go in the Mall food court; and the Ottoman Empire has closed. The Mall is also more packed than I've ever seen it, and I'm told it will get busier. Gary, Howard, Mavis, and Maria seem a little slower with the extra performances, the peacocks a little more manic with all the noise, and the emus a little more deranged with the Christmas season crowds.

Today has shown me that I need to add an appendix to my shoe manifesto about buying women shoes for Christmas gifts. Three times today, men have come in looking for shoes for their wives, two without their wives' shoe size. I had one man come in and say, "My wife's about your size. What's your shoe size?" I sold him a pair of nice black patent wedge heels that would go with just about anything. I selected size 8, the average woman's shoe size, to give him the best odds on the correct size. But I also made sure he was aware of our return policy, and suggested he keep the receipt in his wallet. I spared him a lecture about the importance of a thoughtful gift, but gave him the standard spiel about polishes and protective sprays. I am hoping the thoughtfulness of the polish and spray will lessen the disappointment of ill-fitting shoes under the tree. On the upside, I may still be on track to win western Canada's top seller of 1995. It's good to have goals.

Much of today was spent preparing for the impending Boxing Day sales. Anyone who has lived through one is nervous and filled with dread, even Eugenie who is rarely rattled. We've been training seasonal employees just to re-shelve. Tim has brought in crates of bottled water, and arranged for a special delivery service from McDonald's so we won't have to leave the store (apparently, we might never make it to the food court and back in an hour). We've been instructed to wear only running shoes (I don't have any) and special Boxing Day sale T-shirts (puce green): blech. I've never seen this store so organized. Add candles, batteries, a stockpile of canned goods and we'd be well prepared for a natural disaster. ✖️

HAVE SURVIVED MY FIRST AND, I AM HOPEFUL, last Boxing Day Sale at the Mall. From 8:00 a.m. until 6:00 p.m. the Mall was wall-to-wall people, and Tim was right, we couldn't even get out to make it to the food court; I was grateful for the McDonald's delivery. I sold more shoes today than I did in the months of July and August combined. I didn't even have time to suggest polish. I fear my hopes for being the leading seller of polish in western Canada have been dashed, but I have survived Boxing Day.

I have also survived another MacGregor family Christmas that, for all my grumblings about tartan tableware and Anne Murray Christmas albums, was rather pleasant, especially after the chaos of the Mall. Earlier in December, Tess had told my dad to expect an amazing Christmas gift. None of us expected the gift would be Tess herself. She arrived by cab early in the morning a few days ago, and found us all in our pyjamas, reading the paper, and eating porridge. She took this as a sign that we've fallen into familial disrepair since her departure, and has made it her mission to fix us. In her short time here, she has successfully culled our kitchen cupboards of all expired and stale spices and condiments, and overseen an enforced grocery shopping trip to replenish said spices and condiments ("Do we need nine-dollar nutmeg?" my father reportedly whispered at the checkout. Tess replied, "Just pay the lady, Dad."). She has taken my mother shopping for a wardrobe update (needed and done well) and made my dad get a haircut at a place other than Super Cheap

Cuts. She supervised his haircut so he'd look less professorial (needed, though, still not quite successful I'm afraid). My dad was stunned that his haircut cost twice what he's used to paying. So far, Tess has left Heathcliff and me alone, but I fear she's plotting something.

I haven't been home a lot with all the hours I'm working at the Mall, but I've tried to make subtle inquiries about Tess's social plans. I pretend to be curious about which friends she's seeing, but, really, I'm just listening for one name. She has a new Parisian boyfriend, so I am not sure how an Edmonton boyfriend would fit into her new life. For the record, I have not heard her mention the name I am listening for.

Speaking of men, a small package arrived at Le Petit Chou for me sometime during the past few days, and Maureen forgot to give it to me. Eugenie found it, and I recognized the handwriting right away. Inside was a card with Santa-hat-wearing penguins and a book of *Pride and Prejudice* paper dolls. "Merry Christmas, Miss Austen, Your Penguin Man." This made me happy for the rest of the afternoon. I spent the early part of the evening at home cutting out the dolls, organizing their period costumes and accoutrements, and thinking of the Penguin Man and his Yuletide kindness. I don't have to be in tomorrow until noon so I have spent the evening reading *Emma*. I love re-reading, while trying to pretend I don't know Emma will end up with Mr Knightley. The suspense nearly kills me every time. Oh, novels! What would I do without you? As Henry Tilney remarked in *Northanger Abbey*, "The person, be it gentleman or lady, who has not pleasure in a good novel, must be intolerably stupid."

*S*NOW IS FALLING GENTLY ON THE NEW YEAR. I had wanted to go to a party near campus, but my parents insisted I stay home because Tess was here, and I was needed for party preparations. I wasn't terribly happy spending one of my few days off being a charwoman to my mum's exacting standards and a sous chef to Tess's draconian vision of crudités, but I muddled through. Thoughts of another Hogmanay with the same food in the same dishes, the same argument about whether my dad could or should wear his tartan pants, the same joke my grandfather always tells about a vicar and a sheepdog walking into a pub, the same young Molly stories from Mr MacIndoe, and the same rockhard shortbread Mrs Read brought every year were making me sullen. I will admit to no one, but you, dear reader, that in spite of all of these things—or maybe because of all of these things—it turned out to be one the loveliest nights of my year.

This morning, my dad came back from the Safeway whistling "Scotland the Brave" as he unloaded our evening's provisions. He was excited to tell Tess and me that he had run into Mark Forster's parents near the eggnog, and had invited them to come tonight. He asked me, "Did you know Mark is leaving tomorrow for Europe for six months?" When I nodded, he wondered aloud why I hadn't told him. Tess said, "Nice to see you're still smitten with Mark, Dad. He's a nice guy. Maybe he'll come visit me in Paris."

"Wonderful! You should ask him," my father replied, as he unloaded cartons of eggnog into the fridge, "The Forsters thought he might come tonight." I felt myself blush, but focused on dicing my red pepper to the exact dimensions Tess had specified. I visualized Mark and Tess together again. A sort of Jane Bennet and Mr Bingley reunion after all that Mr Darcy–instigated misunderstanding. A bossy Jane Bennet, mind you. And, perhaps, a more perfect Mr Bingley. I focused on thinking how nice it would be to have Mark in our family again.

After we had done most of our food prep, Tess and I dressed for the festivities. I had decided to try to be more charitable toward Tess and have fun with her. It wasn't her fault that Mark still loved her. How could he not? She was tall, pretty, and much more fun than I remembered. I tried to focus instead on the nicer parts of Tess, like the fact that she had brought me a perfect, vintage, empire-waisted party dress from Paris. It was a beautiful claret-colour and she loaned me a delicate antique necklace she'd picked up on her travels. I realized her "familial renovation" project for me was not only this dress, but also to tame my curls, and put them up in a Regency-era style she'd seen in a book. She did my makeup, and when she was done with me, I felt like Elizabeth Bennet on her way to the Netherfield Ball, where she would dance with Mr Darcy. By the time my father had turned on the bagpipe music that would greet our guests, my afternoon grumbles about the evening were fading quickly.

Our guests started arriving about eight o'clock and there really are no people cheerier than the Scottish on Hogmanay. The Forsters arrived, without Mark, and they seemed happy to see Tess and also me. Leaving the old people to their particular kind of mirth, Tess and I laughed and danced in the kitchen as we prepared our mini-kipper-quiches (Tess's invention) and Scottish-salmon croquettes. Heathcliff was kept busy as bartender, and amused us as he attempted— with appropriate amounts of irony—to replicate moves he'd seen Tom Cruise do in the movie *Cocktail*.

Around eleven-thirty, Tess, Heathcliff, and I stood back and observed my parents' party unfold. Our work was mostly done, and we were ready with the champagne and the traditional midnight supper. We watched our parents laugh and dance with their friends. It was a sight we never could see without a cringey amount of hilarity, but tonight Tess wasn't laughing along with us. "I've missed this," she said, and Heathcliff and I looked at her incredulously. She went to check on her hot hors d'oeuvres, leaving Heathcliff and me to mull over what she said. I watched my dad dance, clad in his tartan tie and matching tartan pants. My mum looked cute swaying to the music in her kilt and red turtleneck, a glass of wine in her hand. Tess called me from the kitchen to help, and I was busily occupied until we were called out for the midnight countdown.

We rushed out and made it in time to join the circle to sing "Auld Lang Syne" at the stroke of twelve. On Hogmanay, our family and friends sing all five verses though we sing it in what my dad calls the "unauthorized version" for the ease of our non-Burnsian guests. He supplies songbooks, so there isn't any awkward mumbling. It wasn't until we got to the line, "We two have run about the slopes,/ and picked the daisies fine;/ But we've wandered many a weary foot, since auld lang syne," that I looked up and noticed Mark smiling at me across the circle. He must have just arrived for midnight. I held his smile as I sang the last two verses. I was thinking about him leaving for Europe tomorrow when we got to the line that says, "But seas between us broad have roared since auld lang syne." For the first time in my lifetime of Hogmanays, I finally understood what this song was about. What if old acquaintance be forgot and never brought to mind? I felt tears well up in my eyes as I sang "for days of auld lang syne, my dear. For auld lang syne. We'll tak a cup of kindness yet, for auld lang syne" to Mark. To Tess. To Heathcliff. To my parents. To dear Mr MacIndoe and adorable Mrs Read. And to everyone in this room. I found it all a little overwhelming, so I told Tess to go enjoy herself, that I could handle the last details of the supper preparation.

By the time I'd got the last of the hot hors d'oeuvres on the table, I was feeling a little more in control of my emotions. I spotted Tess and Mark laughing by the fireplace. They seemed very happy to see each other, and had lots to talk about in terms of Europe. I was happy they had reconnected.

I nibbled Mrs Read's shortbread, which was better than I remembered, while Mr MacIndoe told me how, even though I was all grown now, I was the same wee bairn who read Burns so beautifully. He grabbed Mrs Schultz to confirm how adorable we three wee MacGregors were when our parents took us out of bed in our tartan pyjamas to sing "Auld Lang Syne" at midnight, and then promptly tucked us back in when the singing was done. It was a story I had heard every year, but this year it made me smile and I gave Mr MacIndoe a hug and a kiss.

"Oh, it's been ages since I've been kissed by such a bonnie lass," he joked to the room. I curtsied and started on some tidying and made small chat with the guests, some of whom were getting ready to leave. A few of the diehards were still going strong, and I knew a few people would be sleeping on our couches when we awoke, but our house was starting to empty out, and I sought refuge in the kitchen to start washing some dishes. I stared out the window over the sink, and noticed a gentle snow was beginning to fall. Burns's words about a sea between us were still echoing in my head when I felt a hand on my shoulder.

Startled, I turned to find Mark. I'd never seen him dressed in a suit and tie before and I stumbled to find words. He complimented me on my Jane Austen–style dress and hair. Again, I was at a loss for words. He broke the silence, saying he had a very early flight and that he should be heading home to finish up his packing. I nodded and added that it was very nice of him to stop by and see Tess, and he responded, "Oh, right. Well, I actually I just came to wish the MacGregors a happy New Year. And, also, to give you this." He had a small, wrapped package in his hands. I dried my soapy hands and unwrapped it slowly. It was a blue cloth-bound Oxford: *The Poetical Works of William Cowper.*

"I heard he was Jane Austen's favourite poet. I hope you like it." I pulled back some tears and asked where exactly he heard that Miss Austen liked Cowper.

"I asked the man at Bjarne's Books what a lover of Austen might like for Christmas and he suggested this. I hope you like it."

I didn't know what to say except, "This is perfect. Thank you." I paged through the book, trying to find words to say. He broke the silence by saying he'd better leave to finish packing, and then asked if I'd like to walk him home. I nodded, hurriedly grabbed my coat and scarf and we walked out into the silent snow.

The sidewalks were a little slippery and I still had my dress shoes on. Mark put my hand on his arm. It was only a few short blocks, and we arrived at Mark's house without having said goodbye. We stood at the foot of his sidewalk as snow fell gently around us. I couldn't meet his eye because I feared I'd cry or say something I would regret. Mark said, "I don't think Jane Austen would approve if I left you to walk home alone, would she? Especially in those shoes. I shook my head and we silently retraced the footsteps we had just made in the fallen snow. Now back at my sidewalk, we stood together again. This time I was able to meet his eyes and say, "Send me a postcard?" He nodded and said, "Of course." With "Auld Lang Syne" still in my head, I knew I had just one moment. I stood on my toes and kissed him on the cheek.

"Don't forget," I said with a forced smile.

"I won't. I promise," he responded and kissed me back. He turned and I watched him go down the street until he rounded the corner. He turned and waved once more. And then he was gone into the snowy night.

And now, watching the snow falling faintly through the sky, I've got Cowper beside me and my collected Burns on my lap. I'd opened it to re-read "Auld Lang Syne" but instead I read and re-read:

Ae fond kiss, and then we sever!
Ae fareweel, and then forever!
Deep in heart-wrung tears I'll pledge thee,
Warring sighs and groans I'll wage thee.—
Who shall say that Fortune grieves him,
While the star of hope she leaves him?
Me, nae cheerfu twinkle lights me;
Dark despair around benights me.
Fare-thee-weel, Mark, fare-thee-weel. ❦

January 1996
Third Year, Semester Two
University of Alberta, Edmonton

𝓘 T IS THE FINAL NIGHT OF THE HOLIDAYS AND, as if on cue, my parents' moods have turned frantic. Tess left this morning and Heathcliff is working strange hours in his agronomy lab, so I am left to tend to them alone. Their beginning-of-semester anxieties always manifest themselves in odd ways. Tonight, they are having a disagreement about whether ironing a tie that clearly needs dry cleaning would make it acceptable for tomorrow's class. I was called in as an arbitrator, and promptly threw the case out: no one should be wearing a Stewart-tartan tie on the first day of class, I declared. Case closed. I wanted to say "no one should wear a Stewart tartan tie ever," but that would have made matters worse, so I kept it to myself. But, I record it here for posterity.

I admit I am also nervous about the first day of class. Maybe it's the weather and lack of sunlight, but I'm feeling a little down about my classes. None of my courses seems very exciting, but I will do my best. I have the Romantics with Professor Ronald C. Filbert. Having had more than my fill of them last semester, I am not looking forward to a full course of Coleridge, Wordsworth, Shelley *et al*. Professor Filbert is legendarily dry and uninspiring. I am also dreading Professor Hansel Van Beekveld's nineteenth-century Canadian poetry class as he scares me, and I know he remembers all kinds of embarrassing things about me from my ill-fated play dates with his sons, Prufrock and Pellinore. I have Literary Theory with Professor Brooks Dullardson and a continuation of my Honours seminar with Professor Throckmorton. The one class I am looking forward to is Professor Rita Taylor's "Poetics of Place." Ever since I was small, she has both terrified and nurtured me. I think she scares the best work out of me, and I take anything I can from her. Maybe a plodding semester is exactly what I need. Maybe it will help me to focus, and be more like Elinor Dashwood in my demeanour and activities. I've been far too much like Marianne of late, obsessively reading Cowper. I think I like the book more than the poetry contained therein.

Unlike Marianne, Elinor would ignore *The Poetical Works of William Cowper* sitting on her bedside table. Elinor would not play her Oasis CD. Elinor would never calculate how long it might take a postcard to be written, mailed, and delivered from Europe to Edmonton. Instead, Elinor would spend the next six months edifying herself, focusing on her schoolwork, and banishing thoughts of men who love someone else to the recesses of her mind. When I glanced up to get the approval of Miss Austen from her framed portrait, she seemed reluctant to catch my eye. Maybe she knows my feelings about Cowper's poetry? The portrait of Mrs Woolf beside her, however, met my gaze and raised an eyebrow. She seemed to suggest that my time might be better spent reading her essays. To appease her, I re-read "Professions for Women," where she reminded me: "You have won rooms of your own in the house hitherto exclusively owned by men.... But this freedom is only a beginning; the room is your own, but it is still bare.... How are you going to furnish it? ... With whom are you going to share it, and upon what terms?" It's good that all the dead and fallen leaves are currently hidden under two feet of snow. It will be much easier to be stoic Elinor when the land is frozen and the nights long. Just before I turned my light out, Miss Austen caught my glance and seemed to whisper: "I'd give a postcard two weeks to arrive."

*L*AST NIGHT I HAD BEEN WANDERING AROUND the house from chair to chair trying to find a motivating place to read A.E. Housman's *A Shropshire Lad* for my Poetics of Place class. Finding none, I ended up at the kitchen table. My dad walked by and said, "Oh! *A Shropshire Lad!* We loved that book as undergraduates." I told him I was only eight poems in and already there has been a preponderance of poems about bodies in graves that even I find a bit excessive. "But that's the best part!" he said. He looked around furtively and, finding my mother otherwise occupied, whispered, "My friends and I turned *A Shropshire Lad* into a drinking game. We would start reading aloud at the beginning, and order a shot for every mention of a dead body. We rarely made it past Poem XVI." He then recited the final stanza with a posture and elocution that might befit a schoolboy in a Waugh novel. "We even came up with the phrase 'getting totally Shropshired.' Ah, those were great years." He sighed and faded into a Housmanian undergraduate reverie. After sighing, he looked around and whispered "But don't tell your mother." He smiled and made a strange clicking sound and gesture to signify this secret should be locked in a vault we shared. I inadvertently destroyed this bonding moment by whispering back, "Dad, she already knows you were a nerd." My father's good mood was dashed by my comment, and he dryly added: "I was talking about the drinking, Molly." He started to leave, but before he left the room he turned and said, "I'm not sure what's got into you lately, but you really need to be more careful with the things you say." I did it again. I made another mental note to "be nicer, be nicer, think before speaking, be nicer." So far, my attempts at becoming more like Elinor have failed.

This morning, he knocked on my door to wake me, and recited "Up lass: thews that lie and cumber/ Sunlit pallets never thrive;/ Morns abed and daylight slumber/ Were not meant for man alive." From my newly roused state, I was able to respond, "Housman, 'Reveille.'" I knew by his silence that he paused to smile before saying, "Well done, lass, well done." I think I've been forgiven. I'm not sure if he's pleased I knew my Housman or that he'd raised a child as nerdy as he is. I have to admit "getting Shropshired" is a pretty great phrase. I still feel guilty about insulting him inadvertently. Burns Day is quickly approaching and I'll make it up to him by taking my Burns Day cupcakes to a new level of artistry.

*E*VIDENTLY, I MUST HAVE MADE SOME KIND OF sacrifice to an appropriate god or goddess; my world has been transformed! At dinner with Grandfather Stephenson, my father raised the matter of my procrastination regarding my Adopt-a-Canadian-Poet project. For this assignment, we have to select a poet and read everything written by and about them and then write a "definitive" essay about their legacy within the Canadian poetic canon. Although he refuses to admit it, my father's a nervous wreck about my performance in Professor Van Beekveld's class, and it's driving him crazy that I've not yet adopted my poet. The awkward silence that ensued was broken by Grandfather Stephenson's life-altering suggestion:

"Did you know, Molly, that your great-great-great grandfather was a famous Canadian poet? You could do your project on him, James McIntyre!" Everything in my world stopped. Me? Descended from a great Canadian poet? Even now I can hardly write for the excitement of knowing that I am the literary heiress of a great Canadian talent. Suddenly, my melancholic joie de vivre, my penchant for stylish moody men, and my propensity to cry over the tragic beauty of a fallen leaf all made sense: I am descended from poets! I ran over and hugged my grandfather as I declared my intention to adopt James McIntyre not only as my project's subject, but as my beacon in all things literary. My mother winced audibly and excused herself to the kitchen. My father became very interested in placing six green peas in a straight line on his plate. Heathcliff leaned back in his chair, looked at the ceiling, and chuckled to himself. My grandfather hugged me back, and I saw a tear or two well up in his blue eyes. I thought, "Welcome to my life, James McIntyre! Welcome! Welcome!"

I've been trying to work on my proposal, but in the past half-hour, I've been interrupted three times. First, my mother came in and sat on my bed. She said, "I know you've left things rather late, but there are other poets you could do, you know." I was stunned at my mother's reluctance to have me explore my literary lineage.

"He's your ancestor. I thought you'd want me to know your side of the family," I said. She replied, "I do. But, have you read any of his work? This is a big project and McIntyre, well ... he's a bit ... cheesy."

"Cheesy?!" I snapped. I remembered one of Professor Widgett-Jones's lectures about the elitism of contemporary aesthetics, and tried to pass off a paraphrase of that lecture as my own impassioned defense of McIntyre. For dramatic effect, I decided to add another sermon from another class about the need to embrace one's Canadian heritage, but quickly realized I'd not really paid attention that day. I closed my speech with a statement of my very own that, I have to say, I'm rather proud of:

"One person's cheese is another person's art, Mother." She nodded and then got up to leave. She stood over me and smoothed my hair. She said, "I suppose you're right. Good night, dear."

Moments after she left, my father came in with a stack of dusty anthologies and an eager smile:

"I thought you might find someone in one of these collections that you'd like to adopt. Let's see if we can find someone." He rubbed his hands together and began flipping through the first tome's pages. He stopped, skimmed, and said, "Hmm. This one looks good." Before he could say any more, I interrupted him and said, "Just so you know, I'm not doing any poet who rhymes hill with rill."

"Okay! We can certainly work around that," he said, immediately exposing his ignorance of the Canadian literary tradition. He flipped some pages, read a bit, and then flipped some more. "Hmm, maybe this."

"Keep reading, Dad."

"Oh wait, here's a rill and a hill in stanza twelve." He flipped and skimmed some more, skimmed, and flipped.

"You're certainly limiting yourself by excluding hill and rill rhymes. I suppose hill and mill rhymes are out too?" I nodded.

"Hill and whippoorwill?"

"Nope."

"You are really limiting your choices by excluding hill rhymes you know."

"Yup." He put down the second volume and said, "You're really committed to McIntyre aren't you?" I nodded again. "Well, okay." He got up to leave and said with a funny smile, "At the end of the day, the cheese stands alone doesn't it?" He waited for me to offer an appreciative chuckle for his witticism, but none would be forthcoming. He kissed my head and shuffled off. It's not that I want to be rude to my parents, but it seems they sometimes go out of their way to drive me to surliness.

I had just started back on my proposal when Heathcliff completed the tri-partite interruption. He leaned on my doorframe, and bit into an apple, chewed for a while, and then said, "McIntyre, eh?" He stared at me with his impish look, and I pretended to ignore him. After a few bites, he said, "I do not think I shall ever see a poem as lovely as a brie." He laughed to himself and then wandered away. Why I am related to such freaks? Maybe in McIntyre, I'll find the sympathetic literary forefather who understands my artistic temperament. I hear artistic genius is a recessive gene, so it's no wonder I feel so alone sometimes. I really should have more done on my project for my meeting tomorrow, but I'm tired. I'll wing it and hope for the best. Being related to McIntyre should count for something. 🧀

I WAS THINKING ABOUT MCINTYRE WHILE waiting for the bus. I must have been exuding elation, because people were staring at me like my bliss was interfering with their early-morning moodiness. I expect they were unknowingly, yet subconsciously jealous that they are not descended from a great Canadian poet. Who wouldn't be? I am positively abuzz at the thought of reclaiming my literary kin. I think I have finally found my calling. In all of my classes, there's talk of reclaiming this writer, or recovering that genre; maybe my mission is to reclaim McIntyre, and restore him to his rightful place in the Canadian literary canon. Just as there's an image of Robbie Burns in every home of every Scottish descendent I know, I envision a time when every Scots-Canadian home has an image of James McIntyre placed beside (though, maybe a little below) the Burns portrait, and Scots-Canadian children are read a McIntyre poem before bedtime. I do wonder if my McIntyre reclamation work would interfere with the writing of my historically accurate romance novels, and the eventual penning of my future classic novel, and the development of artistically significant, though temporarily misunderstood, visual art. Maybe I could write a historically accurate romance novel about James McIntyre. I am sure he was beautiful, as everyone on Mum's side of the family is very good looking. I am positive he would have married the most stunningly romantic woman in southern Ontario. Who could help falling for a beautiful, poetic man in Victorian-era

Canada? There are so many things I want to do with my life. Do I have time to reclaim a poet? Then again, how long could it take to reclaim a poet? I'm sure after I dust him off and polish him up, he'll practically sell himself.

This reminds me, I still must get a copy of his book. I think I have time before my meeting with Professor Van Beekveld to stop by the library, and pick up a copy of McIntyre's book. It's called *Musings On the Banks of Canadian Thames, including poems on local, Canadian and British subjects, and lines on the great poets Of England, Ireland, Scotland, and America, with a glance at the wars in Victoria's reign.* It all sounds so romantic! Oh, McIntyre! Even though I've not read a single line of your assuredly stellar verse, I love you already. ⚘

MY HEAD WAS SPINNING AFTER I LEFT PROFESSOR Van Beekveld's office. Once again, I've met with anti-McIntyrean sentiment that is bolstering my resolve to adopt and reclaim him. Clearly, I am onto something monumental, if my efforts are making the Canadian literary establishment nervous. After the usual professorial chit-chat about the weather and the time of the semester, he made an odd remark, which confirms my father's theory that Professor Van Beekveld still resents my father for being fast-tracked to a window office. Eventually, he swivelled his chair away from me, reclined, and gazed at a poster of an Italian vista, taped to the wall where a window should be, issued a long, bored sigh, and took a sip of what appeared to be yesterday's cold coffee. Thus positioned, he said:

"Please. Tell me about your project." I began the speech I crafted on my walk from the library to his office. I began with talk of reclaiming lesser-known poets, and what a great opportunity this project was for me to re-think what makes Canadian poetry Canadian, and what makes poetry Canadian. (I have no idea what that means, but it sounded great and he nodded approvingly. Although, in retrospect, I might have misinterpreted him rocking in his chair as nodding.) I then moved to the lecture I half-remembered about the importance of reclaiming lost voices. All seemed to be going along well until my concluding sentence:

"Thus, I would like to take this opportunity to restore

James McIntyre to his proper place in the Canadian literary canon." He stopped rocking in his chair, put his coffee cup down, and swivelled around to peer at me over his glasses.

"McIntyre? James McIntyre?" I confirmed that yes, I was indeed talking about James McIntyre. He paused, staring at me for an uncomfortable minute. His watery grey eyes locked with mine. The silence was gratefully broken with what began as a wheezy chuckle, but then turned into heaving, asthmatic gasps. He slapped his knee and shook his head incredulously. Rummaging in his desk for his inhaler, he said between puffs, "Your father put you up to this, didn't he? Hamish sure has a sense of the madcap, doesn't he? Always the joker." He paused, waiting for me to join him in a wheezy chortle. When I did not, he leaned back in his chair and asked, "Now that we've got that little joke out of the way, what poet did you decide upon?" Feeling a little like Jane Eyre in her classic moment of defiance I said:

"I'm doing James McIntyre. He is my great-great-great grandfather, and I would like to explore my literary lineage for this project." Had I been standing, I would have stomped my pointy-booted foot for emphasis. He took his glasses off, pressed into his desk, and stared at me as if he'd never seen an undergraduate before. After another moment of his greedy, incredulous gaze he said, "Hamish is related to McIntyre? Do tell!" When I told him I was related to McIntyre's on my mum's side, he seemed much less interested. He rustled some papers as a not so subtle hint that our conversation was over. I thanked him for his time, and got up to leave. As I reached the door way, he called out, "Molly, you're not lactose-intolerant are you? It would be a shame if you got ill from all the cheese you'll be ingesting in the next few months." His wheezy chortle followed me to the stairwell. Puzzled by the recurrence of cheese allusions, I set off toward the library. I put cheese out of my mind until I ran into Susan in HUB Mall. Her mouth was orange and full of an unnaturally orange snack food. She offered me the bag to me, and mumbled "Hawkins Cheezie?" Why is everyone was suddenly talking about cheese? I will seek solace in the poetic musings of my dear Mr McIntyre. 🕸

I CAME HOME FROM SCHOOL A BIT EARLY TODAY to check the mail (nothing), and also to make some Burns Day cupcakes for my family. It's a tradition we started when I was in grade two. It seemed logical to me that if you were to bring cupcakes to your classmates for your own birthday, you should bring them for Robert Burns's birthday too. After that awkward first year, when I had to explain Burns Day to my classmates, my family decided in subsequent years that it was best to keep our Burns Day cupcakes at home. Watching this year's butterscotch cupcakes cool on the rack, I stared at the portrait of Burns that has smiled down on our breakfast table every morning of my life.

My dad started reading Burns to me when I was a very small child, and kept reading him to me because the words made me laugh. Soon, he discovered in me an aptitude for memorizing poetry. On car trips long and short, he and I would work on memorizing Burns's collected works. By grade two, I could recite the first six stanzas of "Tam o' Shanter" and an impressive number of works from *Poems, Chiefly in the Scottish Dialect* (1786). My father also impressed upon me a need to not only know a poem's words, but its date and source. In retrospect, I am not certain why my father thought I (and not my other siblings) should know Burns's oeuvre from start to finish, but I think I'm starting to understand. I think it's the equivalent of Walter Gretzky building a rink in his backyard and taking his boy out to skate: you give your children what you love.

My ability to quote voluminous selections of Robbie Burns has not served me nearly so well as the skills Walter passed along to his young son. People watch with rapturous joy those shaky, home movies of young Wayne skating around his backyard rink. With every awkward step he takes, we think we see glimmers of that speed and stride that brings us to our feet every time he swoops toward the net. On the other hand, I cannot imagine that videos of me reciting "Craigieburn Wood" would garner much beyond a piteous shudder and compassionate recoil. Maybe there are indeed glimmers of the person I have become in that footage, and maybe this is why I hope those films never see the light of day.

Although my career as a Burnsian ingénue began with promise, it ended with both a bang and a whimper. I was in grade four and my Brownie pack organized a talent show. For me, the planets aligned in unfortunate ways. Likely no other parent would have noted that the eve of the talent show coincided with Robbie Burns Day, but this fact did not escape my father who saw it as a clear omen. The talent show featured the usual, ten-year-old-girl fare. Andrea, dressed in an ill-fitting, pink-sequin outfit, tap danced arrhythmically to an Anne Murray medley her dad created on reel-to-reel tape. Elaine played a song very beautifully on her cello. Karen N had trained her poodle to do something other than pee on the gym floor; sadly the nature of the desired trick remained elusive for the remainder of the evening. Julie demonstrated her proclivity for jazz dance and Erin brought out a seventeen-foot scarf and some crocheted kittens as a sort of show and tell of her talents with yarn. Karen R's Disney-themed twirling routine went awry when her baton flew across the room and hit Andrea's little sister Marjorie on the head; Karen R cried more than Marjorie, had to be taken home early. I brought the show to a close—in more ways than one—with my rendition of "Address to a Haggis." When I was done, there was a silence that told me something had gone horribly wrong. The silence was broken by my father standing and shouting, "Brava, lass, brava!" until the rest of audience politely joined in. All in all, I scored a respectable honourable mention in part, I believe, because of the effective lobbying of one of the volunteer judges, who just happened to be my grandfather's curling buddy, Mr MacIndoe. After the last sequin had been swept up, and the last puddle of poodle pee disinfected, I stood by the door waiting to leave. Mrs Jennings, our Brown Owl, was talking to my parents and in a voice not quite hushed enough, I heard her say, "Maybe next year Molly could play the recorder like some of the other girls." I saw my mother bite her lip and nod politely while my dad became deeply interested in something on the floor, until he said with a proud finality, "A little Robert Burns never hurt a child" and then bade Mrs Jennings a good night. The next day at recess Karen L and some other girls came up to me in a tightly formed pack. Karen stepped a little closer than the others and stared at me. She said, "My dad said you're a professor's kid and that's why you're so weird." I didn't know what to say, but I was grateful for the buzzer and the press of kids retreating from the cold. I hung back, pretending to look for something I had lost out on the tarmac. I didn't know why being a professor's kid made me weird, but I felt my face stinging with shame. I knew that I shouldn't be quoting Robbie Burns anytime soon, if ever again. I would like to imagine that no one else remembers my humiliating evening, but I fear I am too hopeful. Just last week, Mr MacIndoe saw me at Safeway, and greeted me by proclaiming, "Fair fa' your honest, sonsie face,/ Great chieftain o the puddin'-race!" across the display of Parker House rolls.

The next year, as suggested, I played "Wild Mountain Thyme" on the recorder, and I won second place. My parents clapped proudly, but there was no standing ovation from my father, nor shouts of "brava, lass!" The next day, my fellow Brownies turned their recess wrath on Erin, and mocked the nine-foot, crocheted caterpillar she'd brought. I hated myself for not being able to bring myself to run to her defense. Their words from last year still clung to me, made my heart pound, so I kept silent. Although Erin and I never spoke of it, we became gym partners for the rest of the year.

After that fateful Burns Day evening, I buried my Burnsian light so deeply under a bushel that I think my father worries I don't remember a single word of Burns. But Burnsian rhymes and rhythms are always in my head. It's only recently that I have felt courageous enough to let that little light shine ever so slightly. I mentioned it to the Penguin Man last summer, and he still wanted to be my friend. Last week, my dad was trying to remember directions somewhere and, for his amusement, I said, "It's up yon heathery mountain, an down yon scroggie glen."

"Aye," he said and gently pulled my ponytail. I'm slowly starting to see my dad's tutorials in the works of Robbie Burns as a gesture of love and of hope, not, as they had seemed for years, a plot to subject me to the taunts or torments of my peers. Like Walter Gretzky, who built the rink for his son, my dad, I see, had hopes for me. There's no denying they're weird hopes, but they're hopes nonetheless. My cupcakes are ready to be iced. I photocopied a dozen miniature portraits of Burns, and coloured each waistcoat and cravat in a different festive colour. I will affix them to toothpicks as decorations. These could be the best Burns Day cupcakes ever. Happy Birthday, my Bard, my Ploughman Poet. 🦢

*H*OPING TO CATCH THE LETTER CARRIER, I LEFT the house a little late today (alas, still nothing). The absence of mail for me means that I can concentrate entirely on my Romantics class. Today Professor Filbert presented our third class on Romantic flora and foliage: we've covered flora and foliage in Coleridge and Keats, and today we commenced our look at Wordsworthian flora and foliage. Professor Filbert opened class today with the comment that Wordsworth's treatment of flowers and leaves is "breathtakingly exciting work." Most of my classmates appeared unconvinced. Behind me, a girl removed her boots and socks, and painted her toenails cotton-candy pink, and four guys played poker for money. In front of me, a woman knit a garishly coloured sweater for an unsuspecting toddler, and, to my left, a neo-hippy attempted to impress women by sitting in a lotus position, pretending to meditate. I saw him opening an eye now and again, glancing to see if that cute girl with the long, dark hair was finally besotted with him. Frankly, I thought she might find soap more of an aphrodisiac, and I pondered whether or not to pass along this little courtship FYI to him. Beside me, a jock-ish guy sketched out football plays with Xs, Os, and arrows. I tried to catch his eye to ask whether the hugs or the kisses were winning, but gave up. Even though I couldn't see Eulalia's face up in the front row, I knew by the tilt of her head that she was blinking with that Doris Day air she has about her. I fantasized about surreptitiously firing my snack of wasabi peas at her oversized head. I can blink as innocently as she, and knew I would emerge without a soupçon of blame, especially with jock boy beside me.

Being a professorial child, I know it is rude not to pay attention in class. Additionally, I know it is un-collegial to fantasize about firing pebble-sized snack foods at over-achieving classmates. That said, I feel I have permission to check out now and then, because Professor Filbert removes his hearing aids at the beginning of every class. Our questions "distract" him, but, as he explained on the first day, he does offer ample opportunity before and after his lectures when we may take full advantage of both his hearing aids to ask any question we like. When he stops lecturing, we vacate the classroom with the same frenzied, angry panic of the squirrel family my father liberated from our attic last summer.

Each class, Professor Filbert brings a stack of notes held together by what appear to be rusty paper clips. I can tell by the way he handles them that his lecture notes are brittle, yellowed, and well worn. They may even predate the invention of the ballpoint pen. Occasionally, he seems surprised and pleased with what he finds when he turns a page. He smiles to himself as if he's turned a corner and run into an old friend. An old friend he's seen around the same corner every semester for twenty-five years, but who is so lovely and charming that it's a treat every term. It is annoying, but it's also sort of cute.

Professor Filbert digressed somewhat from Wordsworthian mulch to talk about Dorothy Wordsworth and her "infirmities." I started to imagine what it would have been like to be Wordsworth's sister, and then began to wonder if she really suffered from hysteria. A more likely cause, it seemed to me, was the fact that she probably had to read six-hundred drafts of "I Wandered Lonely as a Cloud." "Do you like the comma here or here, Dorothy? Tulips or daffodils, Dorothy? Nothing good rhymes with tulips maybe I should go with daffodils. What do you think, Dorothy? Maybe crocus?" And then, twenty minutes later, "Dorothy, can you think of anything that rhymes with crocus? Focus? Locus? Ooh, what about locust? Does locust work?" Did she never say, "For heaven's sake, William, could you kindly stop moping about daffodils and instead wander lonely as a cloud out to the shops and pick up some yeast? This bread's not going to make itself, you know." I wish she would have. I would have.

I stared at the portrait of Wordsworth included in his chapter in the anthology, and noted a marked resemblance to Prince Philip; they have the same smug, pained wince, as if they've just stepped in something unpleasant, and hope no one notices. As Professor Filbert meandered through the instances of indigenous flora in Wordsworth's work, I realized I have about as much desire to ponder Wordsworth's thoughts on dead leaves as Prince Philip's thoughts on what kind of shoes would be best with the perfect, little, vintage black dress I just bought. Even though I do have a passion for dead leaves that rivals Marianne Dashwood's, Wordsworth's thoughts on decomposing foliage do not ignite my soul; he doesn't make me want to exclaim "beauty is truth, truth beauty" the way, say, Keats or Hopkins or Mrs Woolf does.

Instead of interrogating the humble daffodil, I began to develop a new poetic litmus test: could I see myself drinking cappuccinos with this poet after an afternoon of shoe shopping on Whyte Avenue? If I answered yes, I would read, savour, and love the poet. If not, I'd simply say, "Thanks for sharing your work. I have found your artistic production instructional, and, perhaps even edifying, but could you please stand over there with Wordsworth. Thank you." Imagine a day where Miss Austen and I go shoe shopping and café hopping with Gerard Manley Hopkins, John Keats, or Mrs Woolf. What fun! Or, Dante Gabriel Rossetti! I melt at the thought of sipping a cappuccino in a candlelit café with him, staring into his dreamy eyes and swooning at his Zeus-like hair, while he enumerates the ways in which my new Fluevog shoes are the apex of footwear artistry and the perfect match for my new vintage dress. But shoe shopping with Wordsworth? I'd have to spend the entire time talking him out of brown Hush Puppies with rounded toes and athletic shoelaces. It would be best to be upfront with him and say, "It's not me, it's you. I'm sorry, Wordsworth, but this is just not going to work between us." Breaking up with major literary figures is very emotional, but it's what Elinor Dashwood would do. I shall summon some of her stoicism, and attempt to carry on. ❧

WHEN I ARRIVED HOME, THERE WAS, YET AGAIN, no mail for me, and I was in desperate need of some Motown to restore my spirits. It cheered me initially, but then Jimmy Ruffin's "What Becomes of the Brokenhearted" came on. I turned it off, and put on a different record from the set. I'd forgotten record four started with The Marvelettes' "Please Mr Postman." It seems even Motown is ganging up on me today.

I'm still reeling from having dumped Wordsworth yesterday, and am trying to summon the strength to go back to class and face him tomorrow. I know he's quite dead, and it would make no difference to him whether or not I show up to class. It's just that I've never dumped a canonical poet before, and this could be the start of something big. What if I move from dumping Wordsworth to dumping Coleridge, and then go on to dump half of Volume One of the Norton Anthology? What if next semester, I start working my way through Volume Two and dump half of the moderns. What if I jilt all poets in the western tradition except for Burns? Maybe I'd keep H.D., the Imagiste. And Rupert Brooke: he's a cutie keeper for sure. And, I'd need to keep Cowper. After dumping a significant number of poets, I am certain I would go on to dump a good number of the writers we're reading in my theory class, if not all of them. And then I might start working my way through the prose writers. Where would it end? Would I become one of those old women who shuffle about in slippers and socks, carrying canvas tote bags from the public library, and connecting everything to Doris Lessing novels?

I was quite worried about my future, and tonight I outlined my possible downfall to my family in careful detail over dinner. About halfway through my Lessing nightmare (which I'd embellished by adding cat cardigans and bad perms), my mum interrupted and said, "No, darling, I can't see you turning into that. If anything you'll be one of those manicured old ladies sashaying about in satin slippers and whispering about the scandalous happenings at the most recent Jane Austen Society meeting." My father had the good sense to stifle his laughter, but Heathcliff laughed so hard mashed potatoes got lodged in his nasal cavity. Serves him right, I thought. I launched a retaliatory piece of broccoli at his head, and stormed out of the room, much as Marianne Dashwood might have done. Although, for the record, Mrs Dashwood would *never* have said such a thing to Marianne. I have retired to my room in an indignant huff, and will spend the evening with Miss Austen helping Marianne recover from her Willoughby-inspired heartbreak. Sometimes, I think I am only understood by fictional characters.

My semester is perhaps the dullest one I've ever had: Susan is in class when I'm not and I hardly ever see her; Cute Angus has turned his attentions to a girl whose mother, I presume, has not reported him to the dean for plagiarism; and the turtlenecks seem to dominate all of my classes. Even Jason has finally realized he probably gave up his kindergarten juice in vain: even though I promised, we will never get married. Furthermore, the readings have been awful, and my mailbox has been defiantly empty. Maybe I should just start carrying canvas tote bags, styling my hair in a dour, librarian bun, and fully embracing the stoicism of Elinor Dashwood. Perhaps if I did so, I would then find comparative joy in the somnambulist musings of Professor Filbert, the intellectual dodgeball matches of the turtlenecks in Professor Dullardson's class, the accursed hill-rill rhymes of early Canadian poetry, and the droning posturing of the current Honours-English-Alpha-Male. Only Professor Taylor's class gives me hope that there is power and beauty in language, but she seems to be holding something back from me. Even Miss Austen seems to avoid my eye when I look at her portrait. Maybe it's because I still cannot comprehend how Elinor just accepts that Edward is gone, and that he loves someone else.

Maybe if my readings this term were remotely interesting, my mind wouldn't be wandering to Europe, to hostels, to nights out in pubs with fun new people, to walking through winding, brick-paved streets with girls smarter, nicer, prettier, kinder, funnier than I am. Maybe he is with Tess. Maybe he is with someone else. Maybe it's not even a "someone else." Maybe I wasn't even a someone in his mind. All I know is that my mailbox is empty, and he has forgotten what he promised. I want to cry like Marianne over Willoughby, but tears will not help me write all the papers I have due this week. Although Miss Austen keeps avoiding my eye, Mrs Woolf meets my glance. She says, "Stop thinking of men and do your homework, Molly. It's all you should be doing." Maybe this is why Miss Austen won't meet my eye. Maybe I need to put her novels aside. Maybe Jimmy Ruffin's right. Maybe I just need to find some kind of peace of mind. Maybe. ❧

*I*T'S AN ODD DAY IN A GIRL'S LIFE WHEN SHE thinks her mild-mannered, law-abiding father might be a vandal, a criminal even. I know this is a dangerous charge to make, so I will outline my case very carefully. Before I proceed, let me just say this: my father is the most law-abiding person I have ever met. I have never seen my father speed, litter, jaywalk, or sample a single grape in a grocery store. He regularly says things like, "I think you undercharged me for these lemons. I owe you another forty cents." Not convinced? I offer the jury this anecdote. Last summer, my father called Revenue Canada to report that he had incorrectly transcribed the total for medical expenses on his tax form. I was eating a bowl of soup in the kitchen when he called, and I stretched it out so I could overhear the whole conversation. Here are some highlights:

> "Fourteen-fifty, correct.... No, not four-teen-hundred and fifty, fourteen dollars and fifty cents.... No, I believe I owe you money.... Yes. I am calling to report I have underpaid on my taxes.... Do I need to re-file or if I can just write you a cheque? ... Sure, I'll hold.... Hello? Hello?"

When Revenue Canada hangs up on you, it may be possible that you are too law-abiding. This information provides useful context for the shocking tale I now unfold.

Early last week, we were stopped at a red light on the way to campus. My father said, "Good God, Molly, what does that sign on the bus bench say?"

I looked over and read the garish yellow letters out loud. "It says, 'Drive Decent.'" My father stared at it incredulously until drivers behind us started to honk their horns. My father was silent the rest of the trip with one possible exception: I believe I heard him mutter, "Sweet mother of God." Odd, I thought. Later in the week, we stopped by Canadian Tire on the way home from school. I wandered around the store, and then met my father in the lineup. Beside the light bulbs, birdseed, and windshield washer fluid that were on the shopping list, I noticed two rolls of bright, yellow electrical tape. Casually I asked, "What's the tape for?" to which my normally mild-mannered father replied snappishly:

"Since when is it a crime to buy tape? Can't a man buy a roll of tape without a million questions?" He rushed out in such a hurry that I had to collect his Canadian Tire money from the cashier. I thought his behaviour odd, but I didn't think much more about it. On Sunday, while I was rapt in my morning scones and the comings and goings on *Coronation Street*, I overheard this conversation.

"Hamish, you've got to be kidding."

"I'm perfectly serious. I never say anything when you write cheques to save the rainforest, the whales, the ozone, or the chimpanzees. All I want to do is save the adverb. Is that too much to ask? Is it?"

"Oh Hamish. Sigh."

The very next morning, my father and I were sitting at that original red light, and, rather than wincing and glaring at the bus bench as he had done every day last week, my father looked straight ahead. Casually, I looked over to the offending bus bench, and spied an L and a Y made of garish yellow tape at the end of the heretofore offensive word. I read aloud, "Drive Decently?" My head whipped around to stare at my father who inexplicably started whistling "Scotland the Brave" and joyously tapping the steering wheel. Over the course of the week, I have seen more and more LYs in yellow tape on bus benches on the south side. On the north side, drivers are still advised to "drive decent." My father rarely crosses the river.

I'm okay with my dad being a renegade, but what alarms me is that my father's vandalistic motivations are neither political, nor aesthetic, nor anarchistic: they're grammatical. Would I have any hope of being a stylish, cappuccino-drinking, Bloomsburian revolutionary It Girl if my father were arrested for taking a stand against adjectives being used in lieu of adverbs? What if I follow in his footsteps? Just last week, while singing along to "Wonderwall," I corrected the that/who error in the chorus. What's next? Outrage over comma splices? Eventual grammatical vigilantism? Is this the only difference an English major can hope to make in the world? ✾

*A*FTER MUCH CONTEMPLATION, I MUST FINALLY declare that very few places could be less conducive to the poetic soul than the Southgate bus terminal. After re-reading W.B. Yeats' "The Lake Isle of Innisfree" for the nineteenth time for the Poetics of Place paper due next Tuesday, I'm thoroughly depressed that I do not hear "lake water lapping with low sounds by the shore" in my "deep heart's core." The only lapping I hear right now is the ebb and flow of cars on the freeway, the gaseous sound of bus brakes, and the low grumblings and shuffling of people who have nothing in common except the shared anticipation of a tardy bus and a dislike for gusting winter winds. I am also struggling to get through my Walt Whitman readings for my Poetics of Place journal due next week. Maybe if I were Walt Whitman, I could take that multifarious dirge of sounds and voices, and write, "I Hear South Edmonton Singing." But, I'm not Walt Whitman and I don't live in Yeats' Ireland. I am merely Molly MacGregor, and I live in Edmonton. My Lake Isle of Innisfree is a bus shelter at a shopping mall, and my body electric appears to have short-circuited in the snow.

Maybe if I were Walt Whitman, I'd see this bus shelter differently. Maybe if I were Walt, I'd see how that junior-high girl is quietly flirting with a gangly boy who can't sit still or shut up. I'd see that he does not notice her perfect eye makeup. I'd see that he has no idea that prior to his arrival, she peered into an oversized mirror for fifteen minutes fixing her eyeliner with cotton swabs she'd put in her book bag this morning, in the hope she would see him. If I were Walt, I'd notice the boy doesn't know she is in love with him. I'd also see she doesn't know that he is so very wrong for her, and hope she will see this before too many tears are shed.

I'd also follow the rustling of a plastic bag to see to a slightly overweight woman carrying a sensible purse, shifting her blue Fairweather bag from hand to hand. I see someone who is too afraid to get a new hairstyle, but who secretly hopes that one of these days her hairdresser will say "I think we should try something different today. Are you ready for a change?" instead of "Same old?" I'd see the nervous shifting of her shiny bag, and notice how she peeks into it tentatively now and again. I'd wonder if she wishes she'd bought the red instead of the black, the green instead of the blue. Does she hope her husband will say, "Forty dollars? That is a steal. It will bring out the blue in your lovely eyes," or worry that he'll say, "Forty dollars? I thought we agreed we wouldn't spend anything this month." I'd wonder if she thinks, "Maybe this one perfect sweater will make people like me better at work." Or maybe she's just thinking, "This won't go with those pants after all." And then I'd notice that well-dressed married couple and hear the wife say in a not-so-hushed whisper, "No, I'm not mad at you. I'm just disappointed, that's all." If I were Walt, I'd wonder what he'd done. Is he mad she is disappointed, or disappointed she is not mad? Is it better to disappoint the woman you love, or make her mad? I'd notice how they both stare at her finger as she twists her wedding ring.

If I were W.B. Yeats, maybe I could see the beauty of this place. And if I were Walt, maybe I would look up and see my reflection in the windows of the shelter, and I would say, "I celebrate myself, and sing myself." But I am not Walt. And I am not W.B. Yeats. When I look up, I see only a girl from south Edmonton against a backdrop of buses waiting at a shopping mall. The song of myself is hardly a song. I have nowhere to arise and go to now. Innisfree feels as far away as the moon. While I stand on the roadway, or on the pavements gray, I hear nothing but city buses in my deep heart's core. ❧

I'D BEEN SAVING MY INAUGURAL READING OF McIntyre for just the right moment. I did not want to squander the life-altering event on just any afternoon. I must admit, however, that I might have overestimated how soon the perfect moment might have arisen, since I am now uncomfortably close to my deadline, and have not read a single line of his masterful verse. Today probably should have been more productive than it was. Here is a re-creation of my workday.

I found a nice desk on the fifth floor of Rutherford Library North, arranged my notebook and sharpened my pencils, and thought: "I am going to start on my ground-breaking literary work now. Okay, McIntyre, prepare to be reclaimed! Page one. Page. One. Or, in French: la première page." And then my thoughts went something like this:

"I'm hungry. But I should work. I would like a carrot muffin. But I should read some McIntyre first. But muffins are so good. Especially carrot muffins. Read some McIntyre and then you can have a muffin. Carrots are good for you. They can prevent scurvy. It would be hard to read poetry if you had scurvy. On account of the malaise and spongy gums and all. Reclaiming misunderstood poets should not be done whilst undernourished or scurvy prone. I will quickly grab a muffin and then get to work.

"Maybe I'll quickly grab *Persuasion* on my way out in case I have to wait in line for my carrot muffin. Long line at the circulation desk. I read a full chapter of *Persuasion* while waiting to take out my book. No line at Java Jive. But how exactly did Louisa Musgrove fall at Lyme Regis? I will sit here for a moment and review that passage. There is a sun beam shining through the skylights in HUB Mall and I fall into a sleepy reverie. I wonder, how is it that whenever I fall in the snow, no dreamy man says, "'Had not she better be carried to the inn? Yes, I am sure, carry her gently to the inn. I will carry her myself.'" I wonder if Mark has visited Lyme Regis. If a girl fell if he would say, "Had not she better be carried to the inn?" Or would he say, as I hope he would, "Had this girl read *Persuasion*, she would have known to watch her step. Let her find her own way back to the inn for her folly!"

I looked at my watch and realized two things: one, in an hour, I had done nothing to reclaim James McIntyre's oeuvre; and two, our mail gets delivered about now. I wonder if scurvy would be less agonizing than the pondering of the contents of one's mailbox.

WITH NOTHING IN TODAY'S POSTAL DELIVERY to distract my thoughts, I sat down to find solace in this week's required readings. Finding none, I forced myself to start drafting the assignment for my theory class, and within minutes found myself riddled with ennui. I fear I may still have a residual excess of black bile from last semester. Sitting down, I realized I did not want to select a work I felt embodies Bakhtin's ideas of the carnival, and describe why and how. I was bored. I said, "Let me count the ways that I am bored," so many times I felt I owed it to myself to count them. I am bored because Professor Dullardson has no clue who any of us is. I am bored because Dullardson has students' names on a list, and students' faces in a classroom, and never the twain shall meet. I am bored because I know no matter what I write, I will receive a passable grade and the comment "a fair effort." I am bored because my own voice rationally comparing the virtues and failings of Mr Rochester and Mr Darcy, or the leaf imagery in Wordsworth and Coleridge, bores me. I am particularly bored by describing how my favourite foot-stomping scene in *Jane Eyre* is Bakhtinian. Finally, I am most bored because I fail to see how writing this is going to help me become a great novelist. As I looked at my list, it occurred to me that I did not know the source of "and never the twain shall meet," and thought it would both amuse and edify me to look it up. Reference books, I reflected, never fail to cheer me up.

After consulting *Bartlett's Familiar Quotations* and learning it's from Kipling, I ran into Jason and we spent a few moments comparing ennui. He said something that inspired me in ways I have not felt all semester: "People who aren't in our class could hand in papers, and I bet he wouldn't even notice." Initially I said: "Ha ha, yeah," but then I got to thinking. "That sounds like a dare, Mr Richards." And so, I found a solution to my ennui. Behold:

Cal Oucallay

Introduction to Literary Theory

Professor Dullardson

Deconstructing the Motif of the Everyman:

Bakhtinian Theories in Tom Wilson's Ziggy Cartoons

When most people think of *Ziggy* cartoons, they usually think they're silly cartoons with simple punch lines. Harmless fun. If, however, you read these *Ziggy* cartoons through a Bakhtinian lens, nothing could be further from the truth. In this paper, I first argue that *Ziggy* cartoons are actually carefully constructed deconstructions of the Everyman story, and then use Bakhtin's theories of the carnival to show that *Ziggy* embodies social disruption. Finally, I will argue that *Ziggy* cartoons are complex forms of visual rhetoric that ask us to pose difficult questions about gender and gendering in our post-postmodern society.

I will begin my analysis with Figure A. Here, Wilson makes an oblique yet potent, postmodern nod to Bakhtin by placing Ziggy in a travel agency. Anyone who has been to a travel agent recently knows that travel agents always have posters for Carnival Cruises on their walls. By placing TRAVEL AGENT in large letters at the top of the cartoon, Wilson is asking us to visualize travel agencies and the brightly coloured, Carnival Cruise posters ubiquitously located therein. The Carnival Cruise posters summon Bakhtin's ideas of the carnivalesque, thus positioning this *Ziggy* cartoon as a document of social disruption and subversion. That the travel agent suggests Ziggy not go anywhere (thus inverting the whole notion of vacations and the whole travel agent profession) is also an element of the carnival. Lest readers miss this subversive allusion to Bakhtin, Wilson underscores the subversive nature of the travel agent's role in the carnival, by having her say, "I *never* thought I'd be telling anyone this but..." (emphasis mine, np). Clearly the travel agent knows she is being subversive. The fact that the woman is a travel *agent* is very important to note, since it underscores the element of an individual's agency (whether acknowledged or not) within carnival schemata. It is debatable whether we should read the travel agent as highly self-reflective about her agency within the carnival scheme, or if we should view Wilson's artistry as too heavy handed.

Thus, *Ziggy* cartoons are not merely comic artifacts; they are powerful pieces of visual rhetoric that ask key questions about gender and gendering. In Figure A, you will note that the travel agent is highly gendered with her long hair and earrings, whereas Ziggy is highly non-gendered. By creating a gender contrast between the two characters, Wilson is suggesting that the world is a highly gendered place, yet Ziggy stands outside of that gendering. By denying him pants in every single cartoon (and thus denying him the traditional demarcation of masculinity), Wilson is suggesting that Ziggy lives *outside* the world of gender constructions and thus embodies a challenge to hegemonic gender politics. In this way, Ziggy is a free-floating agent of chaos.

Thus, because of these two nods to social disruption, I posit that Ziggy embodies the postmodern paradox: Ziggy is at once Everyman *and* No-man: while Ziggy appears to be every man, he in fact represents no one; thus, he calls into question the validity of the Everyman tradition and, arguably, the entire English literary canon as we understand it today.

Because I am a dedicated user of serif fonts, I used Helvetica, the ickiest of fonts, for this paper. I imagine he will never suspect me. I placed it mid-pile and far from my own paper. It will be very funny when no one selects this paper from the graded pile and he must say "Callooh? Callay? Callooh? Callay?" I would chortle in my joy. ༃

I HAVE RECEIVED MY PAPER BACK FROM Professor Dullardson with these comments:

"Miss MacGregor, I am returning both of your papers together. Your reading of *Jane Eyre* is solidly passable. However, when combined with the carnivalesque act of submitting a chaotically argued reading of *Ziggy* cartoons under a pseudonym, you have conveyed a deep understanding of Bakhtinian carnival. An above fair effort overall. B+

P.S. You forget, Miss MacGregor, that I knew you as a child. Your anonymous papers cannot fool the discerning. ❧

*I*T IS THE FIRST DAY OF READING WEEK. I KNOW I should be sleeping in, or doing something fun this week, but I took the early bus to campus today and basked in the solitude. I love getting to campus early, buying toast from the lovely ladies at Patria, and a dark roast from Java Jive, and watching people walk up and down HUB Mall. Although there was never any doubt that my siblings and I would come to this university, I still find it remarkable to be one of the grown-ups I used to see walking this mall when I visited the campus as a child. I remember loving the idea that you could go to university, and live in the apartments above the mall's stores. Best of all, you could buy an ice cream cone without having to go outside. I loved how the windows' shutters were painted bright colours and covered in posters. Students would lean out of their windows, and have conversations across the mall. It looked like one of those old-world streets where neighbours talked to each other as they hung out their laundry on lines, watered geraniums in terra cotta pots, or pulled bread or wine up from the street in wicker baskets. Whenever we went to campus, I tried to decide what colour of shutter I would want my HUB Mall apartment to have. Red almost always won out, but I thought the "Hang in there" kitten poster I'd want on my shutter would look best on the blue. My parents had to hold my hand to prevent me and my ice cream from walking into pillars, planters, and ramps. They would pull me along: "Come along, Molly, there's plenty of time to daydream later." I might be cashing in this offer now, daydreaming my week away.

As I look around, it appears that there is a more austere regime running HUB Mall now: posters are forbidden and the bright reds, yellows, and greens have been replaced by innocuous shades of blue and grey. Here and there a renegade PETA or Hüsker Dü sticker appears, but the mall has lost its rustic village charm. As I look up to these apartments this morning, I wonder if my parents pulled me along so I wouldn't notice how many of the apartments used the window frames as exhibition spaces to chronicle the residents' liquor and substance preferences and their consumption history. Above me, a rainbow of girly, flavoured vodka bottles on one side of the mall are in a standoff with an army of Crown Royal and Johnny Walker bottles on the other side.

On these childhood visits, I remember watching the grown-ups walk through the mall. I could almost feel the important thoughts emanating from their minds and their urgent work pulsing through their bodies. Some would perambulate as if the act of putting one foot in front of the other down the length of HUB Mall would bring them to the thought or idea they most desired. Others would stride painfully, as if the ideas in their heads would combust and cause irreparable damage to the campus if not released into a notebook, classroom, or laboratory within three minutes. Still, others would walk and talk in groups, making gestures not unlike interpretive dancers. I still see the two Italian gentlemen, older now, strolling up and down the mall, shoulder to shoulder, talking into their hands with a certainty that makes me think they have the mysteries of the world under control. I have always loved walking through this mall and feeling the pulse of ideas and important work.

When I think back to what I thought about university students when I was little, I feel like an imposter now. While the students I saw as a child seemed to be working through world-altering problems, I am mulling the permutations of word choice and punctuation. Would Wordsworth's poem be different if his narrator had "wandered lonely like a cloud" instead of "lonely as a cloud." There are times when I am sitting in my classroom, talking about books and ideas, and I am so very happy that I cannot imagine doing anything other than talking about commas or Shakespearean allusions. Yet underneath this happiness, there's always a glimmer of guilt that I should be doing something more useful with my time. Every minute I have spent talking about iambic pentameter, or sprung rhythm, could have instead been used to feed a hungry child, save a baby seal, or protect an endangered butterfly. Should I be saving the world from larger perils than split infinitives, passive voice, and poorly executed parenthetical citations? There's always a nagging sense of guilt that I should be doing something important as I envisioned those university students doing when I was little: inventing something urgent, not playing with words and aerie nothings. It's as if there's someone still pulling my hand, telling me, "Come along Molly, there's plenty of time to daydream later." Now, as I sit in HUB Mall, trying to get started on my papers, I realize all I do is hold words in my hands, wondering where they should go. ❧

*I*N THE GRAND SCHEME OF THINGS, PACING UP and down in front of the *Edmonton Journal* building downtown does very little to ensure the timely arrival of one's bus. However, pacing, hoping, and walking kept me warm as I waited for the bus to take me home to an empty mailbox. I was reminded of something my granny used to say to soothe the heartbroken Tess: "Boys are like buses, dear. There will be another one along soon enough." She was right: for Tess, there was another boy just around the corner. Curiously, I think of my granny's saying more when waiting for buses than pining over boys. Buses, I have come to think, are more like boys. There are always twenty willing to take you where you don't want to go, but waiting for the one you want is an act of hope, faith, and patience.

Today seemed like the first day we could possibly venture to say there was a trace of spring in the air. Instead of going to Professor Filbert's class this afternoon, I decided to take Robert Herrick's advice and gather my rosebuds while I might. According to my close reading of his poem, I think Herrick would approve of my decision to "be not coy" about my dislike for Wordsworth, but "use my time" to poke around Audreys Books on Jasper Avenue. I stopped by the Herrick section in the library to look at a picture of Herrick, to see if he looked like the sort of man who would excuse me from class to explore an almost-spring day. I was delighted to discover that Herrick looked a lot like a medallion-less Bruno Gerussi and posed this question to his likeness: "'this same flower that smiles to-day,/ To-morrow will be dying,' right, Mr Herrick?" And he said "Exactly, my dear." "Do you think I should skip Romantics?" "Well, they really do drone on, and on, and on, don't they? How are you supposed to commune with nature when they keep you inside with their endless Preludes? Seize the day, my girl!" With Herrick's blessing, I headed across the river, and my afternoon was spent holding the smooth heft of Penguin Classics in my hand.

I read every single back-cover blurb, trying to find my next favourite author. My head is still abuzz with names of people I'd like to know better: Eliot, Dickens, Burney, Waugh, Joyce, and Radcliffe. And places I want to be: The Fens, Bath, Tunbridge Wells, Canterbury, and Bloomsbury. After almost two hours, I left with one pristine Penguin: Dickens' *Great Expectations*.

As I waited for my bus, the tiny hints of spring I thought I saw yesterday were replaced by reminders that winter still has its teeth in our city. I watched silver Edmonton Transit buses troll past, offering to take me to Mill Woods, Castle Downs, Bonnie Doon, Belgravia, and the Highlands. It reminded me of a public transit version of the "Goblin Market": "come ride, come ride." Like the proffered fruit of the goblins, these places sound romantic and appealing, but they're not at all what they seem. If you live in Edmonton, you know our Belgravia is nothing like London's. There isn't a castle, down, or doon to be found, bonnie or otherwise. Edmonton does have the Highlands, but I can't imagine that wherever Robert Burns wandered, wherever he roved, that these northern-concrete Highlands would be those forever he'd love.

When I left the bookstore, I decided not to take an eastward bus to my southbound bus, but instead walked to its stop. At first my mind was full of distant times and places. As I was waiting for a light to change, I stared at Jasper Avenue and wondered how it would be described in the pages of a Penguin. I started also thinking that this time next year I will be a few short weeks away from graduating. I have always thought I would leave Edmonton. Where will I go? And when I am far away, what will I miss? I missed the walk light, and decided to take the long way to my bus stop. I needed this extra time with my city. I imagined what it would be like to prepare to leave Edmonton. I tried to imagine what I would miss.

For all my talk of escaping Edmonton for more romantic places, the thought of leaving suddenly seemed incomprehensible. For the first time ever, I began to doubt if I could exist anywhere else. These thoughts were so overwhelming that I stepped onto a patch of brown grass in a small park and pretended to retie my boot. My bootlaces were fine, but I needed a moment to touch the earth of my city. I needed to press my fingers into the frozen grass and push the love I suddenly felt deep into the ground for safekeeping. I imagined a time when an older version of me might want that moment back again, might, like Burns, want to know that my heart is still here, wherever I go. 🐾

*A*FTER IT BECAME APPARENT THAT THE PERFECT DAY to read McIntyre would not present itself, I finally made myself sit down, and read his collected works. Reclaiming a soon-to-be major poet was more work than I had anticipated. I expected that McIntyre's genius would be such that it would simply leap off the page, and the paper would basically write itself. So far, I have not found this to be the case. Let me chronicle my day.

Before reading McIntryre, I set about to find the required secondary sources about him, but found none. Even the librarian couldn't find anything beyond a few short biographical notes, all of which call him a cheese poet (which doesn't strike me as very nice at all). I became even more convinced that my work restoring McIntyre to his place of glory within the Canadian literary tradition is urgent, especially given my own aspirations. My own literary career, I thought, would be on much more solid ground, if I could build upon my own ancestry. I envisioned the back-cover blurb on my first novel noting my literary pedigree. Maybe there would even be a sticker on the front cover: "Descendent of James McIntyre." Those were my thoughts this morning. Having read McIntyre's work this afternoon, I admit I am somewhat troubled by what I found.

Assuming that reading McIntyre's collection for the first time would be a turning point in my own literary career, I thought good documentation of this encounter would prove invaluable to future Canadian literary biographers trying to make the connections between my craft and his. Allow me, dear reader, to transcribe some of the extensive reading notes I took from my first encounters with *Musings on the Banks of Canadian Thames, including poems on local, Canadian, and British Subjects, and lines on the great poets of England, Ireland, Scotland, and America, with a glance at the wars in Victoria's reign.*

10:02. On the epigraph: "Fair Canada is our Theme,/ Land of rich cheese, milk and cream." Interesting!
10:05. Three poems read. Hmm. Maybe he's just warming up.
10:15. Oh.
10:17. Oh my. Look at these rhyme schemes:

> "Young Dominion so gigantic,
> Where rail cars run at speed terrific,
> Thousands of miles from the Atlantic
> Till in the West you reach Pacific"
> ("Canada's Future").

10:20. He writes about curling. This could prove useful (if you overlook the rhyming couplets)

> "And on the ice men love to hurl
> The polished blocks to skillful curl,
> And curlers all do proudly claim
> Their's is a manly healthy game,
> And in Canadians you trace
> A generous, hardy and brave race"
> ("Canadian Sports and Games and Plays").

10:40. Neat! A poem about Susanna Moodie.
10:41. Ouch:

> "When this country it was woody
> Its great champion Mrs Moody"
> ("Mrs. Moody").

Note the changed spelling of her name for the visual rhyme. Oh, ancestor McIntyre.

11:00. He has a section called Dairy and Cheese Odes. He writes Cheese Odes!
11:03. It's not a value judgment. He really does write about cheese.

> "When Father Ranney left the States,
> In Canada to try the fates,
> He settled down in Dereham,
> Then no dairyman lived near him;
> He was the first there to squeeze
> His cows' milk into good cheese,
> And at each Provincial show
> His famed cheese was all the go"
> ("Father Ranney, the Cheese Pioneer").

11:15. Dear Lord. I am a descendent of a veritable cheese poet! Could the fate of an aspiring novelist be any worse?
11:20. It is worse than I'd thought. I am the descendent of the author of these lines:

> "The land enriched by goodly cows
> Yields plenty now to fill their mows,
> Both wheat and barley, oats and peas,
> But still their greatest boast is cheese"
> ("Oxford Cheese Ode").

And here, dear reader, my notes end. In short, I am doomed. I do not know which is worse: being a descendent of a cheese poet, or needing to create an edited collection of McIntyre's best and most influential poems on cheese by Monday. 🂡

*A*FTER READING MCINTYRE'S WORK, I SET OUT to get a coffee, eat my sandwich, and lament my fate. My lunch was, cruelly, a cheddar sandwich. I had innocently packed it myself this morning, not knowing how caustic cheese would become to me in just a few hours. I felt mocked by a bagged lunch and assumed its mocking would be the beginning of a long line of taunting I would forever endure for being the descendent of the cheese poet of Canada. Coming from Edmonton was strike one for an aspiring writer, but I thought I could overcome that with perseverance. Being descended from the cheese poet seemed insurmountable. Unable to face my fate, I decided to walk around the perimeter of campus while I finished my coffee. Each day there were a few more minutes of daylight and there were promises of warmth. Most of my final assignments nearly done; my mind was finally starting to thaw from the semester.

When I started walking, my first thoughts were about how easy it would be to change poets, choose some famous hill-rill rhymer, and be done with it. I would have to scramble to pull something together for McIntyre anyway, why not pick an easier poet? Logic kept pointing me toward abandoning McIntyre, but something kept nagging at me. I stopped, opened my book bag, and re-read his poem about Susanna Moodie. I read it, and re-read it. I started to walk, repeating the first stanza in my head, his iambs bouncing in rhythm with my steps: "When this country it was woody,/

its great champion Mrs Moody,/ Showed she had both pluck and push/ In her work roughing in the bush." The further I walked along the edge of the river, the more I realized that I, like Mrs Moody (*sic*), have "both pluck and push," and that I needed to take on McIntyre's work in the same way that she took on "this country when it was woody." It was easy to laugh at McIntyre, and that's all critics did. McIntyre needed a champion. I walked toward the river, and by the time I stood on its banks, I knew there had to be more to him than those awful rhyming couplets and dairy-land poems. Whatever it was, I would find it. I will be your great champion, James McIntyre.

HAVE NOT SLEPT IN THIRTY-SIX HOURS BUT I
have finally handed in my McIntyre assignment.
Here it is:

Introduction to "The Poetry of James McIntyre:
Reclaiming an Early Canadian Voice.
An Anthology of Verse"
Selected and Edited by Molly MacGregor

Scanning the scholarly literature for critical responses to
James McIntyre's poetry proves to be a difficult endeavour.
When one does find mention of McIntyre's poetic works,
one frequently finds phrases such, as "the worst English
Canadian poet ever" and "the world's cheesiest poet." In
this paper, I want to acknowledge the poetic limitations
of McIntyre's work, yet I also want to urge us to look
beyond McIntyre's light-hearted and engaging rhyme
schemes, and suggest that his role within the Canadian
literary tradition is not his aesthetic importance, but his
insistence upon writing the Canadian experience as he saw
it. In McIntyre's work, he insisted we not only examine the
local, the mundane, and the minute, but that we celebrate
its specificities as that which makes our nation distinct.
Moreover, McIntyre makes us laugh through his verse. We
are invited to laugh, I believe, *along with* McIntyre at his
verse, his observations, and, most importantly, at ourselves,
our country, and our identity.

Canada is a country that has long prided itself on never taking itself too seriously. Humour is one of the elements that makes Canada the nation that it is, and Canadians are the first to see what is unique and humorous about our nation. Rather than discard McIntyre for his quirky, and at times oddball, rhyme schemes (many of which only work when read with a Scottish brogue), I believe it is important to include McIntyre's work within discussions of the Canadian literary tradition. Throughout his work, we can see a contagious enthusiasm for his country, its past, its present, and its potential for the future.

As can be seen by my edition's table of contents, McIntyre's oeuvre can be divided into two main components: his "dairy odes" and his "patriotic songs." Most of the critical attention McIntyre has received in the past century emerges from his infamous "dairy odes," particularly his "Ode on the Mammoth Cheese." These poems have earned McIntyre titles ranging from the descriptive ("the cheese poet") to the judgmental ("Canada's worst poet"). While many would argue that dairy odes such as "Oxford Cheese Ode" and "Ode on the Mammoth Cheese (weight over seven thousand pounds)" have no serious literary merit, I posit that "literary merit" is not what we should be seeking in McIntyre's poetry. It is unlikely that we were ever meant to read these poems for their literary merit. McIntyre's poems, I argue, have been consciously crafted to celebrate both the distinctness of Canada and of Canadian life. In a true Scots-Canadian way, he reminds us never to take ourselves too seriously, and to see the humour and joy in our daily lives as Canadians.

While most scholarly introductions address the characteristic or representative works, I want to begin my introduction with a work that is uncharacteristically McIntyrean, a short poem tucked midway into the volume called, "In Memorium: Lines on the death of my only son, who died on the 5th of July, 1876, on the anniversary of his mother's death."

His mother from celestial bower,
In the self-same day and hour

Of her death or heavenly birth,
Gazed again upon the earth,
And saw her gentle, loving boy,
Once source of fond maternal joy,
In anguish on a couch of pain.
She knew that earthly hopes were vain,
And beckoned him to realms above
To share with her the heavenly love. (149)

Certainly, this poem lacks the subtlety we often associate
with the literary tradition's finer poets, but we see in
this work a level of restraint and consciousness of craft.
McIntyre's rhymes, diction, and metre are soft, somber,
and appropriate for the topic of the poem, and McIntyre
is able to convey a level of grief without sounding
excessive, maudlin, or overly emotional. I cite this poem,
not as exemplary of fine poetic craft, but as an example of
McIntyre's awareness of craft. In so doing, I want to suggest
that throughout his work, McIntyre was highly aware of
craft, and conscious of the choices he made.

In his collected work, McIntyre offers odes to many of
the fine poets of the English literary tradition that suggests
he was well aware of the literary tradition's greatest poets
and what made those poets fine. As I will show below,
McIntyre's diction, rhyme, and rhythms are overtly and
humourously over-the-top. McIntyre is too aware of the
literary tradition to have made these poetic choices without
seeing their humourous potentials.

Throughout his long collection (just under 300 pages),
McIntyre rarely wavers in his poetic style and form, which
leads me to believe he was highly aware of his particular
and unique contribution to Canadian literary history. The
consistency of style is no accident: throughout his extensive
collection of work, there is little alteration in his style,
suggesting that he was highly conscious of what made
his works characteristically McIntyrean. In this context,
it is difficult to believe that McIntyre was unaware of the
humorous elements in his rhymes, metres, and approach.
His quatrain tribute to Shelley offers a concise example of
McIntyre's particular style:

We have scarcely time to tell thee,
Of the strange and gifted Shelley,
Kind hearted man but ill-fated,
So youthful, drowned and cremated. (120)

Similarly, in "Oxford Cheese Ode," he opens with this
stanza:

The ancient poets ne'er did dream
That Canada was land of cream,
They ne'er imagined it could flow
In this cold land of ice and snow,
Where everything did solid freeze,
They ne'er hoped or looked for cheese. (76)

Characteristically, McIntyre places a local scene of
Canadian life within the context of ancient poets. In this
way, he values Canadian subjects as something worthy of
poetic attention. He takes a quotidian and characteristically
Canadian topic, and locates it within the English literary,
poetic tradition. However, at the same time, he also does
so with an element of humour, undercutting any possible
pretentions, by playfully imagining ancient poets pondering
the Canadian dairy industry.

McIntyre wrote this poem and his other dairy odes
with a full awareness of its potential for irony, parody, and
the gentle, mocking, self-deprecating humour we have
come to see as characteristically Canadian. No other poems
in this collection do this sort of humour as well as "Ode on
the Mammoth Cheese," which I include in its entirety to
convey the full character of this poem. Partial quotations
do not suggest the additive nature of the various metre and
rhyme schemes he has selected.

We have seen thee, queen of cheese,
Laying quietly at your ease,
Gently fanned by evening breeze,
Thy fair form no flies dare seize.
All gaily dressed soon you'll go
To the great Provincial Show,
To be admired by many a beau
In the city of Toronto.
Cows numerous as a swarm of bees,

Or as the leaves upon the trees,
It did require to make thee please,
And stand unrivalled queen of cheese.
May you not receive a scar as
We have heard that Mr Harris
Intends to send you off as far as
The great World's show at Paris.
Of the youth beware of these,
For some of them might rudely squeeze
And bite your cheek, then songs or glees
We could not sing, oh! queen of cheese.
We'rt thou suspended from balloon,
You'd cast a shade, even at noon,
Folks would think it was the moon
About to fall and crush them soon. (71-72)

I think it is a grievous critical misreading to assume that McIntyre was not aware of the humourous nature of the mammoth cheese as a subject for a poetic work. Moreover, as argued above, McIntyre's poems as a whole suggest he was well-versed in the literary tradition, and had to have been aware of the over-the-top nature of rhyme schemes such as "beware of these," "rudely squeeze," "songs or glees," and "queen of cheese."[1] The creative pronunciations of the fourth stanza also show an attempt to draw attention to the forced nature of the rhyme scheme. In order to fully appreciate the work of McIntyre, we need to see poetic works such as these within the tradition of Canadian humour: his dairy odes are at once a gentle mocking of our country and traditions, and a celebration of our country.

The collection of McIntyre's poetic work that I have selected for this anthology is an attempt not only to show McIntyre's contributions to the Canadian literary tradition, but to show that to fully understand this country and its

1 It should be noted that McIntyre's is an occasional user of what I call the "ill-rhymes" which places him firmly within the extensive tradition of "hill/rill" rhymes in early Canadian poetry. His use of the plural form and his volume-wide avoidance of the word "rill" suggest a nod to this tradition as well as an undermining of it. For further discussion of the "hill/rill" tradition in early Canadian poetry, please see my mid-term exam from February. Booklet 2, I believe.

literature, we need new ways of seeing it, and valuing it in our own distinctly Canadian ways. Examining the work of McIntyre with new critical approaches and new eyes will not only help us see our country and its literary tradition in new ways, it will encourage us to see and seek value in parts of our country, our history, our landscape, and ourselves we have long dismissed. 🜨

*M*Y DELAYS IN WRITING MY MCINTYRE assignment set my remaining assignments back a few days and I've been scrambling to get everything done. My last assignment before finals was a short paper on Walt Whitman's *Leaves of Grass*. I thought it would take no time at all. I was wrong. Instead of writing a paper, I ended up handing this in.

> Dear Professor Taylor,
> I apologize for not coming to today's class with my paper on Whitman. Ever since I was a tiny child, you've always seemed to know what I was up to, especially when my parents hosted department parties that lasted past my bedtime. I recall you saying on more than one occasion: "Your youngest child, Hamish, has escaped her bed once more. You'll find her beneath the table, I believe." I always appreciated that you gave me half-an-hour's grace before reporting my trespasses. So, with that history between us, I will simply say, I did not complete my assignment. I could have pulled it all together this morning, I know, but I didn't.
> I'll admit I have not managed my time well, and that I should have had everything read and written before class. I'll also admit I don't have a very good excuse as to why I missed class, and why I still don't have my Poetics of Place paper written. What I

will admit is this: around 11:00, I felt crowded. The press of people, of deadlines, of minor annoyances, the combined weight of my various anthologies and textbooks, the continual presence of words I needed to read, words I needed to write, words I wanted to read, words I wanted to write: all of these seemed too much for me. Reading Whitman for today's class was more than I could handle.

I tried to find a quiet spot to read my Whitman: I read the first stanza of "Crossing Brooklyn Ferry" over and over again on the fifth floor and then on the third floor of Rutherford North. I read these same stanzas over and over again in Rutherford South. I read and re-read them in the desks in the Humanities Building, but I could not get past the lines, "The glories strung like beads on my smallest sights and hearings, on the walk in the street and the passage over the river,/ The current rushing so swiftly and swimming with me far away." The ridiculousness of reading poetry about the poetics of place at an uncomfortable desk in an itchy Irish sweater was making me angry, and so I put my book bag in my locker, grabbed my Whitman, and headed out for a destination I could not predict.

I had no idea where I would end up, but I left the building, guided by something I could not name. I walked north and east and felt the silent, still-wintery air ease the press of words in my head. I told myself it was crazy to leave campus in the middle of the day, but I kept walking with Whitman in my hand. I would be lying if I said the beauty of Whitman's language drove me outside, or that his metaphors demanded that I flee the confines of the institution, and read them *en plein air*. I must be completely truthful—Whitman was annoying me with his ceaseless sentences, his singing America, and his body electric. Eventually, I felt like that philosophy grad student at Dewey's, who ends every argument he can't win with, "Hey. You, me. Outside." And, so, I said to

Whitman, "Hey. You, me. Outside." And Walt and I
walked to the High Level Bridge together.

I was halfway across the bridge when I finally
stopped walking. Standing over the river on this
teasingly cold spring day, I couldn't bring myself to
think about Whitman. I was thinking about the river
that I see every day, but had never stood over: today
was the first day in my whole life in Edmonton that
I've walked above the North Saskatchewan River.
I was thinking about the trees I see every day, but
do not look at. I was thinking about the sky and its
crisp blueness of nearly spring. I was thinking about
standing still over a river, while ice floes pushed
through the water below me, cars dashed behind me,
and bikes sped past me. I was thinking about the
press of people, and words, and ideas, and noise I'd
left behind me. I was thinking about all the poets
I have read who, smugly, thought they alone had
seen beauty in its rarest form: Keats, Wordsworth,
Coleridge, Whitman. But how could those poets say
those things when none of them had seen this river,
these trees, these birds on this day, under this sky. As
I thought about the river, the cool air was working its
way through my sweater, and I felt overwhelmed by
guilt knowing I could not return to campus with my
Whitman unread.

I stared at the photograph of Whitman on the
cover of my book, and felt him laughing at me for all
my struggles reading him this week. "Give in to me,
Molly," he seemed to say, and so I did. I opened my
book to "Crossing Brooklyn Ferry," and read it out
loud to the river. And as I read, I took him at his word
when he said, "It avails not, time not place—distance
avails not,/ I am with you, you men and women of a
generation, or ever so many generations hence,/ Just
as you feel when you look on the river and sky, so I
felt." I can't imagine that Whitman would have ever
thought a girl like me, in a city that would not be a
city in his lifetime, would feel what he felt looking

over a river he would not have heard of, and a sky so big he could not have imagined it. Or that he could have anticipated that a girl like me would say, "yes" as she read, "These and all else were to me the same as they are to you." I finished reading "Crossing Brooklyn Ferry," and began "Song of Myself." I could almost hear Whitman's voice. I could almost feel his arm around my shoulder, pointing to my river, my trees, and my sky when he asked,

> Have you practis'd so long to learn to read?
> Have you felt so proud to get at the meaning
>   of poems?
> Stop this day and night with me and you shall
>   possess the origin of all poems,
> You shall possess the good of the earth and
>   sun, (there are millions of suns left,)
> You shall no longer take things at second or
>   third hand, nor look through the eyes of the
>   dead, nor feed on the spectres in books,
> You shall not look though my eyes either, nor
>   take things from me,
> You shall listen to all sides and filter them
>   from your self.

As I stood and watched the urgent pull of the North Saskatchewan below me, and the push and pull of the ice floes, I understood it wasn't necessarily an American man or a famous poet Walt wanted me to imagine when he said, "I am with you, you men and women of a generation, or ever so many generations hence,/ Just as you feel when you look on the river and sky, so I felt." I was thinking about a girl—a Canadian girl like me or unlike me—a girl from fifty years ago, one hundred years ago, three hundred years ago—who also looked at this river and these trees, and felt just as I felt looking on this river and this sky. Unlike Whitman, these girls never saved these feelings for a girl like me to find. They never wrote them down or passed them along. Those thoughts are gone, but that doesn't mean they're not part of this river, this city, this girl I am. I know a girl has stood looking at this river, and had these very same thoughts about our river and our sky. They are with me, a girl a generation, or ever so many generations hence. Just as I feel when I look on the river and sky, so they felt. I was cold, but unable to leave. Just as I had never seen the trees and river I see every day, I had never before thought to look for the unnamed girls who, like me, "loved well the stately and rapid river" of my city.

Walt Whitman made me ask these unnamed girls, "What is it then between us?/ What is the count of the scores or hundreds of years between us?" and he made me imagine them telling me, "What thought you have of me now, I had as much of you—I laid in my stores in advance,/ I consider'd long and seriously of you before you were born." And he made me see that I could look through my own eyes at my city, and see what is beautiful firsthand, not second- or third-hand. I shall listen to all sides and filter them from myself.

When I first started reading Whitman last week, he frustrated me with his talk of beauty. Shivering in the winter-spring sunshine, Whitman made me say, "I come from a beautiful place too. I see beauty around me. Why are there no odes, no celebrations, no encomiums about the river *I* love?" As I looked into Whitman's eyes on the cover of the book I nearly tossed into that very river, I imagined him winking at me, saying, "Indeed, Molly. Are you waiting for something? Write something, girl!"

I don't know if I can write a paper to prove I understand Whitman, or to know what the phrase "poetics of place" means. But I understand something new. Today I saw beauty in Edmonton, my Edmonton. Whitman made me see my city as beautiful. Before heading back to campus, I knew that I could not write a paper about Whitman. Please accept my apologies. I understand I will get a zero on this assignment, but I have done the math, and think I can still pass your course. I will do better on the final. I promise. ⚘

COMMENTS FROM PROFESSOR TAYLOR ON MY apology for my Whitman paper: "This paper convinces me that you understand the poetics of place more than an analysis of figurative language could. Well done. For the record, I only reported your hiding under a table to your parents because no one, no matter what age, should have to listen to more than thirty minutes of professorial chatter at social gatherings. Walt Whitman and I look forward to reading your own literary works one day. Grade: A."

Comments from Professor Van Beekveld on my McIntyre paper: "Although I am not convinced of McIntyre's aesthetic worth and his place in the literary canon of Canadian literature, you have made a compelling case. Your efforts might have been better focused on a more deserving poet, but you have done the assignment with competence and occasional moments of aplomb. Grade: B"

I HAVE WRITTEN MY LAST EXAM OF THE SEMESTER, and have officially completed my third year of university. In my mind, I envisioned spending my first day off from school and my last day before re-starting at Le Petit Chou, doing fantastic things: painting a watercolour; baking a pie; reading *Vogue* magazine on our back deck with a sophisticated cocktail; planting delicate, blue pansies in our front garden in stylish gardening gloves and an Edwardian straw hat; drinking coffee at seven different cafés on Whyte Avenue; getting a new haircut. Instead, I let my aspirations be dashed by an empty mailbox.

Instead of planting pansies, reading *Vogue*, or baking a pie, I changed into my old Oilers T-shirt and a pair of sweatpants, and made myself a box of Kraft Dinner. I ate the whole thing while dancing to Side A of the first album in the Motown box set. I then danced to Side B while eating a row of Oreos right from the bag. After becoming the fourth Supreme in an imagined gold lamé dress, and singing "Someday We'll Be Together," (complete with hand gestures), I started in on the frost-encrusted ice cream I found at the back of the freezer. By the time Marvin Gaye asked me, "What's Going On?" I was starting to feel ill. I was flat on the couch when The Temptations shuffled into my living room in their black suits and bowties, snapped their fingers and serenaded me. My good friend Levi Stubbs roused me off the couch, and invited me to be a fifth Top for "It's the Same Old Song." I felt better as I sang along and did the swaying lobster step I'd seen them do on TV. I had so much fun I listened to the song again. This time, I sang along with Levi Stubbs, and realized it's a very different song when you sing Mr Stubbs's part. You have to sing about how your heart is in pain, and all that is left is your favourite song. And how every time you hear it, there's just a memory. And now that you're gone, the song is the same. But the meaning is different.

I sat back down on the couch, and listened to the rest of the album as Kraft Dinner, Oreos, and ice cream well past its expiry date raged in my stomach. The album finished, and the needle got stuck in the dead space at the centre of the record. I listened to the static until I heard my parents' car in the driveway. I roused myself off the couch to turn it off. I expect I looked as awful as I felt, because they both looked alarmed and demanded to know what was wrong. I saw my McIntyre paper on the table and showed it to them. It was easier to blame the lowly grade of B, than to explain why The Four Tops had upset me so. I excused myself to my bedroom, put my headphones on, and made myself listen to "Wonderwall" on repeat until I had convinced myself that Mark was gone. While there might be a thousand things I'd like to say to him, the postcard silence could not be denied. I fell asleep and woke later to find my parents making dinner.

They'd seen the Motown box set and were inspired to put on my mum's favourite album while they cooked: *The Marvelettes' Greatest Hits*. I was a little alarmed to hear "Please Mr Postman," when I came downstairs, but smiled when The Marvelettes addressed me as "girl" and reminded me that there are indeed a lot fish in the proverbial sea. We danced together, chopping and stirring. This summer would be a new start. 🕸

May 1996:
Le Petit Chou Shoe Shop
The Mall, Edmonton

HAVE RETRIEVED MY LE PETIT CHOU NAME tag from the bottom of my jewellery box. It seems a little less shiny than it did this time last year, but I remain, "Molly, at your service." I've just finished my first two shifts, and very little has changed in the Mall or at Le Petit Chou. There are some new employees, but many people are still here. Some have changed stores. Most seem to have aged over the year. Eugenie is engaged to someone who works at The Bay shoe department. They are very excited, and I am very happy for them. I asked if this is why Maureen has been disparaging department store shoes lately, and Eugenie shook her head and said, "I'll tell you later." On Maureen's day off yesterday, Eugenie filled me in on the Maureen/Rick fiasco from a few months ago. It appears they broke up after New Year's, and both were quite distraught about the whole thing. Rick had been cheating on her with a manager from Pegasus. It was particularly galling to Maureen that the other woman was a purveyor of footwear from a competing chain. Having purchased a particularly brutal pair of shoes from Pegasus that never stretched out, I could see how this could add insult to injury. On Valentine's Day, Rick had a change of heart, and had a dozen Mylar balloons that read "Some Bunny Loves You" delivered to Le Petit Chou. Maureen was so outraged that her anger never dissipated on the very long walk to Phase One, where Rick had been banished (he'd only been demoted to Phase Two when last I checked in). According to the staff at Mr Large and Burly, heated words were exchanged, and then Maureen, unaware of the flammability of Mylar balloons, took her lighter and lit one on fire. Fire engines were called, head offices were involved. Somehow Maureen didn't lose her job, but Rick is now selling children's shoes at Sears. I was advised to never refer to bunnies in her presence. Eugenie told me Maureen is now dating Gordon, who works at a Radio Chalet.

"Oh, the guy from last summer?"

"No, a totally different Gordon." After my long school year, it's kind of nice to be back in the land of many Gordons. I've been visiting my old haunts, reconnecting with the dolphins, waving to Mall Security, being furrowed at by the Rabid Pekingese, and alarmed by the peacocks below.

I'm enjoying the crime bulletins too. This week it was revealed that roving band of shoplifters are back and have developed a kind of skirt in which they can stash large amounts of merchandise. They captured one woman on film hiding a boombox in her skirt and walking out of a store. I still wonder if they might be interested in some Springtime Canary Yellow polish as we still have all of last year's jars in stock. That things are almost the same is oddly comforting, and maybe just a little depressing. But I'd best not think too much on that. I have quality shoes to purvey.

I RAN INTO MY PENGUIN MAN TODAY. IT'S BEEN at least eight months since I've seen him, and I had no idea he would be in town. He showed up at the store around noon and I was so excited to see him we made plans to meet up for my four o'clock supper break. When he arrived, four o'clock seemed too early for dinner, so we ended up going for a long walk in the newly minted, spring leaves.

"There's got to be some green grass around here somewhere," he said. We walked, and walked, and walked: it's funny how, on the one hand, walking away from the Mall is a very easy thing to do, yet it's also very difficult. It traps you inside with your short breaks and its seemingly impenetrable perimeter of concrete and freeways. But eventually, you arrive at real streets and real houses. As we walked, I began to realize how much I'd missed him. When I heard his laugh, I couldn't contain my smile.

"Tell me some stories," he said, as we spotted real grass and trees in the distance. "I've missed Molly's Mall stories."

"My Mall stories?" I shrugged and laughed, told him my life was sadly pretty story-less. He stopped suddenly, tilted his head and looked me in the eye:

"You claim to be story-less, yet want to be a novelist. Do you see a problem with this?" I shrugged and kept walking. The further away from the Mall, we walked, the more we saw grass and tulips, we began to notice the blue sky. After the long winter and cold spring, the promise of summer seemed too good to be true. I often felt like Orpheus bringing Eurydice back from the underworld—afraid to look back at spring in case it might be ripped from me for all eternity. As we walked, the thrum of the freeway subsided, and I could hear the bustle of robins building nests. We spied a playground, made our way there, and sat on swings too small for us.

"Who's Maureen dating now?" he asked. I'd forgotten that he knew nothing about her spectacular break up with Rick Ghastly, and was eager to fill him in. He chortled at the tiny details I may have exaggerated just a bit. Plus, I told him I had suspicions there was something going on between Tim and Maureen.

"And how's the Rabid Pekingese? What have you done to him lately?" I told him how yesterday, he stopped by the store to ask Maureen if we were having phone issues. I busied myself with a display of high-heeled brogues, fearing he may be on to me. He said, "Last summer I had all sorts of problems with my phone, and I'm having problems again." Worried that I would no longer have the sport of crank-calling him, I interjected, "Funny you should mention that, our phone was randomly ringing too." At lunch, I enlisted the help of Evan at Trendy Togs for Trendy Tots to mention to the fur man he'd been having trouble with his phone. Edmonton Telephone was out to investigate the Rabid Pekingese's phone yesterday, but found nothing. To date I believe I am still humming along under the radar of his suspicion, but I needed to be careful. My Penguin Man said, "You've been busy in your first weeks back, haven't you? Well done." There was a pause in the conversation. I let my feet drag in the warming sand as I swayed on my swing.

He stared at the sky. "Any bridal parties lately?" he asked, and I started on a small re-enactment of last week's attempt to find five pairs of identical shoes in what the bride called "seafoam mint." I hopped off my swing to re-enact the scene. I played the parts of bride, bridesmaid, and a more patient, articulate, and charming version of myself:

"What about these?"

"That's more of a minty mint. I want seafoam mint. Think of a mint in the sea."

"Ah, a mint in the sea...."

"Yes."

"What kind of mint: Spearmint? Wintergreen? Peppermint?"

"Definitely not peppermint. Maybe a spearmint-y, wintergreen-y mint."

"But in the sea."

"Yes, that's it: a spearmint-y, wintergreen-y mint in the sea."

"In the seafoam."

"Right! a spearmint-y, wintergreen-y mint in the sea-*foam*! Oh, you're so good! I'm so glad we stopped here!"

I mimed the group hug that ensued. I then described how, after I located a pair of size 7s in what was determined to be in "a spearmint-y, wintergreen-y mint in the seafoam" green and a pair of 7 1/2s in "a wintergreen-y, spearmint-y mint in the foamy sea" green, the maid of honour tried them both on.

"Neither are very comfortable," she offered, nervously.

"Good! You like them. Let's take them!"

"Umm. No. They sort of pinch—"

"But it's not like you have to wear them all day. Just the ceremony, the pictures, the reception, and the dance. And look at the colour! They're like a mint in the sea!"

"Like a mint in the sea*foam*," I offered, helpfully, I thought.

"I think I already have a blister."

"They'll stretch, won't they?"

Before I could finish "Uh, maybe...," the bride-to-be had extricated her friend's credit card from her wallet, and was boxing up the shoes herself, while arranging with me to find the remaining seven pairs from stores across the country.

"I know the shoes are a teensy bit uncomfortable, but they'll stretch. Besides, they're the ones that are going to make my wedding perfect. That's what we both want, right?"

I did not hear her friend's response. I ended my monologue wondering out loud whether the bride had put half as much thought into her choice of husband as she had into the ideal shade of a shoe that would be hidden under a bridesmaid's long dress. When I finished my narrative, my Penguin Man clapped and said, "Very well done, Miss Austen." I curtsied and returned to dragging my feet in the sand from my swing. "That's what I was talking about," he said and gave me a sideways push on my swing. We noted the time and walked back to the Mall so I could be back in time to let Maureen sneak out early from her shift. Things really haven't changed at Le Petit Chou in my absence, but seeing my Penguin Man put me in a better mood. ❀

WAS REMEMBERING MY BIRTHDAY LAST YEAR: I spent the day at the Mall and the evening alone at home, eating frozen cake with Hodge the Younger and Miss Austen. Although I ended up having a pretty nice day last year, this year's birthday was fantastic. Once again, my parents are at The Learneds Conference (which Heathcliff and I still call The Stupids), and I yet again forgot to take the cake out of the freezer. I had the day off this year, which might be the best gift I could have received. Genevieve and I met for lunch on Whyte Avenue: we looked at shoes and dresses, watched the cute cyclists, wandered around vintage shops and bookstores, drank coffee in the early afternoon and wine in the late afternoon.

We bought the latest *Vogue*, *W*, and *Elle* at Hub Cigar and Newsstand, and went over every page carefully, as we shared a litre of wine. After the first glass, I brought up the Penguin Man. Genevieve listened to me for a while, and then said, "I'm confused. Have you fallen for him or not?" I couldn't answer. I tried to explain what his gift last summer of an Oscar Wilde mixed-genre book really meant:

"It's like getting a bouquet mostly made up of carnations. If someone is in love with you, they don't give you carnations, do they? Carnations don't profess anything. Mixed-genre books are non-committal. A novel or poetry, those are statements." She thought about it for a minute and decided I was reading too much into it. Maybe I am. We continued to flip through pages of ads for shoes that cost more than a semester's tuition, and clothing so expensive we'd be afraid to wear it around food. We ordered another litre of wine, and part way through Genevieve asked, "Whatever happened to Mark?"

I shrugged and said, "He's in love with someone else." Genevieve looked at me incredulously.

"Are you sure?"

"Positive. I have evidence." She held my gaze, and I changed the subject back to the Penguin Man. I paraphrased Miss Austen in his favour:

"It is not everyone who has my passion for dead authors." She admitted this was an excellent point. Susan and Glenda joined us for dinner and we spent the entire night laughing at things that had nothing to do with men.

When I arrived home, it was quite late, and I was still laughing. As I put my key into the front door, I noticed mail in the postbox. Again, nothing from Europe. I sat down on the couch with Hodge the Younger and I ate a piece of frozen birthday cake. Hodge stretched and then sounded his feline yawp. I imagined he was saying, "Happy birthday, Molly. This year is going to be even better." I gave him a snuggle and said, "Very true, Hodge, very true."

*W*E HAD BEEN BRIBED WITH THE PROMISE of breakfast to come at eight o'clock for an all-store, staff meeting. Tim and Maureen, we noted with raised eyebrows, were both running late. It was 8:10 when they both arrived, pretending to be surprised at each other's tardiness, even though we had seen them on Level One orchestrating taking different escalators. We decided it was more fun to let them think they'd fooled us. As for the promised breakfast, Tim said, "Sorry guys. I meant to stop at McDonald's and bring you Egg McMuffins and coffees, but I was running late." He tossed us a Shoppers Drug Mart bag containing a few granola bars, a package of airline pretzels, and leftover Halloween candy. "This will do, right." I noted the absence of a question mark. We gave the pregnant part-timer from Foliage first pick, and she took a granola bar, as did Maureen. The guys from the Prima Donna store played rock-paper-scissors for the remaining granola bar, and the runner-up got the pretzels. The rest of us divided the Halloween treats and, hours later, I am still trying to extricate archival-grade, molasses candy from my teeth.

Tim came prepared with an easel, flipcharts, and fruit-scented felt pens. He took the raspberry-scented pen out of the box, and wrote "Radical New Re-Shelving Mission" on top of the page. This radical new re-shelving mission was going to transform each of our stores into, and I wince to quote, "lean, mean, shoe-provisioning machines." He had many charts and diagrams to illustrate his new scheme, but the gist was that each store would have a "team leader" who would, single-handedly, work through the stock room, and re-shelve each shoe style according to the new scheme, beginning immediately. "You should be finished by the end of your shift tonight," he said. "Tomorrow morning, I will come and inspect all stockrooms, and expect them to all be running like well-oiled machines." I knew before the team leaders were announced that Maureen would have nominated me for perhaps the grossest job I'd ever seen at Le Petit Chou. I admit I was a little disheartened to be chosen a team leader on this project, but it gave me time to think and be alone, two things I rarely get at work.

I spent much of my re-shelving time in the morning thinking about the Penguin Man. I still do not know what to make of him. We were meeting for lunch again today, our third lunch this week. My Austen heroines were full of warnings: he could be a cad like Willoughby! A rake like Wickham! A duplicitous fop like Frank Churchill! An aged bore like Colonel Brandon! Perhaps. But there was something about him I liked.

Just before my lunch break, Maureen ran into the stock room to find me. She was giddy about something:

"Molly, there's a boy here! He's gorgeous! And, I can't believe it, but he's here to see you!" She knew the Penguin Man, so I knew it couldn't be he. Convinced there was some mistake, I finished re-shelving the aqua-blue wedges, and then went out front. I was brushing the shoebox dust off my dress, and shaking dustballs out of my hair, as I rounded the corner back into the shop. I stopped dead when I saw it was the one person in the world who wouldn't care if I were covered in dust. It was Mark.

I know he was talking and I was saying words but I could only hear my heart pounding. Our conversation was a flutter of questions, none of which I can recall. I do remember that just after he asked me if I had a lunch break, the Penguin Man arrived for our lunch date. I introduced them and explained how Mark had just come back from Europe. The Penguin Man invited Mark to join us, but Mark declined saying, "Actually, I need to go to that Aloysius & Flint store right over there, get some polo shirts, and then head home. Jet lag, you know." Mark and I said goodbye and promised to reconnect in the next few days. The Penguin Man and I walked to Café Orleans without saying a word. After we were seated at our usual table, I was still processing Mark's sudden appearance. He hated the Mall. What happened in Europe? And why didn't he send a postcard? The Penguin Man broke the silence with, "Your friend Mark doesn't really seem like an Aloysius & Flint polo shirt kind of guy."

"Pardon? Oh. No. He's not." I can't recall all of what we talked about over lunch. I was distracted thinking about jet-lagged Mark's sudden interest in polo shirts and my absent postcard. But, as The Marvelettes told me, there are many fish in the sea. I made plans to meet the Penguin Man after I got off work at four o'clock on Thursday, and he walked me back to my store. We stood outside my store silently until he said, "Thursday, Miss Austen?" and I replied, "Thursday, sir." I spent the rest of my afternoon converting my store into a well-oiled machine, whilst wondering why Mark is back, why he's wearing polo shirts, and what's going on with the Penguin Man? When I finished my re-shelving, I was no closer to any kind of answer.

When I got home, I retired to my room and looked at the pictures of Miss Austen and Mrs Woolf on my wall. Neither of them seemed willing to meet my eye. I flipped through *Sense and Sensibility* looking for some advice, but Marianne and Elinor seemed preoccupied with their own problems. Elizabeth Bennet also seemed too distracted to pay much heed to my life. There was no point consulting any other novel by Miss Austen, so I scanned my bookshelves. The poets were no help at all, and none of the novels had any advice. My eyes were drawn back to Mrs Woolf's portrait, and she finally met my gaze. I asked, "Why is he back? Why didn't he write to me? And what is happening with the Penguin Man?" Her vaguely raised eyebrow seemed to suggest that I'm on my own on this one, and I fear she's right. Miss Austen darted an eye toward the Cowper book I'd shelved, but would not make eye contact with me. I'd never felt quite so alone. 🌊

*I*T'S BEEN RAINING AND, FOR THE FIRST TIME EVER, I called in sick with a bad cold. After recovering from a lecture from Maureen about my irresponsibility and "letting the team down," I spent all day in my bed trying to finish *Moll Flanders*, the novel I started at this time last year. I finally finished it after dinner. After 373 pages, I remain unenlightened; how is this book to inform my life or character? If my life were a novel, my character would have received insight about herself. She would have said, "Now that I have read the final paragraph of my eponymous novel, my path is clear. I know precisely what to do with my life, where I should go, the vocation I should pursue, the man I should marry, should I choose to marry at all." But I had none of that. Optimistically, I scanned the "Explanatory Notes" at the end of *Moll* hoping for a short explication of what this novel means. Still nothing. Then I smiled to myself, "I wonder where I might find an expert on eponymous novels and eponymity."

From my room, I could hear the *Masterpiece Theatre* theme song and PBS's plea for donations. My dad was downstairs watching *The Jewel in the Crown* episode he had taped on Sunday night. My dad and I loved that show. I brought a bowl of chips for us to share, went downstairs, and snuggled in beside him. I'd brought *Moll Flanders* with me, still thinking about it. We watched the episode, delighting in its intrigue and cliffhanger ending. As the closing theme started, my dad rewound the VHS tape, readying it for next week's episode. He put his arm around me.

"How's Moll?" he asked. I wasn't sure if he meant me or *Moll Flanders*. I said, "I'm not sure how she is. I think she's a little confused."

"About what?"

"Eponymity." I opened the book to the final page and read aloud: "And now notwithstanding all the Fatigues, and Miseries we have all gone thro', we are both in good Heart and Health; my Husband remain'd there sometime after me to settle our Affairs, and at first I had intended to go back to him, but at his desire I alter'd that Resolution, and he is come over to *England* also, where we resolve to spend the Remainder of our Years in sincere Penitence, for the wicked Lives we have lived./ Written in the year 1683./ *Finis*."There was a pause that I broke with:

"I don't know what to do with this. Was it your hope that all I could look forward to is Penitence? Is that all I have?" I heard my voice crack. I didn't want to cry. And I didn't until my dad held me close.

"Oh, Miss Molly. No, not at all. I've never told you this, but the novel I was supposed to teach on the day you were born was Richardson's *Clarissa*, but we were behind, and were still on *Moll Flanders*. Your mum and I talked about Molly versus Clarissa, and I know you think we should have gone with Clarissa, since it's a more romantic sound-ing name. But Clarissa is one of the most tragic literary victims, and I couldn't do that to you. And when I described to your mum about how Moll Flanders led a life of hardship and adventure, and that she not only managed to endure hardship, but that she emerged content and triumphant at the end, reliant on her own wits and abilities, how could we have named you anything else? When we looked into your brand-new eyes, we saw our Molly: determined, alert, prescient, and so utterly charming. Even then you had a hint of impish mischief in your eyes. We knew you were no Clarissa. Besides, *Moll Flanders* was the first novel ever published: it was an original. Like you." After a few minutes of silence, I asked, "Couldn't you have told me all of this instead of making me read the novel?" Thinking I was mak-ing a joke, my dad laughed, and we headed back upstairs.

Before we went our separate ways, Dad paused and made a professorial gesture:

"Technically speaking, *Moll Flanders* isn't your eponymous novel since your name is Molly, not Moll. The novel *Molly* remains unwritten. You can be the author of your own eponymous novel." When I got to my room, I took out a blank notebook, and wrote "Molly of the Mall" on the first page. There might be something there.

WOKE UP FEELING BETTER, AND HEADED IN early for my nine-to-four shift. It was sunnier and it would be nice to see my Penguin Man again. I was also thinking about what my dad said about Moll Flanders. She would never worry over things as silly as whether a man still likes her sister or whether a mixed-genre book is a romantic gesture. Moll Flanders would tackle today, and sell shoes like a polish-wielding juggernaut. And that, I decided, was what I would do too. As a result of my resolve, I had a good day of sales, and sold a respectable amount of polish and protective sprays. Tim has been looking at my sales, and thinks I might be able to make a run for top seller again this summer. Nobody has ever achieved this feat before.

I regretted how I'd acted at my last lunch with the Penguin Man, and determined to be more cheerful and talkative this time. He arrived at the end of my shift. He needed to be at work at the hotel lounge at five. It was a perfect day outside so we took another walk to the park. He was telling me about his weekend gigs, and amusing me with stories of the weird mall people he encounters. We made our way to the swings again, and I liked feeling sunshine on my feet and spring wind in my hair. We sat in silence on our swings for a while, but I could tell my Penguin Man was formulating a sentence. Maybe it was the sentence he was working on last time. When he finally spoke, he said, "Are you going to say yes when Mark asks you out?" I was so startled that I just about fell off my swing.

"Mark?"

"Mark."

"Mark? Why would he?" I thought about mentioning the promised postcard that never arrived, or my theories that he was still in love with Tess, or that he'd fallen in love with a Louisa Musgrove in Lyme Regis, or met a Marianne Dashwood in Hertfordshire, and forgotten all about me. But his next statement brought my musings to a bruising halt.

"Because he's absolutely and completely in love with you."

"But you only met him for three minutes."

"I know."

"It's obvious you've been reading too much Henry James."

"It's obvious to everyone, except, apparently you, that he adores you. I'm never wrong about these things. I know that he's going to ask you out, you're going to say yes, and you're going to be happier than you can ever imagine."

"With Mark?"

"With Mark." A long pause ensued. I kept swinging and looking straight ahead. My Penguin Man's gaze was fixed on me and I didn't want to meet it. Finally, he got off his swing and stood behind me giving me gentle pushes. "I met a woman over the winter. Lisa. I asked her to marry me last month. She said yes. We're getting married in the fall."

I wasn't sure why I felt a lump forming in my throat, but I was glad he could not see my face. The shock of his news made me worry that I had fallen in love with my Penguin Man and not even known it. He returned to his swing, and saw my tears. We both looked straight ahead. A child was walking with his new black-and-white puppy, hoping, I think, we'd notice how cute the dog was. We did notice, and concentrated on the puppy until one of us had to break the silence.

"Molly, you didn't think...."

"Think what? Oh! No, not at all. I'm so happy for you! Congratulations!" I made sure that there were exclamation points at the end of every phrase. I hopped off my swing, and stood to give him the kind of hug you'd give someone if you wanted to pretend you were really happy for them, and not in love with them at all, which I realized I wasn't at all. He held on to me and said, "I know. I know."

"What do you know?" I squeaked. My tears—inexplicable to me—seemed perfectly logical to him.

"You're the first person I've ever met who loves Penguin Classics as much as I do. And that's rare." He left a space for me to smile and laugh, and I did so politely. "But I also know, you're barely twenty-one years old and I'm not. You have so many things you need to do, and so many things you want to do. I've been to the Fens, I've seen the Arno, I've had my heart broken, I've tried to be an artistic genius, and failed. I've fallen in love with all the wrong people and, now, finally the right one. I also know your life is going to be spectacular. You will write your novel. You will travel. You will understand how beautiful you are. You will do things you'll regret. You will do things you are proud of. You need to do all these things; but you can't do those things with me." He paused and added, "But I think there's someone else who wants to do those things with you. And you need to call him."

"You seem to have thought this way through very carefully," I observed.

"You have no idea."

"You'll still be my Penguin Man though?"

"I will still be your Penguin Man, and you will still be my Miss Austen."

"Am I still going to have to read Hemingway?"

"Absolutely. I'll expect a book report on my next visit."

We walked back to the Mall in what a novelist might describe as "a contented silence." When we got to the place where our paths would diverge, he said, "I will see you again very soon. And I'll want that book report." He leaned in to kiss my cheek. I could only nod and look down at my shoes. As I turned to catch my bus, he caught my hand. "There are so many things you can't see. You're going to be the heroine of a most amazing novel. Write it all down, Miss Austen. Promise me." I promised. "And one more thing: call Mark." I nodded and looked away. Mark. ✸

WHEN I GOT OFF THE BUS, I WAS FULL OF WORDS. I dashed home and called Mark's house. He didn't answer. I didn't leave a message. Genevieve, Susan, Glenda, and I were going to Andante tonight to see a band and I thought about asking Mark to join us. Susan has a crush on the drummer, and we were all going for moral support. I called him back a few minutes later and when the answering machine kicked in, I thought better of it. I needed a girls' night out, and even though I wasn't sure if I would tell anyone about the Penguin Man or Mark, seeing my friends seemed like a great way to improve my mood. By this time, I was quite certain that the Penguin Man was probably just being nice about Mark, so I wouldn't be too devastated about his engagement to a girl he had never mentioned. If the Penguin Man had been right, Mark would certainly have called me by now. I told myself, "It's best to move on." Mrs Woolf nodded, but Miss Austen continued to be evasive.

I stood in front of my closet for some time trying to decide what to wear. I settled on something decidedly un-Mall: a sparkly, black sundress and my new pointy Fluevog shoes with silver detailing. I looked in the mirror on the way out, and saw a glimmer of the self I had not been for some time. At the last minute, I stashed a pair of ballet flats in my bag in case the new Fluevogs inflicted their characteristic cruelty on my feet. I had missed being non-Mall Molly, and from the minute Genevieve picked me up, I started feeling like myself again.

It was a perfect, early summer night, and the patio doors at Andante were open. Music spilled into the street, laughter and cigarette smoke swirled around me as I was embraced by the press of the crowd. My bare shoulders and arms were basking in the unaccustomed warmth, desperate to believe that summer had indeed arrived. I was surrounded by people I knew and loved, and my laughter came easily. I paused for a moment to sip my pint of Big Rock porter and take everything in. Glenda was amusing a group with one of her stories; Genevieve was listening intently to a beautiful man, unaware, I think, of how utterly taken he was with her; and Susan was enmeshed in the circle of the band members' girlfriends. I could tell the drummer had told everyone about Susan, and they were excited to finally meet her. At one point, all four of us made eye contact with each other and we each raised our glasses. I'm not quite sure what the other three raised theirs to, but I raised mine to the arrival of summer, to pretty sundresses, to my darling friends, and to everything that made tonight special.

Seeing everyone so happy made me smile, but as the night wore on, my long day caught up to me, and I was feeling tired. Acquaintances were talking to me, but I couldn't hear them over the music. I nodded as they talked, but comprehended very little. The crowd was building, and hands on my shoulder and on my back were gently pressing me one way and then the other. Pretending to listen to my acquaintances, I found my thoughts wandering back to my conversation with the Penguin Man and the image of Mark walking away. Maybe later tonight Genevieve could help me think it all through. Or maybe this was something I needed to sort through myself. Words had been failing me all day, and I wouldn't know where to begin. I used a waitress coming through with a tray of drinks as an excuse to extricate myself from the conversation. I had been feeling lonely for weeks, but somehow, right then, I just needed to be alone. I wished I smoked to have an excuse to separate myself from the crowd, and to stand alone for a few moments. I walked to the edge to the parking lot to look over the Edmonton skyline.

It was the time of year when the northern lights would

sometimes silently thunder across the sky, and I wondered if tonight would be one of those nights. Even without the northern lights, tonight was spectacular: oranges, pinks, and reds spread seamlessly across the dome of the sky. As I looked across the river, I looked at my city from an angle I rarely see. I stood on a cement block to see over the trees: lights blinked atop the high-rises downtown, and the glow of streetlights hung over the river valley like a fog. It wasn't Mrs Woolf's Bloomsbury, or Miss Austen's village, or Emily Brontë's moor, but it was my city. It belonged to me and I belonged to it. As the sky gloamed, I thought it best to return to Andante as my friends would begin to worry.

Walking into the club, I let the press and warmth of the crowd, the pounding of the bass in my chest, and the sparkle in my sundress take over again. In my absence, Susan, Glenda, and Genevieve had settled at a table across the room, and, spotting them, I attempted to make it across the crowd. Navigating the space upstream seemed more difficult than it should have. I waved at Glenda and Genevieve, and they waved back at me, frantically pointing, I thought, to the door. Assuming they wanted to leave, I pressed my way back outside, and turned to look at the sky as I waited for them. The sun had fully set, and the moon and a smattering of stars glowed warmly above me. I was so engrossed in the stars, that I failed to hear footsteps approaching. I jumped at the hand that gently touched my shoulder and the voice that said,

"Molly?" I knew the voice instantly.

"Mark?"

"Molly."

"Mark."

For whatever reasons, Mark left me completely speechless. Maybe I thought we should be at our poetic best right now, but we stumbled around the obvious situational topics for quite a while. He was fine. I was fine. I was here because Susan loves the drummer, he was there because he's a friend of the bassist. Susan and the drummer do seem well matched. It is a beautiful night. The sunset was spectacular. Seems like summer is here. My dress is very cute. My shoulders must be cold. He really didn't need his jacket. I was fine. Really? No, actually my shoulders were cold. Thank you. How are you really? I was a little tired and so, he admitted, was he. He offered to drive me home, which I accepted. He then remembered his friend had driven. We laughed. He was tired. Still jet-lagged. One of us suggested walking. It was a long walk, but it was a beautiful night, and I had ballet flats stashed in my bag. A walk would be perfect. While Mark said goodbye to his friends, I gestured across the room to my friends that I was leaving. Using the ultra-secret-girl code of signals Genevieve gave me the "call-me-immediately" sign, Susan the "I told-you-so" sign, and Glenda the "he-is-very cute" sign. Mark had a funny smile on his face that made me wonder how ultra-secret the girl signals really are. He guided me through the crowd and into the quiet air.

Getting away from the crowd was a relief. He didn't seem to want to talk about Europe, and so I left my questions for another day. As we walked down the train tracks in the moonlight, we didn't talk about much. We laughed about tiny things, exchanged gossip about our friends, and talked about everything other than ourselves. The walk was a long one, but we were at the edge of the University Farm before we knew it. Although there weren't cars anywhere in sight, we stopped for a walk light at the intersection closest to our neighbourhood and were silent. We were two blocks from my house, and I had to ask what I'd wanted to know all night.

"How was Aloysius & Flint?" He looked confused so I added, "You said you couldn't go for lunch because you needed to buy polo shirts." The walk light illuminated, but we stood still.

"Oh. Right. No, I just went home."

"Why didn't you come for lunch with us?"

"I was feeling pretty tired. And I didn't think your boy-friend really wanted me to come along." The "don't walk" light flashed and turned to red. A car waited beside us for the light to change again. "He seems nice, by the way. What's his story?"

"He's a musician. He reads a lot."

Mark nodded and said, "Of course." The light changed and we let the car pass us before we crossed the road.

"He likes Steinbeck and Hemingway. He's fond of Cajun

food. He only listens to music before 1989. And he's engaged to his girlfriend, Lisa. They're getting married in the fall." Mark's pace slowed as he processed what I was telling him.

"Your boyfriend's engaged to someone else?"

"He's not my boyfriend. He's just a guy who likes to talk to me about novels. And Penguin Classics at that." Mark said nothing until we were at the edge of my yard. Heathcliff was sitting on our front porch. We all nodded acknowledgment and then Mark and I stood fully engrossed in the new buds on our neighbour's privet hedge.

"What are you doing tomorrow? Free for a walk?" he asked. I had the day off and was free all day.

"Of course." Mark looked at me, then at Heathcliff, who was captivated with the sky. He pushed an errant strand of my hair behind my ear.

"Meet me at the bench at ten o'clock? I have something for you." I nodded and our fingers caught and lingered. He kissed me on the cheek quickly and I watched him until he turned the corner to his street. I joined Heathcliff on the porch. It was almost two o'clock in the morning and he was staring at the sky.

"Looking for something?" I asked, gazing up.

"The northern lights. It's very late in the season, but the conditions seem right for them. Someone saw them earlier this week so I thought I'd watch for them." In silence, we stared up at the sky. Heathcliff said, "This sky is magnificent even without the northern lights. I could stare at it forever. Last night I saw hints of Jupiter. It should be at its brightest soon." As someone obsessed with fescue and plants, I'd only ever seen him look down, never up. But he knew as much about the sky as he did the earth. We stared on in silence until I said, "Can I ask you something? Why do you love fescue so much?"

"It's not all fescues," he explained, "just the ones that grow here. Indigenous fescues. I like that they've evolved so they can survive this climate. You can plant them other places, but they'll never really thrive the way they do here." He walked over to a section of garden he's cultivated since childhood, and picked a stem of grass. "This is plains rough fescue. I love how it smells." He handed me the stem of grass, and I caught a barely discernable scent. "Alberta's the only place in North America where all three kinds of rough fescue grow. That little stem in your hand likely descended from seeds that date back to the end of the ice age. It's like a time capsule of our whole region's history. If you know the story of fescue, you know the story of Alberta. It's pretty magical when you think about it." I'd never thought to think about a blade of grass like that before. I stared at it intently. Maybe this is what Whitman meant when he leaned and loafed, observing a spear of summer grass. "Nowhere else in the world will you see a fescue growing like this one. And nowhere else in the world might you see that," he said, pointing upward.

As if on cue, a dash of phosphorescent green danced across a corner of the sky. More greens followed, and soon the sky was awash with waves of yellow and hints of purple swirling like flames across the expanse of our sky. There was nothing either of us could say about the spectacle before us. It was if the sky had put on a performance for those who waited and watched. On this particular night, it was just for Heathcliff and me. And when it was over, we heard not a sound. I'd never heard such silence in my city before. Heathcliff and I sat until we heard the morning's first birds, which I took to be my cue to head inside and go to sleep. Just as I was about to get up, Heathcliff said, "You know Virginia Woolf and Jane Austen never saw the northern lights from their front porches, right?" I nodded, dusted off my dress, and opened the front door. I looked back one more time, and Heathcliff turned to look at me. "Do you also know that Woolf and Austen never assumed their big brothers didn't see them kissing Mark Forster by the privet hedge?"

"That's Mrs Woolf and Miss Austen, to you," I retorted, and swatted him gently with the stem of fescue I still held in my hand.

It wasn't until I got into my room that I realized I was still wearing Mark's jacket. It fit so nicely. I didn't want to take it or my sundress off. I fell asleep in both while thinking of what today had brought and what tomorrow might bring.

*B*ECAUSE I'D BEEN UP SO LATE, I OVERSLEPT, AND had to run to meet Mark. I was five minutes late and found Mark looking anxious, and then relieved to see me. We sat on our bench at the top of the hill, and noted how almost before our eyes the leaves were filling the river valley with new green. The horses from the stables below us grazed on the new spring grass, more than once kicked their heels in the air, and galloped up and down the pastures. I told him about seeing the northern lights, and staying up with Heathcliff until the early morning birds chirped.

"Last night was so magical, in so many ways."

I started to dread that I'd said something wrong because Mark was quiet for a few moments. But then he spoke, straight ahead, not looking at me.

"I went to the Mall the other day because I had so many things I had to tell you. But then when I saw you with that other guy, I panicked and lied, and said I had to go shopping. I don't know why I picked Aloysius & Flint. Maybe it's because the only other store I saw was the fur store, and I knew you'd hate me if I shopped there. As I walked to my car, I was convinced I'd lost my only chance with you. By the time I got home, I told myself I could get over you, that you and I could go on being wonderful friends, and that it would be fine that you were with someone else. But last night, when I saw you in your sparkly dress, with my jacket on your shoulders, I knew I was wrong. It wouldn't be fine. And then you told me he wasn't your boyfriend, and so I can tell you this now. I went to the Mall to tell you that I came home from Europe early to give you this. I know I missed your birthday last week, but I bought it on your birthday." He handed me a parcel he'd hidden in his messenger bag. He'd wrapped it in William Morris wrapping paper. I whispered, "The chrysanthemum pattern. My favourite." I unwrapped it carefully so as not to rip the paper. Inside was a stack of about twenty postcards from across Europe, written but not mailed, and a book. It wasn't a novel as I'd expected, but a well-worn copy of *Let's Go: England*. "Thank you, Mark," I said, unclear why he left Europe a month early to give this to me.

"Go to the section on Hampshire. I've marked it." I flipped to the section and found a small pink envelope with my name written in his neat script tucked in its pages.

"Mark, I don't understand."

"Open it." Inside were two entrance tickets to Jane Austen's House Museum in Chawton, good for a year.

"I still don't understand." He turned to face me and took my hands in his.

"Molly, from the minute I arrived in Europe, I kept thinking, 'Molly would love this' and 'Molly should see this.' Everywhere I went, I wrote you a postcard that didn't even come close to what I wanted to tell you. I wrote you letters in my head about everything I saw. And then I started thinking 'I wish Molly were here to see this' and then, 'I wish Molly were here.' That's all I could think about. I was in England around your birthday, and thought, in honour of you, I'd go to Jane Austen's house and call you from a payphone outside the museum. I went to Chawton, found the payphone I'd use to call you, and walked around the town thinking about how I would describe it to you. As I walked around, I couldn't get over how wrong it felt for me to be there without you. I sat outside Jane Austen's house and realized, it wasn't just Chawton. It felt wrong to be anywhere without you. I went to the museum, bought two tickets to the house, and then went to the payphone I'd found. Instead of calling you, I called the airline and booked my ticket home."

I was, perhaps for the first time in my life, entirely bereft of words. He continued, "I couldn't send you the other postcards because what I really wanted to say to you was this: It's up to you whether I'm your Colonel Brandon or your Willoughby, your Mr Darcy, your Mr Knightley, or even your Mr Collins. But you need to know you're my Marianne Dashwood, my Elizabeth Bennet, my Emma Woodhouse, my Catherine Morland, my Fanny Price, and my Anne Elliot. And, if you'd let me, I'd like to take you to Jane Austen's house next spring after you graduate." I didn't know whether to say, "Mark, I love you," or "Mark, you've read all of Miss Austen," which, I realize, in my books might amount to about the same thing. I settled on:

"Mark, you've read all of Miss Austen," and then followed with my second choice. "Mark, I am so in love with you." And, dear reader, I do confess, although there was no rain dashing against window-panes, nor great swoops of wind, we did kiss tremblingly on the cliffs above the North Saskatchewan, under the cloudless, blue Alberta sky. 🕸

Acknowledgements

A faithful crew of family, friends, and community have been essential for me while writing this book. I am grateful for the love, support, and friendship of many but I would particularly like to thank:

Linda Zagaglioni, for giving Molly her first audience; Gwendolyn Ebbett, for making many wonderful things possible; the University of Windsor, for being a supportive, caring, and exciting place to be; and the Royal Scottish Country Dance Society of Windsor, for being my Windsor family.

I am deeply grateful for and indebted to:

NeWest Press's Claire Kelly and Matt Bowes, for making everything work flawlessly, and Kate Hargreaves, for her meticulous design work. I will be forever grateful to Merrill Distad for his gallant championing of Molly and his exquisite editing.

Molly's first readers, Susan Holbrook, Griff Evans, and Dayna Cornwall, who offered invaluable feedback, steadfast encouragement, and devoted friendship.

The Whyte, Martin, and Jacobs families, especially:

Marguerite Whyte, Melvina Jacobs, and Elmer Jacobs, who are deeply missed.

My dad, Jerome Martin, who taught me about fescue, words, and the beauty of Penguin Classics.

My brother, Paul Martin, whom I adore and admire beyond words.

My husband, Dale Jacobs, who makes me grateful every day for having a group project in Mediæval literature. *Pulchra es et sapiens.*

And, finally, my mum, Merle Martin, the funniest person I've ever known and also the most generous, passionate and tenacious. Without her, this book, among many other things, would not have been imagined, let alone completed.

HEIDI L.M. JACOBS was born and raised in Edmonton. While attending the University of Alberta, she worked a variety of retail jobs, including selling shoes. She is currently the English and History Librarian at the University of Windsor.

Nunatak is an Inuktitut word meaning "lonely peak," a rock or mountain rising above ice. During Quaternary glaciation in North America these peaks stood above the ice sheet and so became refuges for plant and animal life. Magnificent nunataks, their bases scoured by glaciers, can be seen along the Highwood Pass in the Alberta Rocky Mountains and on Ellesmere Island.

Nunataks are especially selected works of outstanding fiction by new western writers. Notable Nunatak titles include *Chorus of Mushrooms* by Hiromi Goto; *Icefields* by Thomas Wharton; *Moon Honey* by Suzette Mayr; *Dance, Gladys, Dance* by Cassie Stocks; and *Paper Teeth* by Lauralyn Chow.

We are proud to have published fifty books in the Nunatak First Fiction series and are excited to continue highlighting new voices in the years to come.

Chorus of Mushrooms: 20ᵗʰ Anniversary Edition – Hiromi Goto
Icefields – Thomas Wharton
Moon Honey - Suzette Mayr
Whipstock – Barb Howard
Talon – Paulette Dubé
The Wheel Keeper – Robert Pepper-Smith
Touch – Gayleen Froese
Running Toward Home – Barbara Jane Hegerat
Paper Trail – Arleen Paré
Wonderfull – William Neil Scott
Gerbil Mother – D.M. Bryan
Cleavage – Theanna Bischoff
Fishing for Bacon – Michael Davie
Ruins and Relics – Alice Zorn
Seal Intestine Raincoat – Rosie Chard
Crisp – R.W. Gray
Extensions – Myrna Dey
Dance, Gladys, Dance – Cassie Stocks
The Shore Girl – Fran Kimmel
Belinda's Rings – Corinna Chong
The Paradise Engine – Rebecca Campbell
Love at Last Sight – Thea Bowering
Shallow Enough to Walk Through – Marissa Reaume
After Alice – Karen Hofmann
Blind Spot – Laurence Miall
The Guy Who Pumps Your Gas Hates You – Sean Trinder
Things You've Inherited from Your Mother – Hollie Adams
Meadowlark – Wendi Stewart
Friendly Fire – Lisa Guenther
Paper Teeth – Lauralyn Chow
Lost Animal Club – Kevin A. Couture
Border Markers – Jenny Ferguson
59 Glass Bridges – Steven Peters
To Me You Seem Giant – Greg Rhyno
The Melting Queen – Bruce Cinnamon
Only Pretty Damned – Niall Howell
Molly of the Mall: Literary Lass and Purveyor of Fine Footwear
– Heidi L.M. Jacobs